CORY'S DILEMMA: MISSING THE BEAT

DANGEROUS MUSIC

SUSPENSEFUL SECRETS
BOOK 1

DAN PETROSINI

Print ISBN: 978-1-960286-16-1
Naples, FL
Library of Congress Control Number: 2023903980

ACKNOWLEDGMENTS

A special thanks to Julie, Stephanie and Jennifer for their love and support.

OTHER BOOKS BY DAN

Complicit Witness

Push Back

Ambition Cliff

1

Cory plugged in a code, and the smell of bleach hit him as the door opened. It was late, after 1 a.m., and he was tired after bartending. But money was tight, and studio time after midnight was cheaper.

Time was melting away. He was thirty-two in an industry that prized youth. There weren't many breakout artists who came of age in their mid-thirties.

A janitor on his way out passed him as he hit the first step. Trudging up, he wondered if this was his last shot to make it. He had excellent chops; all he needed was a break to prove his father wrong. Walking down a hallway lined with studios, he noticed the live room's red light was on.

He peered in the window. Jay Bird, a hit machine, was alone in the room used to record full bands. Sitting at an ebony piano, the megastar was playing chords and notating them.

Cory watched. When Jay Bird paused, Cory knocked and opened the door.

"Hey, Jay."

Jay Bird slurred his words: "Cory. What's going on here this late?"

"Polishing a couple of my tunes. I'm auditioning for Sharp Five tomorrow."

"You'll crush it, bro."

"I hope so."

"When you make it big, you still gonna play on my stuff?"

"Definitely. I'm super thankful for all the sessions you've given me."

"I might have given you the first one, but you earned the rest. You know, I got the chills from your solo on 'Joy River.'"

"Thanks, man. Look, I don't want to keep you from doing your thing. I'll see you later."

"Be well, brother."

Cory headed to his studio, wondering how it felt to be at the top of the music industry. Jay Bird had blown past Bruno Mars in the number of albums sold and swept the Grammys three years in a row.

Pushing open the door to his studio, Cory couldn't get his head around how it came so easy to the star.

Unpacking his Martin acoustic, he strapped it over his shoulder and strummed a couple of chords. Cory tuned it and stepped into the vocal booth, putting on headphones. He sang two verses then cleared his throat. His voice sounded dry, almost scratchy. He put his guitar down and went for water.

The light was still on in the room where Jay Bird was. Peeking in as he walked by, he stopped short. The superstar was slumped onto the piano.

Had he fallen asleep? Cory didn't want to disturb him, but something was off. Opening the first door, he leaned over the soundboard and knocked on the window. No movement. He swung the door open.

"Jay? You all right?"

Cory approached, stepping over the pencil the musician had used. "Hey! You okay, man?"

Jay Bird's forehead was leaning on the bottom of the music rack. A stream of foam dripped from his mouth, puddling on the keys. Had he overdosed? Cory shook him. His head lolled. He put his fingers on his neck. It felt cool. He couldn't find a pulse.

Pulling his phone out, he saw a stack of manuscript paper lying on the grand piano. He shuffled through them. There were eight songs that appeared complete and two others with sixteen bars of music.

Cory looked around. He was alone. He scooped the papers up, folded them, and stuffed the music in his jacket. He went into the sound booth, checking the recording equipment. Nothing was turned on.

Cory ran to his studio. He shoved the manuscript papers into his backpack. On the way back, he dialed 911. "I need help. My friend's foaming at the mouth. I think it's an overdose."

"Is he breathing?"

"No. I tried to check his pulse, but there's nothing."

"Do you know CPR?"

"Yeah, but he's sitting up, leaning against a piano."

"Lay him down and try to revive him."

"Okay." He noticed a double-reel tape player with cords running to a series of microphones on booms.

"I want to confirm the address, One Forty-Six West Twenty-Ninth Street, is that correct?"

"Yes, Mirrortone Studios, on the second floor."

"Okay, help is on the way."

Cory went to the reel-to-reel. It wasn't on. He rewound it and hit playback. It was blank. Jay Bird hadn't recorded anything.

The star wasn't breathing, and with no one around, it seemed safe to keep the new material. Then he remembered the drug EMT responders gave to reverse drug overdoses.

Cory eased Jay Bird onto the floor. He wiped Jay's mouth with a shirtsleeve, pinching his nose, and administered mouth-to-mouth. After a minute, he paused; there was no response. He used his hands to compress the chest area. He had to be certain no one would question his attempt to resuscitate the fallen star.

Waiting for the ambulance to arrive, Cory made a call to the management office that handled Jay Bird. It was the middle of the night, but in the music business someone always monitored their celebrity cash cows. And Jay Bird was one helluva heifer.

Cory stood in the hallway as the sound of the approaching siren grew louder. He put his hands in his pockets to keep them from shaking.

2

Cory watched as the medics hit Jay Bird with an injection of Naloxone. They strapped a face mask on him and forced air into him with a resuscitation bag. Cory shifted positions to see if it was working.

Ten minutes passed. Cory wondered how long they'd keep at it. Nothing they were doing seemed to be working. He knew Jay Bird abused drugs and drank too much. He and many others thought there was a chance it would come to this.

Cory couldn't believe it. The guy was bigger than Bieber and Katy Perry combined and had flushed it down the toilet. How could he be so stupid?

Even though he had nothing to do with the overdose, Cory rehearsed his story. The police would be asking questions. He could have acted quicker, but that was all. He'd leave that out and keep it to seeing him playing when he arrived and noticing he was slumped over when he went for a drink of water.

The medics looked at each other and shook their heads.

One stood, and the other removed the mask from Jay Bird's face. It was too late. They couldn't revive him.

Cory trembled and wiped a tear from his cheek. As the medics pulled a sheet over Jay Bird, the star's manager, Ronny Dee, rushed in. Dee stopped in his tracks when he saw the covered body.

"Oh no, God. Don't tell me he's gone."

"We're sorry, sir."

"Oh, Jay, what have you done?"

Cory hung his head. "He was slumped on the piano. When I saw him, he was, was gone already."

CORY AND HIS WIFE, Linda, were in bed.

"I still can't believe it. I saw it with my own eyes, but it's hard to accept Jay Bird's dead."

"It's so sad. What a waste."

"It's crazy, just the day before yesterday I was laying down a line for one of the tunes on his new album. He was right there, in the control booth. I opened the door just a minute to say hi, and he told me he loved my soloing, and now he's gone."

Linda put her head on Cory's chest. "Life can change so quickly, it's scary."

"I know, but he did it to himself with the drugs."

"Are you sure that was it?"

"Yeah, the last couple of times I saw him, he was high as a kite. I heard that's why the new album was taking so long."

"Didn't anybody, like his manager or agent, realize he had a problem?"

"Oh, yeah, they had to. I'm telling you, in music, they

look the other way. More people than not in this business are doing something."

"What a shame. You better stay away from that stuff."

"Don't have to worry about me."

"I still don't understand why nobody intervened."

"You know how much money he was making for everybody? They were afraid to mess things up."

"That's ridiculous. The man is dead, and now they have nothing."

"I know."

"What's going to happen now?"

"I'm sure the album will come out. It'll probably top the charts on sympathy alone, not that he needed it."

"But what about you? I don't want to seem selfish, but you got a lot of session work from him."

"I know. There's a new kid, a girl from Queens, supposed to be the new Taylor Swift; she just signed with Columbia. I'm going to talk to Davey about working with her. We'll see what happens."

"I hope it works out."

"You know, this whole thing just shows you can't depend on anyone else. I got to make it on my own. Then we'd control our destiny, you know?"

"You're trying. I'm sure you'll make it; you compose such beautiful songs."

"I've been writing a lot of new stuff."

"That's good."

"I got to say, some of it's pretty damn good. Maybe the best I've written."

"I'd love to hear them."

"Maybe tomorrow. I want to clean a couple of things up first."

"Whenever you're ready."

"Let's get to sleep. Ava is going to be up in a couple of hours."

Linda fell asleep but Cory couldn't. Images of Jay Bird slumped on the piano continually popped into his head, interrupting his thoughts on what to do with the music he'd taken. He worried that someone had been there earlier. Had Jay Bird really been on his own the entire time?

He'd check with the network of musicians that played with the star to see what they knew. He was certain the studio didn't have cameras in the recording areas as he'd signed his share of nondisclosures before working sessions.

———

SLIPPING A POD INTO THE COFFEEMAKER, Cory said, "Can you take Ava to preschool?"

"I can't. I'm gonna be late for work if I do."

"Oh man, I'm beat. I just couldn't sleep after what happened last night."

"Take a nap when you get back."

"I have to take Mrs. Ponte to the doctor."

"Again?"

"She's got nobody else."

Linda looked at her phone. "All right. I'll get Ava there on the early side."

"Thanks."

"Come on, pumpkin. Mommy's going to take you to school today."

Cory kissed his daughter and said, "Daddy will pick you up later. Have fun today."

"Bye, Daddy."

As soon as the door closed behind them, Cory went to the

small room that served as Ava's play area and his place to practice and write music. He dug into his backpack and took out the manuscript paper he'd taken.

He shuffled through the pages, stopping halfway through the pile. Cory took his prized Gibson Hummingbird off the wall and strapped the acoustic guitar on. He set the handwritten sheet music on the stand and strummed the chords to the tune. Halfway through, he got excited and began singing the melody. After eight bars he was hooked.

The middle of the tune had a difficult passage. The rhythm was hard for him to sing. He wondered whether the song's bridge was easier to play on the piano. He played through the section a couple of times and got it under his fingers. Hearing how it sounded made it easier to sing.

He started at the top, playing the chords and singing. It sounded good. The lyrics were nothing but fluff, but he'd played on enough tunes with meaningless and repetitive words to know that had nothing to do with it becoming a hit.

Cory shook his head. How did Jay Bird write such catchy tunes? The guy was a hit factory. Cory slipped the next page on top and played the chords. It was totally different, but he liked the dark sounds of the minor chords.

Cory read the lyrics. It was about love found and lost. A timeless theme, but this version used a puppy who'd run away to convey emotional pain. He thought it was weird, but when he started singing it, the fresh approach grew on him. It wasn't hooky, but he felt it could be another winner.

He put the next sheet on the stand. Unlike the previous two, this one had a title: "A Handle on You." The lyrics were about controlling someone. He began strumming the chords when the door to the apartment slammed shut.

Cory swept up the sheets as Linda came in.

"Rushing to leave, I forgot my lunch."

"Sorry."

"What are you doing? I thought you were going to try and get some rest."

"I don't know, I just felt like writing. You know, maybe the emotions from what happened will come out in a song."

3

———

AS SOON AS HIS WIFE LEFT, CORY TOOK THE STOLEN MUSIC out and played through each song. He thought six were amazing and two others better than average. The opening sections on the two incomplete ones were pop oriented, and he felt he could complete them.

Cory took out blank manuscript paper and copied each of the tunes. He double-checked to ensure he had everything duplicated and played the copies as a final test.

Satisfied they were the same, he fed the originals into the shredder, bagged the snippets, took the bag outside, and dumped it in the trash.

Cory didn't get the relief he'd expected by destroying the originals. He made a call. "Ronnie Dee, please."

"Who's calling?"

"Cory Lupinski."

"Mr. Dee is extremely busy. What is this about?"

"I'm the one who found Jay Bird last night."

"Oh my God. I'm sorry, hang on."

"Ronnie Dee."

"Hi, Mr. Dee. I-I just wanted to reach out and tell you

how sorry I am about everything. And you know, see how you're doing."

"We're devastated. It really hasn't sunk in yet."

"I know, it's really crazy. I keep seeing him in my head, you know?"

"Seeing him lying there, it's haunting. I just wish we could have done something to help him."

"I got there too late. I saw him when I came in. I saw him through the window, popped the door open and said hi. That was it. He was working, well, not working but playing, and later when I went to get some water, that's when I saw him hunched over."

"These damn drugs. I warned him about it several times. Tried to get him into rehab but he wouldn't go, said he was cutting back on his own."

"Wasn't anyone else with him?"

"Not that we know of. As you know, Jay liked to compose alone."

Cory fist-pumped. "I wish I would've left earlier or something, anything to help him."

"You and me both. Now we've got to pick up the pieces and find a way to move on."

"At least you've got the new album."

"I don't care about the music. I've lost a dear friend; I have a hole in my heart."

Cory knew the manager had spit out a canned response. He also knew the manager was truthful. He didn't care about the music: what he cared about was the money he would be missing out on.

"I know what you mean. I played on almost every one of his recordings. He was a good guy. I'll miss him."

"You and me both. Look, as you can imagine, I've got a lot of things that need my attention. Thanks for the call."

"DADDY! I can't talk to my dolls if you keep singing."

"Do me a favor, honey. Can you watch a little TV? Daddy is working on a super important song."

"But I wanna have a tea party."

"Just for ten minutes, okay?"

Ava frowned.

"How about a little scoop of ice cream before serving tea to your friends?"

"Yay! Ice cream!"

Cory spooned out some ice cream, put the TV on, and went back to practicing the songs. He was getting more comfortable each time he played through them. He had three that he loved and was trying to piece together a strategy.

Should he go all-in, try to get a record deal using all the tunes, or should he use one or two to secure a contract? He preferred the piecemeal route. He'd get more mileage out of it by stretching the material over a few recordings.

Though he preferred the slower release, he knew attaining blockbuster status wouldn't be possible unless he somehow penned a hit or two to go with the material he'd taken.

Cory took out two of his recent compositions and compared them to the ones he'd stolen. The difference in the openings was startling. It made him remember what someone at Motown had said: "You gotta grab them in the first four bars: give them something to remember right away."

The lyrics contrasted markedly from what Cory wrote. Cory liked to tell a story with his. Jay Bird's bordered on childish but were snappy. Maybe he'd have to dumb it down. If he could. He remembered his dad saying to keep things simple.

Cory grabbed one of his compositions and sat at his desk.

He closed his eyes and thought of simple phrases for a new opening line. He wrote and wrote, ripping up page after page. Nothing had the Jay Bird cadence to it.

He reached for the other song he'd crafted and began writing new lyrics for it. Cory was scratching out a line when his wife came in.

"You gave Ava ice cream?"

"Uh, yeah."

"She said you were in here all day."

"Not the whole time. I had some stuff in my head I had to try and get out. You want to hear something?"

"Maybe later."

Cory reached for his Gibson. "Hang on a second. I need to see what you think."

He rifled through the pages, picking out his second favorite song from the stolen ones. Cory strummed the guitar and began singing.

"Wow. I really like that."

"You do?"

"Yeah. You wrote that today?"

"Nah, I've been working on it for, like, two weeks."

"I think it's the best song you ever made. Even better than 'Mr. Sunshine.' I really like it."

He wrote "Mr. Sunshine" right after they met. That meant she thought he hadn't written anything better in ten years. It hurt hearing the assessment, especially from the love of his life.

"I've been writing like mad. I have a couple of others." He reached for another of Jay Bird's tunes.

"Maybe later. How was Mrs. Ponte?"

"Doctor said she's doing okay. I have to bring her back next week."

"Good. I never asked you; how much did you make last night? The rent is due Tuesday."

"It was a little slow at the bar, only picked up sixty-four bucks in tips."

"You have any gigs coming up?"

"Just two, but one is a good one, six hundred for the session. And I'm pitching that new record label tomorrow."

"But even if they sign you, it'll be a while before we see any money."

"Gee, thanks for the support, hon."

"Sorry, I didn't mean it that way. It's just that if we want to have another kid and stop living like this, maybe we have to think about making some changes. Maybe put the music on hold, you know, for a little while, until we save up."

She's sounding like my father. "Come on, I don't want to talk about that again. Right now, I need to get back to polishing the audition tunes."

4

————

AS SOON AS CORY WALKED INTO THE STUDIO, DONNY BLAKE said, "Here he comes. The man of the hour."

Cory's best friend and monster player was tuning his electric bass. "How you doing, Donny?"

"Good, man. What's with the new look? You trying to get into the Jonas Brothers band?"

Cory's agent suggested he get a hipper haircut to make him look younger. "Can't get stale, you know."

"Man, I still can't believe you were there when Jay Bird crashed. It must have been otherworldly."

"It was super eerie. I can't shake it."

"When them drugs get their claws in you, it's tough to get away. What a waste."

"That crap is bad news."

"Hey, enough of the negative vibe. You ready to light this place up?"

"I hope so."

"You'll do it, man."

"I'm starting to doubt it, you know. Everybody's got an opinion on what to do. One day they're telling me I'm not pop enough, then the next day they say to do it in a folk style."

"Just stay true to yourself. Do it the way it speaks to you. If you don't, you're not gonna own it."

"Thanks, man. Let me get set up and say hello to everybody."

They did a soundcheck, and after making minor adjustments, Robin Day, the man paying for the session, arrived. Wearing a puffy yellow vest, the A&R guy for Sharp Five Records entered the booth. He waved at Cory and signed some papers.

Cory strummed his guitar to quell his nerves. The sound engineer took a seat behind the control panel. Day and a producer from the label stood behind him.

"Is everybody ready?"

Cory and the other musicians nodded.

Cory addressed the band, "All right, let's kick this off. Don't rush it, lay it back, guys."

The red light went on and Cory said, "One, two. One, two, three, four."

Cory thought the introduction sounded good and sang the first verse.

The producer cut in. "Hold it. Let's do that again but without the intro."

Cory counted it off. It felt awkward without the eight-bar intro, but Cory settled in, disappearing into the music. As he started the chorus, the audio engineer broke in. "That's enough."

Singing, Cory turned toward the window. The engineer was waving his arms.

"Let's run it again, but they want to change it up."

Pulling his headphones off, Cory said, "What's the matter?"

The producer said, "Not that it's bad, but it's just not there. I want to try something, all right?"

"Sure."

"In this take, I'd like you to be more soulful. You gotta communicate the emotions of the tune on a gut level. You have some nice lyrics, but you have to connect more. You get what I'm saying?"

"I guess."

"This tune doesn't have a hook, you know. Not that it's bad. I kinda like it. I just don't know how big an audience will get what you're doing. If we add more feeling, it could be the magic we're looking for."

"Okay." Cory put on the headphones. Closing his eyes, he began singing.

"Hold up. That's not it."

"But—"

"You got anything else you wanna run? Something pop oriented?"

"Yeah, 'Empty Pool.' The third one on the list, it's super hooky."

"All right, everybody. Let's run it. We're going use a click track for this."

Cory cracked his knuckles. He really liked this tune and wanted to play it first but felt everyone needed to warm up and find a groove before running it. Having stopped after eight bars of the first song, they were neither warmed up nor in a groove.

The red light came on and a click track counted down, cueing everyone in. Cory had written the song to fit the register of his voice and was into the chorus when the engineer cut in.

"They feel it's not working."

Cory said, "We didn't even get to the bridge yet."

The producer said, "We need to grab the listener right off the bat."

"It's got a build to it."

"Let's run it again. But this time, add a run toward 'and she goes' and hold the last note in bar four."

"Like this?" Cory added a string of notes before the phrase.

"Yes. But give it some zing. All right?"

"You got it."

"And put the guitar down. I want you focusing on the vocals."

Cory rarely sang without playing. He'd played many sessions without singing but never the reverse. "But I don't feel comfortable that way."

"Getting out of your comfort zone is where things happen, man."

Cory leaned the guitar against the wall and cleared his throat. He flashed a thumbs-up. As the click track counted down, Cory's heart rate went up. He muffed the opening line, and a second later the engineer broke in.

"That's a wrap for the day."

"Can't we do one more take?"

The producer said, "The muse ain't showing up today."

"But—"

Robin Day stepped into the room. "Let's give it a rest. When it's not happening, it's better not to push it. Call the office next week, we'll see if we can have another go at it."

The heat rushed to Cory's face. They hadn't given him a chance, cutting the session to less than an hour. As a sideman, he'd been on sessions lasting eight hours. The record company never spared a dollar pushing the artists in their stable.

Packing his guitar up, Cory wanted to hide. He knew they

weren't interested in him. He didn't have what they or anybody else wanted. He thought of his father as Donny sidled up to him. "Hey man, don't get down."

"They rushed the whole thing. It made me tense."

"It's impossible to make music when you're nervous."

"I don't know, man. Maybe my old man was right, I'm never gonna make it."

"Don't say that. It takes time, you know that."

"What did you think of the tunes?"

"I liked them, but we've been on a couple of Sharp Five sessions together. It's not really what they do. Everybody's into the pop stuff. It might be simple, but they sell the shit out of it."

"They sure do."

"You're doing the Gilberto session, aren't you?"

"Yeah, that's at five, in studio B, right?"

"Yep, I'll catch you later."

Cory was about to leave when the drummer, Freddy, said, "Cory, you got a second?"

"Sure man. What's up?"

"I'm not just saying it because I have a favor to ask, but I really liked the material today. I don't know why we couldn't work out whatever the suits were looking for."

"Thanks, man. They don't make it easy."

"I know, it's what I'm worried about."

"What's going on?"

"I'd love to have you on the demo I'm doing, but with the new baby, I just don't have the scratch to pay you. I feel terrible—"

"Don't worry, man. I'm happy to help you out."

"Really?"

"No problem. Text me the where and when."

Cory stopped into a Starbucks. He didn't want to blow

four bucks on a coffee, but he needed to eat up some time. If he showed up too early, his wife would know he had failed. He took a seat in a corner and called Dave. They said his agent was unavailable, but Cory knew Dave was dodging him.

Sipping his coffee, Cory wondered if that had been his last chance. He'd failed again, and though music was a major industry, it was run by a small circle of people. His options were limited.

5

———

BEFORE HE WENT INTO THE GILBERTO SESSION, CORY CALLED his wife.

"Hey, how you doing?"

"Good. How did it go?"

"Pretty good."

"Really? Are they going to sign you?"

"I think so."

"Oh my God. That's amazing. When do you think it will happen?"

"I'm not sure, these things take time."

"What did Dave say about it?"

"I haven't been able to reach him. I think he's flying down to Nashville."

"Oh Cory, I'm so excited. You see? All the years of hard work paid off."

"Don't get carried away. Let's see what happens, okay?"

"All right. Wait till I tell Ava."

"Look, I gotta run. We're getting ready. I'll see you tonight."

Cory shut his phone off and went into Studio B. The only

person in the room was Mike Sosa. Cory had played with the tasteful drummer a dozen times.

"Hey, man, how's it going?"

Sosa was adjusting the drum kit. "Yo, Cory, good to see you're on this."

"You ain't kidding. I can use the cash."

"I gotta say, that session we did over at Threshold was a good time. You played your ass off. I loved what you were doing."

"Me? The polyrhythms you were laying down were amazing. I was struggling to find the downbeat of one."

He smiled. "I never worry about you. Your time is impeccable."

"Thanks, man. I appreciate it."

"You get a record deal yet?"

"I wish. It's not for lack of trying."

"That's crazy, man, you're better than ninety-five percent of the cats out there."

"Not according to the A&R guys."

"You know, you should go see the guys over at Sharp Five. You'd be a good fit for them."

"They didn't think so."

"You went to them already?"

"Auditioned with them earlier. They cut me off before I had a chance to show them anything."

"The suits can't see the end of their own damn nose. I'm sorry, man."

"It's all right. I'm not giving up yet."

"That's the spirit, man. Keep writing, something will click."

"I know. I got a bunch of new tunes I'm working on. Stretching out a bit on them. They're more mainstream."

"Good luck with it, man."

Besides Gilberto, Donny Blake was the last one to come into the studio. He spotted Cory and said, "You again? Am I having déjà vu, or did I just play on your audition down the hall?"

Cory stiffened at the mention of the earlier session. "Hey, when is our fearless leader gonna get here?"

"He's here somewhere. I saw his limo downstairs."

"Limo? Must be nice."

"He needs one; he's barely old enough to drive."

A couple of people filed into the sound booth and the door to the studio swung open. A woman came in and handed out sheet music. "We laid out a spread in the hallway. If anyone wants to get something before we start, now is the time."

Cory was hungry but never ate before playing. No one took her up on the offer, and she left. Cory looked over the sheet music. It was simple. It also wasn't handwritten like his compositions. He wondered what software they were using when Gilberto, outfitted in an aqua blue jumpsuit, stepped in.

"Hey, everybody. So exciting to see all of you." He bowed. "I'm really pumped about this new album. I think it's something special. Everybody ready to roll?"

A sea of heads nodded.

"Okay, then. Let's see what we can make of this. Keep in mind, the vibe for this project is chilled." Walking to the piano, he continued, "I want everyone relaxed. Let's have some fun with it. Okay?"

Gilberto swung his legs over the piano bench and tinkled the keys. "Everybody, pull up 'Momento.' Donny, remember the bass line you cooked up?"

Donny played a funky line. It was uncomplicated and repetitive, but Cory knew it was infectious.

Gilberto said, "Man, that's it, sounds good. Keep it

going." He signaled the booth and said, "All right, everybody, we're going to launch straight into it. One, two, ah, one, two."

———

CORY OPENED his neighbor's mailbox and grabbed the mail. He unlocked Mrs. Ponte's door, setting the mail on the counter. The old lady was sleeping in a recliner. He shut the TV off and left.

Climbing the stairs to his apartment, Cory thought about the session. It wasn't difficult, and he'd made an extra hundred bucks. He slipped inside. It was after nine and Ava was sleeping. Linda was on the couch. He put his guitar away and sat next to her.

"I got to tell you something, but how'd the recording go?"

"It was easy. All bubble gum stuff. I can't understand how big this Gilberto guy is. He's playing to stadiums now."

"I like his music."

"You do? It's super repetitive."

"I know, but it's fun. He's getting very popular. He was on that singing show as a judge the other night."

"He's just not that good. He can barely play the piano."

"Maybe, but I'm sure he's making a lot of money. Did you get paid?"

"Yeah, they gave everybody an extra hundred." Taking the check out, he thought it should have been more.

Linda took it. "We could use a few more of these."

He took her hand. "It's going to be okay. Where's your wedding band?"

"The silicone started to shred."

"They're supposed to last forever."

"Maybe we can send it back and get a new one."

"I'm sorry. You deserve a real one. I just didn't think things would go like they did."

"It's okay. I don't care about things like that. I just want a better life for our family. The only thing that bothers me is Ava's going to be six, and she's sleeping in our room. We can't keep living like this."

"I know. Don't worry. I got something going. I really feel it's going to work out this time."

"I hope so, but promise me if it doesn't that you'll get a steady job, one with benefits. We don't need much, just a three-bedroom place."

"Three bedrooms?"

Linda smiled. "Yep, I'm pregnant."

6

Cory bolted upright.

Linda whispered, "What's the matter?"

"Bad dream."

"What was it about?"

"Nothing."

"Tell me." She reached out. "You're sopping wet."

"I'm all right." He swung his legs off the bed. "Go back to sleep."

Cory snuck a look at Ava and straightened her blanket. He threaded his way to the bathroom thinking over the dream—the scary possibility that Linda would have triplets or twins. It ran in her family.

Cory washed up and went to the galley kitchen. He turned his phone on and grabbed a glass of water. Plugging a question on multiple births into the search bar, he held his breath.

"Shit."

The answer was an ultrasound at ten to twelve weeks would show whether a pregnancy involved multiple births. Linda was just eight weeks pregnant.

He weaved his way back to bed but stared at the ceiling.

As an only child, he wanted another kid, someone Ava could pal around with. But the timing wasn't right. They'd have to move. Maybe they could last a year after the baby came, but no longer than that. And if they had twins, forget about the cost of a larger apartment; he wouldn't be able to afford the baby formula.

Linda would push him to get a regular job, and Cory understood where she was coming from. The thing that scared him more than the money was giving up the music. With a full-time job and responsibilities of fatherhood, there was no way he'd be able to keep gigging.

Cory realized he had six, maybe seven months to do something before it was too late. Every day counted. He came up with a plan and would get started in the morning.

CORY WALKED AVA TO SCHOOL. "Daddy, look at that squirrel." She pointed as it scampered up a tree.

"He's fast."

"How does he do that?"

"They have tiny claws that dig into the bark of the tree."

"Does it hurt the tree?"

"Nah. Trees don't feel anything. You have the food for Miss Cybill?"

"Yep, she's going to like it today. I put an Oreo in with an apple and sandwich."

"Super nice. Come on."

Cory held her hand and they crossed the street to a small park.

"Dad, she's still sleeping."

"It's okay. Just put it on the bench."

Ava walked over and placed the bag of food by the homeless woman's feet.

"Perfect spot." He took her hand and they walked away. "What're you doing in school today?"

"Miss Murphy is going to teach us about the moon and stars."

"Super. I wish I could learn that."

"You can come."

"I can't. I have a lot of work to do."

"Are you making more songs?"

"Yep. I'm working on a record."

"When are you gonna be on TV?"

Even though the approval he'd gotten performing as a kid fueled him to pursue music as a career, Cory said, "Being on TV is nice, but there are a lot more important things in life."

"Like what?"

She sounded like him as a kid. "Being the best father I can be for you."

"You're the best, Daddy."

Cory kissed her. "And so are you. There's your friend Maria. I'll see you later."

He watched her walk into school and hustled home.

Cory took out the tunes he'd stolen and got to work. He was lost in splicing parts of the tunes into ones he'd written when the doorbell rang. He looked at the clock. Three hours had gone by. He stuffed the pilfered copies into a drawer and answered the door.

"Hey Donny, thanks for coming over."

"No problem, brother. Where you want me to set up?"

Cory scooped up a couple of toys in the main room. "Right here. It's a little tight."

"Compared to some of the places we've played, this is a Las Vegas stage."

"Remember that gig at the Corner Bar on Seventy-Second?"

"Oh God, Frankie had to play with just a snare."

"Yeah, it was a frigging closet. I was sitting on my amp."

"The good old days."

"Hey, got some news for you. Linda's pregnant."

"Wow, congrats. When is she due?"

"Not for like seven months. We'll have to move, so I'm really hoping I can get some kind of deal."

"It'll work out."

"While you're setting up, I'm going to check on my neighbor. She's not feeling well."

"You're a good dude."

When Cory came back, Donny said, "How is she?"

"Fine. You ready?"

"Yep. You said you had new material?"

Cory took out the altered music and they played through the first one. Cory said, "What do you think?"

"I don't know. It's a little Frankensteiny. The bridge doesn't fit. The melody doesn't jive with the rest of it."

"I see what you mean. I'll work on that. Maybe I'll send an audio file to you. Let's run the next one."

After playing the second one, Cory said, "Is that better?"

"The first sixteen are catchy. Now that I think of it, how about this bass line?"

Donny played a reggae type rhythm. Cory said, "Interesting. It could work. You want to try it?"

"It feels like the chord progression in the chorus needs a better transition. It doesn't flow, you know. It's good, but it needs to be better."

They reworked the midsection of the tune, but neither of them was happy with it. Donny said, "You know, it might be better to let it sit. Come back to it in a day or so."

"You're right. Let's try this one."

"Oh, what a cool name: 'Tree on the Moon.' Where'd you get that from?"

Cory didn't want to tell him from a children's story he had read to Ava. "I don't know, it's about something surviving in the worst conditions, and I just thought of the moon."

"I like it."

The title was the only thing Donny seemed to approve of. Cory had played with the chords, and Donny picked up on the dissonance. Cory knew he'd rushed rewriting the tunes, and it showed.

"I'm sorry I wasted your time, man."

"It's not wasted. We ran the tunes, and there's some stuff to work out. It's all good, man. It'll come together."

"I hope so."

"It will. I'm feeling like you're straddling something, you know? Your normal stuff is like in there, but there's this other side to you that's emerging. I always love your stuff, but this new stuff, if I was you, I'd run with it."

"Really?"

"No doubt, brother. It's a winning style."

7

———————

Tired, Cory made a cup of coffee and called the agent for Sharp Five Records again. As the days passed without a callback, the chance there was interest signing him faded, and the question about what to do with the stolen music grew in importance.

Cory gave up trying to rework the music. Donny was right; it didn't feel natural. He had what he thought was a golden ticket but hesitated using it. Cory sat in front of his laptop, wishing he had someone to talk it over with.

He reached into his drawer and pulled out the file with the tunes he'd copied. He flipped through them wondering whether it was wrong to take the songs if the creator was dead. Jay Bird had made a point of telling everyone he'd been abandoned as an infant and had no family.

Cory typed a question into Google: 'If someone dies without a will and has no family, who gets their assets?' He read through the results, clicking on one from New York State. It said that if there were no known heirs, the money would go to the state.

He wasn't sure how much money Jay Bird had left

behind, but wasn't it crazy to add to it? New York would waste the money like they always did. Cory would at least make sure some good came of it, provided they became hits.

There was no assurance the songs were any good. How many times had he been at a session where all the 'in the know' people believed they were recording a number one hit? At least half the time they were wrong.

Jay Bird had been good to him. It wasn't that they were friends, but the star respected Cory. Using his material felt like a violation of the regard the dead man had for him.

But Cory would bring life to the songs Jay Bird had penned. Isn't that what artists wanted, to have their creations enjoyed by people? He couldn't see a way to give any credit to Jay Bird without arousing suspicion. Plus, it would diminish the career boost he hoped for.

Cory thought about creating a foundation for kids who were sick, funding it with a portion of the proceeds, if it was successful. He liked the idea. Between paying to help his mother-in-law and a foundation, was it really bad if the money was used for good?

———

CORY STOLE a look at Ava and slipped into bed.

"She's something else."

"Ava's our angel." Linda took his hand and placed it on her abdomen. "I think I can feel the baby."

"It's too early, isn't it?"

"I read some women, in their second pregnancy, can feel the baby around nine weeks."

Cory pulled his hand back. "You think it's twins?"

"I don't think so. That would be crazy. Wouldn't it?"

"You got that right. You're going to the doctor's tomorrow, right?"

"Yes. But insurance won't cover an ultrasound yet. It's too early."

"These coverage rules are frustrating."

"Tell me about it. My mother's going to go into hock if she ever needs a kidney transplant."

"Don't get yourself worked up. It'll hurt the baby."

"You're right. I wish you could come tomorrow."

"Me too, but I got the Robinson Brothers session tomorrow."

"That's in New Jersey, right?"

"Yeah, at Van Gelder Studios."

"Your friend Eddie still working there?"

"Yeah, he's been there from day one, helped make some great jazz records. It's a pain in the ass getting there, but they're paying for an Uber, so me and Donny are going together."

"That's good."

"I read something today that got me thinking. Say somebody robbed a bank, but instead of keeping the money, they gave it to, say, a hospital to help people with cancer. Would that be wrong?"

"Of course, you can't just go around stealing, no matter who it benefits."

"Because the money belongs to someone else?"

"You can't take from one person and give to another. It's not right."

"Say nobody owned it."

"That's ridiculous, it belongs to somebody."

"Well, how about someone dies but they have no family. None at all. And they have a hundred thousand in cash at the bank. Somebody at the bank knows there aren't any heirs, and he sends the money to a homeless shelter. Did he do anything wrong?"

"I don't know where you get these ideas from."

"I saw something like that on the internet. I think it was in Minnesota or something. What do you think? Would that be wrong?"

"I guess not."

"That's what I thought too."

Cory couldn't sleep. It wasn't from worrying but planning. He went over the personnel playing tomorrow. He was sure his friend would let him use a studio to cut a demo. Donny said he was good with playing on it. He could use a drum machine if the drummer gave him a hard time, and if Tony wouldn't play piano, Cory would cover the chords with his guitar.

It was for a demo, not prime time. Cory only needed to communicate a sense of what the tunes were.

STUCK in traffic crossing the George Washington Bridge, Cory was quiet. Donny said, "You all right?"

"Yeah, fine. Just thinking about how Linda's doctor visit went."

"I'm sure it went okay."

"I know."

"Did Chase ask you to record anything?"

"Yeah, I'm gonna lay down solos on two tracks."

"You're doing it?"

"Sure. He's a good guy and needs the help."

"But he isn't paying."

"I know. It's all right. You're not playing on it?"

"My old man told me a long time ago not to play for free. Said it degraded the work we put in."

"He's right, but I can't say no."

"Mr. Goody Two-Shoes."

"What did you think of the stuff I sent over?"

"I gotta say, the tunes for the demo were good, really good."

"You think they'll work?"

"For sure, they're perfect for pop radio. You really surprised me; I didn't see the commercial stuff coming from you."

"I've been working on it for eons."

"You never said anything."

"It felt like a sellout, you know?"

"No, it isn't. I'd like to hear more. Didn't you say you wanted to lay down seven tracks?"

Cory didn't have an answer and shrugged.

"You should've taken advantage. There isn't another studio where they'll let you do it for free."

"I wanted to get home, you know, with Linda's appointment and all."

Donny's phone rang, and as he answered it, Cory fingered the demo thumb drive in his pocket.

8

AVA RAN TO THE DOOR. "DADDY'S HOME!"

"Hey, pumpkin." Cory put his guitar down and picked her up. "How was school today?"

"I made you a picture. Let me show you."

He put her down. "Mom! Where's the picture I made for Daddy?"

Linda came in. "Here you go."

"Wow! This is nice. I like the sun; I can feel the heat. Let me guess—who's this girl over here with the dog?"

"That's me, silly. Can't you tell?"

"It looks exactly like you."

"When can we get a puppy?"

"I really want one, but with the new baby coming, we may have to wait. Let's see what happens."

"Aww.

"Don't worry. Why don't you put the picture on the fridge? That way, I can see it all the time."

"Yay."

Ava ran off and Cory said, "How'd it go at the doctor's?"

"Good, said I have to be careful about getting diabetes."

"You didn't get it last time."

"That was almost seven years ago."

"Oh, she say anything about twins or anything?"

"She put the odds at fifty-fifty."

"Fifty-fifty? That's—"

"Don't worry, we'll figure it out if we have twins."

"COME ON, monkey. It's time for bed."

"Can Daddy read to me?"

"Sure. What book do you want? *Green Eggs and Ham?*"

"No, the one about the koala bear."

"*The Koala Who Could.* That's one of my favorites. Let's go."

Reading aloud, Cory wondered if the book about taking risks was the universe's way of sending him a message.

Cory tucked her into bed, kissing her good night. Linda was on the phone with her mother. Cory opened his laptop and pecked out an email to his agent:

Hi Dave,

Tried calling you a couple of times. I know Sharp Five isn't interested, but I wanted to let you know that I've gone in a new direction musically.

I got the message about the pop-oriented stuff everyone seems to want and wrote some songs that are perfect for radio play.

I'd really love to talk this over and have you listen to them all. Everyone who listened really dug them. I've attached one to give you an idea of what they're like. Give it a listen.

Let me know, Cory.

He inserted the USB drive and transferred "Tablet Blues," a song he considered the strongest of the bunch. Cory's finger hovered over the send button. It was wrong to do this, he thought. But how wrong? He knew it wasn't ethical, but he'd paid his dues, and it wasn't like he was taking from someone else. There was no loser, was there?

Linda put a hand on his shoulder. "What are you doing?"

"Just some email." Cory hit send and closed the laptop. "How's your mom?"

"WELL DONE, Miguel. You really nailed last week's lesson. This week, I want you to work on pentatonic scales. Start with C and go around the circle of fourths. You don't have to learn them all in one week."

"Okay. That's it?"

"If you have extra time, practice the strumming patterns on page twenty."

The student's mother said, "Say thank you, Miguel."

"Thank you, Mr. Lupinski."

"No problem, pal. I'll see you next week."

As the kid thumbed through the exercise book, Cory headed to the door, saying to the mother, "Miguel is like a sponge. I wish I could learn that quick."

"He really likes to play. I'm so grateful you're teaching him."

"No problem."

"I wish we could pay you, but—"

"Don't worry, it's fun for me."

Back in the apartment after giving guitar lessons, Cory's cell rang.

"Hey, Cory, it's Dave."

"Hi."

"Hey, I'm sorry I've been tied up. Things have been crazy busy here."

Dave lied so easily, it eased Cory's concern. "I understand. So, how are you doing?"

"I got your email, and I gotta say, the track blew me away. I mean, I knew you had it in you, but, you know, you really changed things up."

"And you thought I wasn't listening."

"Glad I could help. You said you had a couple more tunes."

"Yeah, I've been writing every chance I get."

"Are they like the one you sent?"

"Definitely. I kept them in the pop genre."

"Well, you got my attention. If they're as good as this one, we got something to work with. If not, it'll be tough to convince the label to put up any advance money into a recording. They'd push for a straight royalty deal."

"No worries. The others are all in the same style."

"Sounds good. How do you want to handle it? You want to come down? We haven't seen each other in a while. It'd be good to spend some time together. How about you get here around noon, we'll have a listen, and then I'll take you for some lunch?"

Dave had never even bought a hot dog for Cory. "I don't have the time today. Maybe I'll send them over later."

"Oh, when are you going to send it?"

"I don't know."

"I'm going to be going out later, have a bunch of appointments, and I'm not in tomorrow at all. Maybe not even the next day. I'm extremely busy, and I'd like to hear what you have before things get crazy again."

Cory wondered if Dave was aware of how transparent he was being. He wanted to call out his phoniness, but he realized he wasn't any better. "I'll get them to you right away. Check your email in five."

After he sent the files, Cory paced the apartment. If Dave didn't like the tunes, what were his options? Jay Bird's former label was the natural, but Cory didn't want to take any chances.

There were three other companies he thought about, but what if everyone passed? He flopped onto the couch. He couldn't bear the thought of shelving his dreams for a nine-to-five gig.

9
———

Though Cory had taken the RR train into Manhattan, he felt like he was floating. When a lady saw the wide smile on Cory's face as he stepped into the elevator, she slipped out. He tried to remember what Dave said on the phone. Was it—*We got to lay this down and get it out there. I think it'll go platinum?*

Dave was at the elevator to meet him and slapped him on the back. "How are you doing, buddy?"

"Good." A wall of gold and platinum records led to a glass conference room overlooking Central Park. "Place looks different."

"Really? Last time we redecorated was about three years ago. Let's go to my office."

Dave slid behind his desk and Cory settled into a chair that had a view of the building next door.

"This is a new office, no?"

"Yeah, when they built the conference room, I had to move, lost my view of the park. But it doesn't matter. I'm hardly here anyway."

Cory knew the downgrade meant his stable of artists

wasn't producing. "That's a nice shot." He pointed to an overhead shot of a band on a stage in Central Park.

"It's pretty cool, isn't it? Let's try and get a picture of you like that out there."

"Be nice."

"Oh, I forgot to tell you, Iggy is going to produce yours."

Cory's heart beat faster. "Good. Like I said on the phone, I want certain players in the studio when we cut the album."

"I know. I already reached out; everybody is on board."

"Good. What about having everybody sign nondisclosure agreements?"

"NDAs? Why? Didn't you file copyrights?"

"Did it this morning."

"Then you don't have anything to worry about."

"It's going to take some time to get the music out, and I don't want anyone talking."

"Today we can get it to market as fast as we want. We just need to get the marketing lined up to get it to soar."

"I get it, but I'd feel more comfortable if everyone signed."

"If that's what you want, I'll get it organized."

"Good. You sure your guys are going to want to put it out?"

Dave leaned forward. "I'm sure they will, but if they pass, I'll take it to Semi-Tone. They got a huge hole to fill with Jay Bird gone."

"No, not them."

"Why not? They're a perfect fit."

"I don't like those guys. They're too arrogant."

"Believe me, they're going to have to get real after losing Jay Bird."

"I don't care, anybody but them."

"We'll worry about that if and when we have to. Just leave it to me."

"Okay."

"Everybody is available tomorrow, which is no small feat. I blocked out a couple of hours at Mirrortone Studios for tomorrow."

"No, I don't want to record there."

"Oh, come on, man, you know it's the best one in the city."

"I gotta have the right vibe to do this, and after what happened there . . ."

"I see. Let me check with Platinum. See if we can get Studio K."

"Good, I love the sound of the Yamaha grand they got there."

———

CORY POPPED a Rolaids in his mouth before pushing through the door. Dave and Iggy were huddled with the sound engineer. Cory ran his hand over the scores of buttons on the control board. He'd played a bunch of sessions in the studio, but it was the first time he saw it through the control room's window.

His eyes bounced around the wood-floored room. Donny was setting up, and Paulie was tightening a cymbal. He caught a glimpse of Joanne's inner thighs as she swung her legs onto the piano bench. With her looks, Cory thought, if she could sing, she'd be bigger than Diana Krall and Eliane Elias combined.

He counted the horn players; they were all there.

Gerry Riley walk into the studio and Cory said, "What's he doing here?"

"Vince couldn't make it. He flew out to Chicago to meet up with the Pinkletons. Their rhythm guy got into a bad accident."

"But I wanted Vinny."

"Gerry's a monster. You know that. He played on all the Jay Bird stuff."

"Isn't there anybody else?"

The producer said, "Gerry is right for this. And we don't have time. Come on, let's get something down."

Wishing he had the power to throw a hissy fit, Cory said, "All right."

THE SOUND ENGINEER'S voice came over the speaker. "Okay, that's a wrap."

Cory looked at the clock. Nearly four hours had gone by recording seven songs. Cory had stolen eight but held one back. If this album did well, he wanted to have a tune to use in a second project.

Grinning, Donny stuck his fist out. "Well done, my man."

Cory bumped it. "You think so?"

"You kidding? I can see your fan club already. A sea of teenagers in braces."

"Very funny."

"Seriously, man, it sounded good. Real good."

Gerry Riley walked over. "Yeah, he's right, thanks for having me on it."

"Glad you made it. You sounded good, supporting everything."

"Thanks. You know, I gotta say a couple of the tunes, especially the first two, reminded me of Jay Bird."

"Really?"

"Definitely. I was with him a couple of weeks ago, and man, what he was working on was just like what we recorded."

"Yeah, well, I started writing some for him, and since he's no longer around, God rest his soul, I decided to use it myself."

"But Jay Bird never played anything he didn't pen."

"I'm just telling you we worked together."

"That's strange, man. I'd been with him from the jump, and he never collaborated. And he could've worked with anybody. People sent him tunes like crazy, but he wouldn't even look at them. I know for a fact a bunch of them charted, but he didn't care. He needed complete control."

"Sounds like a good position to be in. Look, I've got some stuff to do in the booth. I'll see you around."

"I'll be around. You can count on it; it's not going to be easy to get rid of me." Riley's laugh sent a chill up Cory's spine.

10

Dave was talking nonstop, and the sidewalk was packed with people in motion. Cory couldn't concentrate and caught about half of what his agent was saying. A car pulled up to the curb and Cory said, "It's my ride. I'll see you later."

Dave said, "Okay. Again, that was great, man. I'll call you after I talk to the marketing gurus."

Cory climbed into the Uber. Before the driver pulled away from the curb, his mind cranked up. Did Gerry Riley know he'd stolen the tunes from Jay Bird? What was it he said? He was with Jay Bird when he was working the song out?

Riley said Jay liked to work alone. So, he probably didn't contribute to the song. Did he see it or hear it? Would Jay have shown him, or would he have somehow seen it when Jay wasn't around? Riley had great ears. If he'd heard it, he'd remember some of it.

Cory wondered if Riley had said anything or would say something. Some songs, especially those with similar rhythms, chords, or bass lines could feel like another tune.

But Riley was an accomplished musician; he'd know the differences. Was he signaling he knew?

If he had a strong suspicion, what could he do about it? It was his word against mine, Cory thought. He had no proof, and Jay Bird was dead.

Cory leaned his head against the seat. It was all going to be good. It was probably just a coincidence. He closed his eyes and pictured himself performing at Madison Square Garden. He was on his way. The only thing that could possibly be better would be if his father could see he'd been wrong and that he was making it.

Wondering what his father would say, he remembered what Riley said when they parted: that he'd be around and it wouldn't be easy to get rid of him.

What the hell did that mean?

"Daddy! Can we hear your song on the radio?"

"I hope so. But we'll have to wait a little while."

"Why? When you do it yourself, we can hear it right away."

"It's just a different way of doing it. They want to make sure it's the best it can be. They play around with it."

"What do you mean?"

"Well, even though everybody is playing together, they record each instrument and my voice separately. Then, during playback, if the guitar is too loud or my voice too low, they can fix it in the mixing process. Sometimes they add violins or want to record a part over. That way just one player has to go into the studio, not the entire band."

"When can I tell my friends it's on the radio?"

"How about I ask them tomorrow?"

"Okay."

Linda said, "Ava made brownies to celebrate."

"Super. I'd really like one now. Can you get a brownie for me?"

"Mommy, can I have one too?"

"Yes, you can. Get the paper plates and napkins."

Ava took off. Linda said, "How did it go?"

"Really good. I think this is it."

"Oh, I really hope so. You've been working so hard for this."

"You can't believe how everyone changed. It's like I feel all of a sudden they respect me; they're listening to me. It's weird, even the players are different, and I've worked with them all before."

"I get the record guys, they're in it for the money. They follow the trends, but you always said that the musicians were supportive of you, always gave you compliments."

"I know, but something is different. I can't explain it. Even Donny wasn't himself."

"Come on, you guys grew up together."

"I know, it's nothing big, just a feeling."

"Maybe it's in your head. Now that you feel like you created something that's going to be popular, you're seeing it differently."

"Some of it, sure, but you see how quick they arranged the session? And they got Iggy to produce it? That guy is behind a ton of megahits. I feel like I'm in a dream or something."

"It's real, and you deserve it."

"I played in a lot of dumps."

"Yeah, and what about practicing eight hours a day. You've paid your dues."

"That's for sure. Finally, things are going to change. Look

at this place. We're all sleeping in the same bedroom. I got nowhere to play. It's terrible. I—"

She grabbed his hand and kissed it. "It's not that bad. We made it our home. I don't regret it for a minute."

"You're right."

"Come on, let's celebrate."

"You know what? I'm so wired, I could use a drink. It's a good time to take out that fancy scotch my father used to drink."

The family had a little party and watched *Finding Nemo* together. When the film ended, Cory put Ava to bed and they talked about the meaning of the movie

Cory walked into the kitchen and picked up the bottle of Chivas Regal.

Linda said, "You're having another one?"

"Why not?"

"Because you were slurring your words reading to Ava."

"It was a big day for me. Just a teeny bit more."

"Don't overdo it."

He sat down next to her and asked, "Do you think a lot of songs sound alike?"

"What do you mean?"

"When you hear certain tunes, does it make you think, that sounds like XYZ?"

"Sometimes when it first plays."

"Some introductions and chords can be similar."

"A lot of times, I say to myself this one is the type of song so and so would make."

"Yeah, that's what I think it is, the style of the song."

"Probably, but what about that lawsuit against Ed Sheeran? It's for, like, a hundred million dollars. They say he copied from Marvin Gaye."

Cory froze.

"Cory?"

"Oh, sorry. I was trying to remember the tune's name."

"'Thinking Out Loud.' Sheeran won a Grammy for it."

"Yeah, that's it. I think I had too much to drink. Let's go to bed."

Cory had never considered the possibility of a lawsuit. The only risk he weighed was the embarrassment of being labeled a thief and forced to give up playing. The fallout from being found out wouldn't be limited to his career; the damage to his personal reputation would be life-changing. How would he ever explain it to Ava and Linda?

11

———————

Dave led Cory into the conference room. Cory wanted to look at the view of Central Park, but the people sitting on the window side of the table stood, blocking most of the greenery.

As the introductions were made, he didn't realize the marketing and promotion department was so large. A reed-thin woman in a black jumpsuit shook his hand. Her perfume was too sweet.

"Marcy Anderson, director of talent branding. Good to be working with you."

"Thanks."

Marcy said, "Okay everyone. Let's get started. We have a lot of work to do and, as usual, a short time frame to do it. Sebastian will give us a quick demographic overview of Mr. Lupinski's audience."

"The pop genre, at fifty-six percent, has the largest audience. We believe Mr. Lupinski's core listeners will be female weighted, and they will tend to be on the younger side, ranging from thirteen to twenty. The majority will be from the suburbs, from families above the median income level. Naturally, there'll be people who cross over, but other than soccer moms, we don't believe it will amount to a significant segment."

Marcy said, "Thank you. We know what to do with this. No disrespect, Cory, but Lupinski isn't going to cut it. We need a stage name."

"Sure, whatever you think would help."

"I need suggestions."

A flurry of names were bandied about and shot down. A woman with the brightest lipstick Cory had ever even seen said, "Why not keep it simple. Just CL."

Marcy said, "CL. I like it, but it reminds me of CeeLo. It wouldn't be clear enough as a brand."

"Good point."

A man in a black T-shirt said, "What about Cory Loop? It's snappy and fun."

Marcy said, "I really like that. How about you, Cory?"

He couldn't believe they were talking about him as if he weren't in the room. "It sounds good."

"I agree. It stays connected to your family name and it's fresh, hip, you know? I can see the kids grabbing on to it. I think we'll go with it. Todd, run a check for any conflicts or negative connotations in the foreign markets, to be sure."

"Will do."

"I want everybody thinking of a title for the album. We don't have much time."

"Why not title it with his stage name? Cory Loop."

"That's a tired and, frankly, lazy idea. Think it over. Meanwhile, Cory needs a look. He's more mature than some of the others in the genre, so we'll need to create a timeless look. Bryan, you have any ideas?"

"I'd lean toward using colors in the wardrobe. Maybe

neon colors under a dark jacket. It's energetic and no one's doing it."

"I like that."

"I'm looking at the artist, and I think wearing a hip pork pie hat would be cool. It could be a signature kind of thing."

"Hm. Try it."

"He's got the perfect chin and mouth to carry a soul patch."

"I like that combo."

"What about hair? Any coloring? Streaking? What kind of cut?"

"I'd keep it a bit long if we're going with a hat. We don't want to hint he's wearing a hat because he's going bald."

Cory put a hand to his head.

"Good point. Todd, we're going to talk about marketing now. Why don't you take Cory down to the stylists?"

CORY CURSED the city's ever-present traffic as the cab crawled along Sixty-Eighth Street. He told the driver, "I can walk faster, let me off here."

Cory paid the fare and jogged three blocks to Weill Cornell Medical Center.

Linda did a double take when she saw Cory. "What are you wearing?"

He pecked her cheek. "How's she doing?"

"Better, she's on dialysis, and they gave her some diuretics for the swelling. It's helping. She's breathing much better."

"That's good."

"I'm so glad you're here. She'll be happy to see you."

"What happened?"

"When I called her, I knew something was wrong. She was so confused, I had to go over. As soon as I saw her I called 911. Her legs were swollen worse than I've ever seen and she had trouble breathing."

"She'll be okay."

"She's depressed. The doctor said if she doesn't take care of herself, she'll need a transplant."

"We'll get her help, someone to live with her to make sure she takes her meds and does what she needs to."

"She doesn't have the money for that."

"Don't worry, we'll help her. Just get it going."

Linda hugged Cory. "Thanks, but we can't afford that."

"The way the record label is acting, we won't have money problems anymore."

"Did they dress you like that?"

He stepped back. "Why? You don't like it?"

She shrugged. "I can see your ankles."

"They took ten years off me." He tugged at the lime green shirt under his black, lapelless jacket.

"Not exactly, Mr. Big Shot."

"It's like a makeover place. They want to give me a new haircut and get porcelain veneers."

"They're paying for it?"

"Yeah."

"I'd love to get veneers one day."

"Whenever you want, I'll get them for you. Come on, I want to see your mom."

"Tell her about what went on today. She always gets a kick out of your stories."

12

———

Two Months Later

Cory hung up the phone and ran up the stairs to his apartment. He pulled one earbud out and flung open the door. "Linda! Put on Z100."

She poked her head out of the kitchen. "What?"

"Dave just called. He said 'Tablet Blues' is going to get airtime today. I got KTU on. Put Z100 on your phone."

She fiddled with her iPhone and music played. "What are you wearing?"

"Oh." He took off the pork pie hat. "The stylist said it would make me look hip."

"Not just that, the jacket. What is it, lamé?"

"I got no idea. You don't like it?"

"It's flashy. And what's under your lip?"

He ripped off a patch of hair. "It's a fake soul patch. They want me to grow one. They want a certain image, you know, for the tour and all."

"Image? More like a complete makeover."

"I know. They got me going to another hairstylist tomorrow."

She shook her head. "I hope Ava will recognize you."

"It's not that bad. I think it looks pretty good."

She put a hand on her belly. "You're getting a new wardrobe, and I can't fit into my clothes anymore. I'm going to need a tent."

Cory wrapped his arms around her. "You know, I always thought you looked sexy when you're pregnant."

"Yeah, sure."

"I'm not kidding. It's kind of a turn-on for me." Cory massaged her neck and worked his hands down to her breasts.

"I'm in the middle of cooking."

Cory pressed his growing manhood into her. "Let's go in the bedroom." Hands on her buns, he followed Linda to the bedroom.

Linda wiggled out of her pants and crawled under the covers. In the middle of taking his pants off, Cory said, "It's on! Listen." He put one bud in Linda's ear.

He pulled his pants up. "I can't believe it! It's really happening. I can't wait for Ava to hear it. Damn! I should've recorded it so she can hear it."

"Where you going?"

"To get your phone. I don't want to miss it when Z100 plays it."

As he walked out of the bedroom, Linda said, "But I thought . . ."

———

Ten days after "Tablet Blues" debuted, Cory's cell rang.

"Hey Dave, how's it going?"

"Guess who's sitting at number five on the Billboard charts?"

"Are you kidding me?"

"Nope. 'Tablet Blues' just climbed to number five. It's the fastest rise I've seen in a long while."

"Man, this is surreal. Hang on a second." He pulled the phone away and said, "Linda! 'Tablet Blues' is number five on the Billboard chart."

"Oh, my God, that's amazing."

"Sorry, had to tell my wife."

"No problem. Look, we got to move fast and ride this wave. We're going to release 'Spring Water' as a single, and a great opportunity just opened up. Freddie got a call from *Good Morning America*. Slade was supposed to perform Wednesday morning in their Bryant Park series, but he checked into rehab and canceled."

"You want me to fill in?"

"Absolutely. The timing is perfect. It's a gift from the music gods."

"Is everybody gonna be available?"

"Trust me, nobody is going to miss this opportunity."

"We'll need to rehearse. We only have two days."

"Relax. You only need to do two songs on air. They'll do a short interview, and then you open up with 'Tablet'—"

"I got to talk? What are they going to ask me?"

"It's all softballs. I'll have Mallory send over a couple of clips. We'll tell them about how quickly you charted, the fastest-since type of stuff. Believe me, they'll use it."

"Okay. So, after that, we'll do 'Tablet Blues.' Then what?"

"They'll go to a commercial break and then do an unrelated piece of news before you come back on. That's where you're gonna do 'Spring Water.' The rest of the show, you can do whatever you'd like from the album."

"Okay. I'm going to call the players."

"Look, I think it's time for you to get a manager. There's

a lot of stuff that's gonna be coming at you, from a lot of different directions. You're going to need help, or you're gonna be overwhelmed."

"I told you I can't afford that."

"Of course, you can. How do you think you charted? The royalties are gonna start rolling in. 'Tablet Blues' had nine hundred sales yesterday and over two thousand downloads."

"How much do I get out of that?"

"Well, the streaming stuff is like, a nickel for every hundred downloads. The sales, you do a lot better, but the money is in the live shows. We're setting up a nice tour for you. You'll be on the road just when the rest of the album gets released."

"How much money will I make touring?"

"If you do, say, twenty shows, with an average of ten thousand people, at a hundred a pop, that's a million a show. So, the gross would be twenty million."

"Twenty million? Dollars?"

"Yeah, but that's the gross, and half goes to the arena so, that's ten million, and there's a lot of other expenses. A manager has a better handle on it."

"That still sounds good."

"It is, but like I said, you're gonna need a manager and an assistant."

"An assistant?"

"Definitely. You need somebody to screen access."

"Wouldn't the manager do that?"

"No, separate roles. Don't worry, I have a great guy, Lew Stein. He's tough, but you tell him what you want and you'll get it. We'll work together to get the best deals for you. Now, for an assistant, Tracy Burnett is perfect. You'll love her. I'll reach out to them and set something up."

"Okay."

"Now, get ready for the show."

Cory hung up. His mind was spinning. Too much to do, too much to think about. A manager, an assistant?

Linda wrapped her arms around him. "I can't believe you made it."

"I'm whirling. So much to do. And I'm going to play on the *Good Morning America* show at Bryant Park."

"Really?"

"Yeah. Wednesday. Slade was supposed to play it, but he went into rehab."

"Oh my God, that's like two days away."

"I know. Look, you gotta keep Ava out of school that day."

"We can come?"

"Uh, I didn't think about that. I was figuring you'd watch it on TV."

She unraveled her arms. "Oh."

"What's the matter?"

"I thought you'd want us there. That's all."

"Of course, I do. I never thought about it. I mean, I just got off the phone."

"Forget it. It'll be one big hassle going to the city."

"You sure? It's a super opportunity to play on national TV."

"It's too bad that it's at someone else's expense."

"What do you mean?"

"Slade going into rehab. That's sad."

"It's not my fault. What am I supposed to do, not do it because somebody screwed up? I gotta worry about me."

"You're doing a good job of that. I got to go to work."

Cory thought over what she had said about it being at somebody else's expense. It wasn't Slade he thought about but Jay Bird. He didn't see how it mattered. Jay Bird was gone, also a victim to drugs. And he left no family that would benefit from his body of work.

He brushed off any concerns about taking advantage, but his wife's behavior puzzled him. Where was she coming from? He discounted jealousy. Maybe it was her having to work. That didn't make sense. His success would enable her to quit and take care of the kids.

Cory's concern faded when he factored in the possibility it was hormonal. It made sense, he thought. He had to prepare for the show. He pulled his cell out to start calling the band, realizing that his rhythm guitar player was still on tour with the Pinkletons.

Riley was a good player, but Cory had concerns he knew something. Was it his paranoia, or did Riley somehow know Cory hadn't written the tunes?

13

THE TV'S GLOW WAS THE ONLY LIGHT IN THE APARTMENT. Cory tiptoed in and plopped on the couch next to Linda. He kissed her cheek, putting his hand on her belly.

"How you feeling?"

"He's been kicking all day. Can't wait till this little guy comes out."

"We're more than halfway there." He put his head to her abdomen and sang, "Calm down, little man. I know you're anxious to see us, and we're super excited to meet you."

"Ooh, did you feel that?"

"He knows it's me."

"What happened today?"

"It was crazy. Before the rehearsal, I met with this manager, Lew Stein. Dave recommended him. Then an assistant, Tracy Burnett. I hired both of them."

"You're not making enough to pay two people. How much is that going to be?"

"Lew gets ten percent—"

"Ten percent? That's way too much."

"He's going to do a lot. You had to see the stack of papers

that had to be dealt with. Every band member needs a contract, and all the places we're hitting on the tour. There's insurance to deal with and transportation and hotels. It's an endless amount of things I have zero interest in doing, if I could even do them."

"But doesn't Dave handle any of that?"

"No, he's dealing with getting the music out there, you know, marketing, and he sets up the concert venues, but the paperwork and all the other arrangements, Lew is going to handle."

"And what's this assistant going to do?"

"Tracy's great. Just like all the personal stuff I got to deal with, the appointments and scheduling, and she's going to protect me."

"Protect you?"

"Everybody keeps saying that people are going to want a piece of me as I get famous, and she's like a gatekeeper. She said she'd be like a chief of staff. She'll deal with the players so I don't have to get in the middle of stuff that would mess up the creative side."

"So, you're going to be famous, huh?"

"You know what I mean. Everybody, even small acts, got someone to do the dirty work. If we're on the road, somebody has to deal with the transportation, food, and laundry kind of things. What time we got to be where, you know, stuff like that."

"I guess so."

"Look, if this goes like it looks like it will, we'll be moving out of here super soon. I'm thinking maybe you should start looking at places now. Get a feel for what will work for us."

"Really?"

"Sure, why not?"

"There's a new place going up in Prospect Park."

Cory frowned. "Let's shoot for something in the city."

"Manhattan? I don't want to take Ava out of her school."

"It'll be easier for me, give me more time to spend with you and the kids. Besides, she's only in kindergarten."

"But we'll get so much more for our money in Brooklyn."

"It's not that big of a difference from what Tracy said."

"You talked about where we should live with Tracy?"

"It was nothing. She asked me a bunch of questions to get a feel for us."

"Well, I don't want you talking about our personal life with her."

"Oh, come on, Linda. You don't even know her. She's just trying to help."

"Tell her to stick to the business side of things."

IN THE PAST, getting rehearsal space and organizing the players was challenging for Cory. This time, Tracy secured the studio and contacted the band members. He needed to remember to tell Linda how easy Tracy made it. Tracy held the door, and Cory walked into Studio J with his guitar.

Cory saw the horn section stood in groups in a far corner of the spacious room. Sax players talking to other sax players, and trumpets huddled together.

Cory put his guitar down. "Hey, Donny."

His friend was tuning his bass. "Hey, man. This is a nice space."

"Yeah, it's pretty cool, ain't it?"

"A long way from Tommy's garage."

"You got that right." Cory pointed to the drum set. "Where's Paulie?"

Donny plucked a note. "Boys' room."

Cory nodded toward the piano. Joanne was sitting on the bench talking to Riley. "Is it me, or is she getting better looking by the hour?"

Donny tightening a string. "No doubt, she's got the goods, man."

Cory overheard Riley saying, "Yeah, and the turnaround in the first ending is something Jay Bird used all the time. It's the same thing with the key change. Jay always set it up like that."

Cory said, "You guys got everything you need?"

Joanne smiled. "I'm good. Just do me a favor and ask the horns to keep it down. I want to be able to hear when I'm forty."

Cory knew that, even among professionals, the issue of volume topped a player's complaint list. "I'll make sure and say something. How about you?"

Riley said, "I got more than I need."

"Okay."

Walking toward the horn players, Cory wondered what Riley meant. And what were the references he made about the musical devices Jay Bird used? Was he trying to convince Joanne the tunes were Bird's?

At the end of the rehearsal, Tracy sidled up to him. "You all right?"

Cory said, "Just a little uptight." He couldn't tell her Riley had distracted him.

"You think you'll be all right tomorrow?"

"We'll pull it together. The crowd will force us to focus."

"You been sleeping?"

"It's been tough. Between the pressure and excitement, I can't get more than an hour or two at a time."

"It's the adrenaline rush. I've seen it a hundred times. No

matter how successful you are, a certain venue or a TV thing or a joint project with a megastar, it gets to everybody."

"It sure does. I hope I get a good one tonight."

"If you want, I can get you something to help you sleep."

Cory knew between the big show and what Riley said, he wouldn't sleep. "That's a good idea. What do you have?"

14

———

Six Months Later

A black Lincoln Navigator pulled up to a glass tower on West Street. A pair of legs led by stilettoed feet emerged. They were owned by a shapely woman in a short dress. Cory, thankful for the break from two months of touring to get back home, came out next. He could see his wife holding their newborn in the lobby.

Cory rushed inside. His son was screaming. "Sorry, the traffic from La Guardia was a nightmare." He kissed Linda's cheek and took the baby. "Hey Tommy, how are you? Don't cry, Daddy's here."

She whispered, "What's she doing here?"

"Hello, Linda. So nice to see you again," Tracy said.

Linda sucked in her belly. "Yes, it is. How have you been?"

"Excellent. You're going to love this place. Oh, here comes Eduardo now. He's the best Realtor in the city."

Little Tommy's face was beet red. Linda said, "Let me take him. I'll get him to settle down."

They met the Realtor and waited for the elevator as Tommy wailed away. Tracy said, "Come here, little one."

Linda said, "No, it's okay. He'll be fine."

Cory said, "Let her take him. Tracy is great with babies."

She took Tommy from Linda, and before the elevator arrived, the baby quieted down.

"You see, what did I tell you?"

The Realtor gave them details of the listing as they rode up. When the doors opened, he said, "You're really going to love this apartment. I'll leave you alone. Feel free to roam about."

A view of the Hudson River filled the floor-to-ceiling windows. Cory felt he could reach out and touch Lady Liberty. It was an apartment the way Grand Central was a train station.

Linda said, "How much is this place?"

"About twenty thousand a month."

"That's ridiculous."

"It's got four bedrooms. Ava can have her own room, and we can set one up as a guest room for your mother. And they all have their own bathrooms."

"It's way too much money."

"Don't worry, we can handle it."

"Are you sure?"

"Yep."

"It is nice."

Tracy walked over with Tommy, who was sleeping. "So, what do you think? It's pretty incredible, isn't it?"

Linda said, "We'll have to talk it over."

Cory said, "Why? I think it works perfectly for us."

"I'm not rushing into anything. We need to think about this."

Tracy said, "Why don't you talk it over. We don't leave

for Frisco for another four days. If you decide you want it, I'll get it done for you."

<hr>

Cory rolled the stroller in front of Lincoln Center. "For Christmas this year, we're going to go to see *The Nutcracker*. You're going to love it."

Ava said, "Yay!"

Linda said, "Don't make promises you can't keep."

"I'll be here. No way I'm going to be doing any shows around Christmas."

"Daddy, can't we come to California with you tomorrow?"

"I'd really like you to, but we're playing a different place every night. There's a lot of moving around. It would be hard on Mommy and Tommy."

"We can get a nanny to help."

Linda said, "A nanny? Where did you get that idea?"

"Patty said all the famous people get nannies to help."

"No stranger is going to bring my children up. That's Daddy's and my job."

Cory said, "We could always get someone to help around the house, so you don't have to do everything. If we take that apartment, it's miles bigger than our old place."

"I don't know how we can afford it while we still have to pay for the old place plus the one we're in now."

"Lew said he made a deal on the old place. Said it wasn't safe for us any longer since they couldn't control the onlookers."

Linda said, "I feel bad for Mr. Romano. He was good to us."

"Me too. Lew said he would give him five thousand to

give him time to rent the place and pay the cost of the Kmart cop he had there."

"Daddy, what's a Kmart cop?"

"A silly way to say a security guard. So, what do you say? Are we getting the apartment?"

"It's really nice."

"You said I'd get my own room. Can we paint it pink?"

"Absolutely. Let me text Tracy and tell her to bring over the lease tonight."

"Yay."

Cory sent the message and said, "Now, let's find a toy store so we can get you something."

"Yay! And a stuffed animal for Tommy."

"And Mommy needs some new clothes."

"Not until I lose the baby weight."

"That's okay, get something now, and when you slim down, you'll get some more."

"We'll see." Linda tapped her phone. "Toy World is on Seventy-Second Street."

"That's a long walk. Let me go get the car."

Loading the Tesla SUV with their shopping bags, a pair of teenage girls came up. "Are you Cory Loop?"

"Yep. How are you girls doing?"

"Oh my God. We love your album!"

"Thank you."

"Can we take selfies with you?"

"Sure."

Cory stood in the middle, and the girls clicked away. A small crowd began forming and Cory was surrounded. He was signing autographs when the Tesla's window rolled down. Linda said, "Come on, Cory. We gotta go. Tommy needs to be fed."

"Sorry, guys. I gotta go, but it's was super meeting all of you."

Cory hopped into the car, and as it drove off he said, "Wow, that was weird. I can't believe those girls recognized me without the hat."

"Daddy's famous!"

"Not too famous to change a diaper." Linda handed Tommy off.

"Never. Ava, help me a little. Then we'll grab something to eat. I'm starved."

As they changed the diaper, Cory said, "Why don't we head down to the West Village? There's a tiny place on Christopher Street, I Sodi. It's the best Italian food in the city. I went there with Tracy. It was amazing."

After placing their orders, Cory picked up a piece of bruschetta. "Wait till you try this, it's incredible." His phone pinged with a text. He looked at the screen and dropped the bruschetta.

15

———

"CORY, ARE YOU OKAY?"

"Daddy, are your new teeth bothering you?"

"No, I'm fine, honey."

"I thought you were hungry. You haven't eaten a thing."

"My stomach's acting up. I'm going to order a bottle of wine."

"Wine? You just said your stomach's bothering you."

"Are you sick, Daddy?"

"I'm fine. Let's get out of here."

Though the message, *I know*, was ambiguous, Cory knew exactly what it meant. Someone was aware of what he'd done. He thought it was Riley. What did he want? Was he looking for more money? Could this be about trying to get a raise?

Cory wanted to fire him from the band, get rid of him so he never had to deal with him again. Riley had no proof the songs weren't composed by Cory. Cory took his phone out and wrote a text to Lew. He told him to let Riley go, that their musical styles clashed.

Cory was about to hit send when he thought it might be

better to have Riley close by. Keeping an eye on him might be the best way to handle this. Once he was sure it was him and that he had no evidence, he'd get rid of him. As they pulled up to their temporary living quarters, Cory deleted the text.

———

Tracy raised a glass of the champagne she brought over. "Here's to your new place. May it be filled with laughter and joy."

Linda clinked glasses with her and Cory. "Well, one thing is for sure, we know it's going to be filled with dirty diapers."

"Thanks for putting this together for us."

"No problem. I've got to get going. We're leaving tomorrow, and I've got a lot of packing to do."

"I wish we had another day."

"You and me both. I'll see you tomorrow."

Cory walked her to the door.

"Do you know anybody that can do some checking around?"

"What do you mean?"

"I'm getting strange messages from someone. I'd like to know if it's who I think it is."

"They're not threatening, are they?"

"No. I just want to know who it is."

"I have contacts in the security industry."

"But I want this kept quiet."

"Of course. What do you have?"

Cory handed her a note. "Here's the number. Let me know who it belongs to."

"No problem. I'll get it checked out."

He whispered, "You have any more of those sleeping pills? I'm down to the last two."

She dug a bottle out of her bag. "Make sure you don't take them with alcohol."

"No worries."

THE CHASE CENTER crowd was on their feet as Cory led the band off the stage. He tore off his hat and opened his sweat-soaked shirt. Tracy was offstage with water bottles.

"You're not doing an encore?"

"No." He grabbed a bottle and took a gulp. "That's it for tonight." The band took waters and headed to the green room.

Tracy said, "What's the matter?"

"We sounded like crap."

"No, you didn't. It was amazing. The crowd loved it."

"Well, I don't think so. I got off to a rocky start and never recovered."

"It was great. Don't be so hard on yourself."

"And it wasn't just me. Riley blew a couple of chords."

"I didn't hear anything out of place."

"I need a drink and a shower."

"There should be a bottle of the Wild Turkey Honey Bourbon you like."

"Wild Turkey? I told Lew I don't drink that crap anymore. Make sure it's Pappy Van Winkle from now on."

"Sorry. If I knew, I would've made sure. Let me see what I can do."

Stripping off his shirt, Cory walked into his dressing room. "Forget it."

Tracy poured him a glass of bourbon.

"Three ice cubes."

"I know." She handed him the glass. "Try and relax. It really was a great show."

He drained the glass. "This is nowhere as good as Pappy Vee." He handed the glass off and went into the bathroom.

Cory's mind raced as the water beat on his back. Right before he'd gone on stage, another text had come in. This time it said: *I know what you did. You're a fake.*

It had thrown him so off that he'd flubbed the opening lines of the opening song. From there on, the demon in his head kept telling him he wasn't good enough. He couldn't wait to get offstage and cut a tune out of the set list.

Cory thought that during the show Riley seemed to be looking at him more than was necessary as the leader. Was he trying to gauge his reaction? The timing of the text couldn't have been worse. Who else would've known, almost to the minute, the time the band was going on stage? It wasn't a coincidence.

Cory had to find out who was behind it and determine whether it was a baseless taunt or if it posed a real threat.

He put on a pair of silk lounge pants and came out toweling his hair. "Can you make me a drink?"

Cory plopped onto a chair and put the TV on. Tracy handed him the booze, saying, "I understand this is an important tour, but you're too tense."

He took a slug. "I got a lot to deal with."

She put her hands on his shoulders and massaged his neck. "Stop worrying, you got this. Trust me. It's going to be all right."

Cory stiffened. "I better get dressed."

Tracy pouted. "Are you sure about that?"

"Believe me, I'd love to, but . . ." Cory headed into the bathroom. He splashed his face with water to combat the dizziness. He grabbed his phone and hit speed dial.

"Cory?"

"Yeah."

"What's the matter? It's the middle of the night."

"I don't know, I just needed to hear your voice."

"Tell me what's wrong?"

"I don't know. Things are moving too fast. I'm not sure of anything anymore."

"We're here for you, Cory. I know things are changing quickly. I feel it too. But if we can slow things down, it'll get better. Don't worry. We'll figure it out."

"Is that Tommy crying?"

"Yeah, he just woke up."

"Go ahead. Take care of him. How's Ava?"

"She's good. We love you, and we'll talk in the morning, okay?"

"Sure. Love you. Bye."

Cory looked in the mirror as he buttoned his shirt. Linda was right, he could slow things down, take control.

"Cory? You okay in there?"

He opened the door. "Yeah, I'm fine. I want to go back to the hotel."

"Did you forget about the backstage party?"

"Do I have to go?"

She smiled. "Definitely, everybody is expecting you. The label flew in a bunch of media big shots."

"Ugh."

"Come on, you need to eat anyway, and I put together an incredible spread."

"All right, but I don't want to stay long."

"That's okay. Hey, I forgot to tell you, my guy called about that number you wanted to trace."

16

Cory's heart rate sped up. "What did he find out?"

He held his breath waiting for Tracy to answer.

"My contact said the number was just a mirror one."

"A mirror?"

"The caller uses a fake number to hide the real one."

"He has no idea who it is?"

"No."

"Now what am I going to do?"

"Block the number, at least they won't bother you from that number."

He took his phone out and blocked the number, even though he knew it was a waste of time. "I want you to keep an eye on Riley."

"In what way?"

"I don't know. I get the feeling he's the one who's hassling me."

"Why would he do that?"

"Just do it, okay? And not just him, anybody says something or does anything a little strange, I want to know about it. Immediately."

"Sure. But if you tell me what's going on, I'd be more effective in helping you."

"Not now." He drained his glass and said, "Let's get this damn party thing out of the way."

Cory and Tracy walked silently in the underground corridor to a large area behind the stage.

The security guard said, "Nice show, Mr. Loop."

"Thanks." Cory turned to Tracy. "Let's have someone get him something to eat."

"Will do."

The cocktail party was in full force. Lew Stein, with two teenagers in tow, made a beeline for Cory.

"Cory, this is my niece Janice and her friend. They're huge fans."

"Nice to meet you."

"Oh my God. I can't believe we're here. Can we take pictures?"

"Nothing I'd like more."

"Hurry up. Cory has to say hello to everyone."

Cory posed with the girls and signed autographs for them. He said, "Lew, why don't you show them the stage? They'll get a kick out of it."

"Can we?"

As the manager led the girls away, Tracy said, "See the guy with the long sweater? He covers the arts for the *Chronicle*, but his column is syndicated, even *The New York Times* carries it. We have to say hello."

"I'm not doing any interviews."

"All I want to do is build a bridge tonight. I'll reach out later about doing a piece on you."

It took them ten minutes to handshake and chat their way thirty feet to the columnist. "Cory, I want you to meet Herbert

Trout. He's my favorite journalist. No matter where I am, I make sure to read anything he writes."

"Tracy sure knows how to pump up an ego."

Cory shook Trout's hand. "Nice to meet you."

"Same here. You're quite the phenom."

"It's been a longer journey than everyone thinks."

"I'd love to hear about that. What I say is, it takes at least ten years of hard work to become an overnight success."

"I put more than ten years of practicing eight hours a day before I even picked up a decent gig."

"It'd be nice to talk about that."

Tracy said, "You tell us when, and we'll work out the details."

"Let's chat next week."

"Absolutely. Which of Cory's songs did you like best?"

"The entire performance was entertaining. I appreciated the lack of an elaborate effects show. To me, they tend to distract from the music."

"Thanks. That's not who I am."

"Where do you get your song ideas from?"

"Oh, I don't know, they just come to me."

"That's quite a gift."

"I write a lot, most of it gets tossed."

"Well, we have that in common."

Cory forced out a laugh.

Tracy said, "I hate to break this up, but the label execs want a piece of Cory."

Walking away, Tracy said, "See? He's going to do a piece on you. That's great."

"I don't know about doing it."

"You got to. It'll help get you to the next level."

"I don't need to get anywhere."

"You'll sell more and command higher ticket prices for your shows."

Cory said, "We'll see. Right now, I need a drink."

"Wait till you talk with the record guys. You've had a couple already, and I don't want them to see you buzzed. And don't forget, you got to be on the morning show set at seven a.m."

"I know, but I'm really tight. Get me one more."

CORY SAT in a director's chair in front of a backdrop of the Golden Gate Bridge. Cables snaked all over. He faced a semicircle of cameras draped with overhead microphones. Tracy was off to the side, talking to the production people.

Cory checked the time. Ten minutes to go. Putting the phone away, a text chimed in. Cory opened the message: *Good Morning, Mr. Pretender.*

He stared at the number. Who was this? It was clear whoever it was, wasn't going away. He typed back: *Who is this?*

Your partner.

What do you want?

Some of the money you're making from stealing.

I didn't steal anything.

I told you I know, and you're going to pay to keep it quiet.

Keep what quiet?

That the songs on your album were taken from Jay Bird.

That's crazy.

I'll be in touch. Soon. Real soon.

17

———————

Cory's head was pounding. He closed the drapes and flopped on the couch. He closed his eyes and was drifting toward sleep when his phone rang. It was his manager.

"Hey, Lew. What's going on?"

"What happened with the morning show?"

"Nothing."

"You were disconnected. It didn't come across good."

"It was all right. I had a late night."

"Were you hungover?"

"No, I wasn't."

"I heard you were knocking it back pretty good after the show."

"I was fine."

"You've got to be careful. You got to remember, kid, there's a lot of eyes on you. We need things to go smooth, real smooth. That way, on the next album we'll get triple the royalties you're getting now."

"Sounds good. What did I make last night?"

"Not sure of the final figures yet, but the total amount was five million. Your gross cut is about forty percent. But next tour, things keep up this way, we go to fifty-five percent like the hot acts."

"Super. That's a ton of money."

"Don't spend it all, kid. We got a lot of expenses that come out of it."

"But we got another five dates to do."

"Yeah, except for the Staples Center, they don't seat anywhere as many as last night."

"I want to send some money to my wife."

"Tell me how much, and I'll wire it."

"I don't know. How about twenty thousand?"

"Make it ten, you don't want her spending too much."

"You're right. Sounds good."

"Consider it done. Look, I gotta run, but remember, don't screw up with the booze or the women."

"Hold on a sec. Since you mentioned, the . . . ladies. I want to ask you something. Say you made a mistake, and the person you did it with was threatening to tell your wife. But they said if you paid them, they'd keep it quiet."

"You in a jam, kid?"

"No, just asking."

"Never pay. It's a mistake."

"Why?"

"They'll come back for more. It'll never end. You can't let something like that happen, you understand?"

"Yeah, it's for a friend, not me."

"Either way, don't do anything stupid, kid. You'll regret it."

"Don't worry. I won't."

"And do yourself a favor: lay off the booze, and stay clear of drugs. They'll drag you down faster than anything with big tits."

Cory paced the hotel suite trying to figure out what to do.

Would he be contacted again? It seemed inevitable. He reviewed the messages, convinced they'd probably ask for money in the next text.

He unscrewed the cap off the bottle of Pappy Van Winkle. Cory poured a glassful and sipped it without ice. The slow burn felt good. He drank some more, believing he'd figured a way out of the situation.

He thought about what his manager advised. Lew said not to pay, but he had plenty of money now. Whoever was about to extort him had to know that asking for a large amount wouldn't work. Maybe he could pay until it got to a figure that was too high or he was too big a star for any damage to stick.

If the payment request was too high or too close in time to a previous one, Cory would cut it off. The blackmailer wouldn't want to end a good thing, would he? Cory drained the glass thinking it was a plan with a reasonable chance of working. He'd pay as long as it was reasonable.

Cory poured another glass and put the TV on. The news mentioned the date, and he realized it was his father's birthday. He wished his dad were still alive; he wanted him to know that he'd hit the big time.

His old man was a tough taskmaster, but they'd had a good relationship until it had gotten off track well before high school. For some reason, Cory felt his father lost confidence in him.

Feeling sad, Cory took a sip of bourbon and wondered what had happened. He remembered his father slapping his face when he learned that Cory had been bullied into handing over his lunch money in middle school.

That was it, he thought. His father had lost respect for him because he'd allowed himself to be bullied. It was a tough lesson, but Cory hadn't allowed anything like that to happen again.

Topping off his glass with amber liquid, Cory realized this was another attempt to bully him. It would never end if he allowed it to happen. What his father had said years ago amounted to the same thing Lew just said.

They were right, Cory thought. Screw him, or her, for that matter. You're not getting shit from me. I'm Cory Loop.

He took his phone out and tapped out a text: *Go to hell. I'll never pay you a damn penny. If you contact me again, I'll go to the police.*

It felt good. Cory raised his glass. "Here's to you, Dad."

He took a sip, relishing the cherry and vanilla flavors when a text message sounded. Cory read the message and hurled his glass against the wall.

18

———

Cory stared at the message: *Keep your eyes on the news.*

He wondered what it meant. Were they going to go public? Based on what? The short-lived rise he was enjoying would come crashing down.

His family would be embarrassed, and he'd be laughed out of the industry. It'd be worse than what happened to the lip-syncing duo Milli Vanilli.

Cory typed a response: *Don't do anything stupid. I'll pay. How much do you want?*

Ping: *Too late.*

What do you mean too late???

Cory waited for a reply. He grabbed another glass and filled it up. He drank half before typing: *Answer me.*

No reply came. He tapped out another message: *You there? Answer me!!!*

There was a knock on the door. "Leave me alone!"

"Cory, it's Tracy."

"What do you want?"

"Open up. We're leaving for the airport in five minutes."

He flung open the door and walked away. Tracy said, "You're not ready?"

"I'm ready."

"Where's your luggage?"

"Do me a favor, will you? Stop asking so many goddamn questions."

"Is everything okay?"

"Fucking fine."

"We got to go."

He emptied his glass.

"It's a bit early to be drinking."

"Yeah, well, I got a lot of shit on my mind."

"What about your clothes and toiletries?"

Cory pulled a hoodie on and headed out the door. "Get someone to deal with it."

On the ride to the airport, Cory had his earbuds in. It wasn't that he was listening to music, he just didn't want to talk. Approaching the terminal, his phone vibrated with a call from his manager. Cory swiped the call away.

Tracy's phone rang. "Yes, he's right here. Okay." She handed the phone to Cory. "It's Lew."

"Can't it wait?"

"No. He said it's urgent that he speak with you."

"Yeah?"

"We got a problem."

"What now?"

"I just got off the phone with a contact at *Variety* magazine. She received a call from someone claiming to have information that would prove the music on your album wasn't yours."

"What? Who said that?"

"I asked the same question, but she won't reveal the source."

"That's crazy. What proof do they have?"

"I don't know, she was just feeling me out, to get my reaction."

"Geez."

"My question is if there's any truth to this."

"No way, man."

"You wrote all the tunes?"

"Yeah. It's bullshit that people can make accusations like that."

"Well, this type of stuff happens from time to time. People target celebrities constantly, especially ones that rise as quickly as you did. Everybody wants their fifteen minutes of fame."

"What are we going to do?"

"We may have to get out in front of this. But let me call her back and categorically deny the allegations. Maybe threaten a lawsuit."

"Handle it. Do what you have to. I don't want to deal with this shit."

Cory hung up and sank into the seat. Tracy said, "What's going on?"

"Nothing."

"Don't tell me nothing. Lew said it was urgent. What's going on?"

Cory told her about the threat but cut off any discussion. He tried to figure out who was behind this. The word had gotten out quickly. Was it Riley?

He said, "Look, I want you to check into something, but you can't let anybody know."

"Okay. What?"

"Can you find out if Riley has any connections at *Variety*?"

"You think he's the one?"

"It's a good possibility."

"Why would he do that? He's part of the band. It doesn't make any sense to destroy things."

"Can't you just do what I ask?"

"Of course. I'm just trying to understand why you think it could be him."

"I have my reasons. Just check him out."

CORY AND TRACY were at a table in Cory's suite. They were FaceTiming with his manager, who said, "I just got off the phone with my contact at *Variety*. I did my best, but they're going to put something out—"

Cory said, "How can they?"

"Hold on. She said they would mention the rumor in a short piece while stating that at this point it was unsubstantiated."

Tracy said, "But merely putting it out there gives it meaning. How can they print something without two sources?"

"The press has been doing that for years. Look, we got to hit this head-on and put it to bed. If they have proof, then it's a different story. Cory, is there any truth to this?"

"No."

"Not even something that could be construed that Jay Bird or anyone else had a hand in creating these songs?"

"No."

"Look, kid, if there was even the slightest collaboration, you can always co-credit the music. We can say it was a minor contribution by Jay Bird. He's not around to challenge anything anyway."

Tracy said, "Why do that? If they don't have any proof, it's his word against someone who is dead."

"I'm just throwing out options if we have a problem. This can get ugly fast. The press will be all over it if there's something there. Is there anything we have to be concerned with?"

"How many times do I got to say no?"

"Okay, just trying to be sure. We'll put out a statement. We may have to do an interview or two if it doesn't die down."

"I don't want to do any interviews."

"Let's see how it goes."

A BLACK SUV pulled up to a side entrance of San Diego's Pechanga Arena. Cory and Tracy hopped out, walking between the barriers that kept the press and fans away. Cory waved as hundreds of flashes from fans' phones went off.

Microphone in hand, a journalist hung over the railing. "Hey, Cory, can you comment on the plagiarism story? Who really wrote the material on your album?"

Cory waved and put his head down. Once inside, he said, "What the fuck was that? How did this get out already?"

"Garbage like this always leaks. Don't let it upset you. We'll deal with it."

They pushed through the door to Cory's dressing room. He pulled out his phone. Ava wanted a picture of his dressing rooms. He snapped two pictures and froze. A text from an odd number had arrived.

19

The phone slipped out of his hands. Tracy bent to pick it up, and Cory shoved her out of the way. "I got it."

He stuffed the phone in his pocket. "How long till we go on?"

"At least an hour, but the kids from the shelter will be here any minute."

He cracked open the bottle of bourbon and poured a glass.

"You should eat something."

"Not hungry."

Tracy sat down. "I know you're under a tremendous amount of pressure. You have to find a way to let it not get to you."

"I'm okay."

"Maybe, but I think you can do better. You're not eating properly and you're drinking too much. It's starting to show."

"What are you talking about?"

"Your color's off, and you've lost a couple of pounds."

"You try going out there under those lights. I sweat off five pounds a night."

"I know, that's why you have to start taking better care of yourself. I can get a chef to prepare proper meals for you, no matter where we are."

"Okay, do it."

"Good, but you also have to cut back on the drinking."

"Stop nagging me, will you? I need an assistant, not a mother or another wife. Do your job and find out if Riley is behind these frigging rumors."

"I'm trying, but I can't find an obvious connection."

"Do I have to do this myself?" Cory's heart started pounding. "Lower the air in here, I'm sweating."

Cory retreated to the bathroom. His hands trembled as he splashed water on his face. What was happening to him? He wondered if the tightness in his chest meant he was on the verge of a heart attack.

Cory sat on the bowl. Everything was falling apart. Karma was getting even.

"Cory, you okay?"

"Yeah."

"The kids you invited are here to say hello."

THOUGH HIS LEGS WERE HEAVY, Cory was the first one off the stage. Tracy bowed to him as he exited. "Great show."

"Are you kidding me? Tell Lew to fire the sound guy."

"Why? Cooper is the best."

"Did you see me signaling to him about the mix in my monitor? I was waving like a fucking bird out there. I couldn't hear myself. And the horn section, they either lower the damn volume or they're gone too." He started to walk away and turned around. "You got that?"

"Yes. I know you're upset, but it really sounded good to me."

"What do you know?"

"I'm just saying . . ."

"I'm gonna shower."

Tracy trailed behind Cory to the dressing rooms. He pointed in the direction of the band's dressing rooms. "Who's Riley talking to?"

"That's Petey from *Rolling Stone*."

"Tell Riley I want to see him."

"When?"

"Now!" He slammed the dressing room door behind him.

Cory poured a drink and took it into the bathroom with him. He showered and came out with a towel around his waist. Tracy and Riley were picking at a cheese platter.

"Hey, Cory. That was a monster show tonight."

He shrugged. "My monitor feed was garbage."

"Yeah? Mine was fine. What's going on?"

"What were you talking to the guy from *Rolling Stone* about?"

"Nothing."

"Don't tell me nothing. What did you tell him?"

"He was asking about the tour, you know, the stops we're making and how it is to play with you."

"What did you tell him about me?"

"Nothing, just that it was fun playing with you."

"Are you sure about that?"

"Hey, man, I don't know what's going on here. It was just a bullshit conversation."

"Did you tell that bitch at *Variety* that I didn't write the stuff on the album?"

"Me? No way, man."

"A couple weeks ago, in the studio, you were talking to

Joanne. I heard you say some shit that the songs resembled what Jay Bird did."

"When was this?"

"At Platinum, when we were laying the album down."

"I don't know what you're talking about."

"You told her, I heard it myself."

"I honestly don't remember anything like that, and whatever I said wasn't nothing more than small talk."

"Yeah, right."

"It was. I swear."

"Give me your phone."

"My phone?"

"Give it to me!"

Riley handed his phone over. Cory scrolled through the messages. "Someone's trying to destroy me. If it's not you, who is it?"

"Hey, man, I didn't do anything."

He tossed the phone back. "I'm watching you. If it's you, I'll find out."

Riley turned around and headed for the door. "You're paranoid, man."

Tracy shook her head. "He's right, you know. You're acting paranoid. You can't let one rumor, especially in this business, throw you off. The gossipy bullshit comes with the territory."

"I don't trust him. He wasn't my first choice anyway."

"Can I make a suggestion without you jumping down my throat?"

"Go ahead."

"If you have a problem with the talent, let me or Lew deal with it. Otherwise, you're going to poison the music."

Cory knew it was a good idea, but said, "I want to be alone. Give me an hour to unwind."

"Sure, but please don't get smashed. You have to make an appearance at the party."

Cory poured himself another drink and got dressed. He had to get past this. Paying whoever it was would at least reveal who it was and would end his fear about being exposed.

He didn't think they were bluffing, but what proof could they possibly have? It had to be a musician. They had bigger ears than elephants, and many had an ability to recall exactly what they heard.

If all they had was somehow hearing what Jay Bird had written, the proof was just aural. It wasn't evidence. The more he thought about it, the more likely it seemed. Why hadn't he realized it before? Cory settled on fear as the answer. He'd gotten so worked up, he couldn't see the obvious answer.

He put his feet up and lit up a joint. It was going to be fine. His plan wasn't going to be upended by some punk who thought he could blackmail him.

He tapped out a text: *If you have proof, it's time to show it. Otherwise, stop harassing me.*

20

THE KNOCK ON THE DOOR WOKE CORY UP. "WHO'S THERE?"

"It's Donny. You got a minute?"

Cory got off the couch and went to the door. Donny said, "Hey, man. You okay?"

"Yeah, actually I'm feeling the best I have in a couple of weeks."

"Good to hear it. I was getting a little worried about you."

"Everything is good. You want a drink?"

"Nah, I'll have something at the party."

"Suit yourself." Cory poured a glass.

"What's going on with you and Riley?"

"Nothing."

"Nothing? He came in all upset, said you were accusing him of being the one who leaked to the magazine."

"Between you and me, I was never a fan of his. I mean he can play his ass off, but something about him, I don't know."

"He's a solid dude, man. I'll bet my Gibson on it not being him."

"Whoa. Laying your baby on the line?"

"I own four Gibbys."

"Me too."

"Great musical minds think alike."

"You sure you don't want a drink?"

"No thanks. You really dig that stuff, don't you?"

"I always liked Pappy, just couldn't afford it."

"Don't overdo it."

"I won't. How'd you think it went tonight?"

"Honestly?"

"No, lie to me."

"The last couple of shows, there's been too much tension. Nobody is relaxed. Everybody is on edge."

"Why?"

"Look, brother, we've known each other a long time, right?"

"Yeah, grammar school, Mrs. Johnson's class."

"So, don't take this the wrong way, but you've been a bear, man. I know you got a lot of pressure and all, but don't take it out on the band. You should be looking to the music as a way to blow off steam. Does that make sense?"

"I guess. I've been uptight. I feel like everything and everybody is coming at me and, you know, being away from home. I hate to complain, but it's not exactly what I expected, you know?"

"Just relax and enjoy the ride, bro. It's all going to be good. We'll be back in New York in a couple of days."

"Believe it or not, maybe it was the run-in with Riley, but I was feeling a hundred percent better right afterward. I realized how lucky I am to be here."

"Me too, bro. I'm really happy for you."

A text chimed in. Cory stared at his phone.

"You all right, bro?"

"Uh, I don't know. I . . ." Cory ran to the bathroom and vomited into the toilet.

"Holy shit! Let me get a doctor or something."

"No. Wait." Cory stuck his mouth under the faucet.

"No, man, don't take chances. You were fine one second, then, bingo, you got white as a ghost."

"It's something I ate."

"You want me to get Tracy?"

"No. I'm fine. Go ahead, I'm going to wash up. I'll see you at the party."

"I'm going to stick around, make sure you're okay. Take your time. We'll go together if you're up to it."

Cory put the lid down and sat on the toilet. He put his head in his hands, trying to figure out what to do next. He pulled his phone out and scrolled through the images he was sent.

They all featured Jay Bird in the studio. The sheet music Cory had taken was visible in the background. Cory zoomed in on the compositions. There was no way to defend his claim he had composed them.

Who had taken these pictures? It had to be a musician. Nobody else would have put it together or even thought to examine the sheet music. Someone must have heard the songs. Someone close to Jay Bird recognized the tunes. They probably had been in the studio with him at one time, took the pictures, and when the album came out, had gone over them looking for proof.

Why hadn't Jay Bird stood a little more to the right when the pictures were taken? Cory shouted, "Fuck!"

"You okay?"

"Uh, yeah, banged my elbow."

Cory realized the who part was less important than the

what. What did they want from him? It was money, for sure, but how much?

His finger hovered over the message he tapped out: *How much do you want?* He amended it to: *How much do you want for the pictures?* and hit send.

21

———

As soon as the door to his hotel suite closed, Cory pulled his phone out. He stared at the message he'd received when Donny was in his dressing room: *The pictures aren't for sale. You're going to pay to keep them out of the press.*

Cory considered asking how much they were demanding but was afraid of the answer. He was making a lot of money and could afford it. But these people knew that, and the aggressive text scared the hell out of him.

Cory wondered whether to call Lew. He might have a way to deal with this. He thought it through; his manager had mentioned being against paying anyone, but this person had proof, evidence that would be difficult if not impossible to refute.

He'd be exposed as a fraud or even worse, a thief. Was it too late to claim he'd worked with Jay Bird on the tunes? The dead pop star had a reputation for working alone. He'd need someone credible to confirm they'd worked together.

Laying on the bed, he kicked off his shoes and tried to think of someone who would be willing to corroborate a nonexistent relationship. He got up, pacing the room. He thought about his friends but couldn't think of a way to start the conversation. Cory opened the nightstand drawer. He pushed his socks aside and pulled out a bottle. He shook two pills out and dry swallowed them.

He sat on the bed. A text chimed in. Cory held his breath, taking his phone off the nightstand. It was Linda. She wanted to know if he could talk. He went to the bathroom before calling his wife, wondering if there was a way she could vouch for him.

"It's so good to hear your voice."

"I know, I miss you. How are the kids?"

As Linda filled him in, Cory stretched out on the bed. The pills were starting to hit him.

"Cory?"

"Yeah."

"I asked you how the show went."

"Oh, it was okay."

"What's the matter?"

"Nothing."

"Cory? Cory? You there? Hello?"

22

———

The hotel manager opened the door and Tracy rushed in. She shook Cory. "Cory, wake up. Wake up!"

The manager said, "Shall I call 911?"

"No. He's getting up. He'll be all right. He's just exhausted, been on the road too long."

"Are you sure, ma'am?"

"Yes. Thanks, you can go. And please, don't say anything about this. We really like your hotel, and we'd like to come back."

"Absolutely, ma'am. Good night."

"Hold on a second. Can you get room service to bring up some coffee and a couple of sandwiches?"

"Yes, ma'am, right away."

The manager disappeared, and Tracy propped Cory's head up. "What did you take?"

"Sleeping pills."

"How many?"

He held up two fingers.

"You can't be using them when you drink. It's dangerous. You scared the hell out of your wife."

Cory closed his eyes. "Damn."

"Can you get up? You got to move around."

He struggled, and Tracy supported him as they walked into the living area. "I want to sit."

"Let's circle around one more time."

"I gotta call my wife."

"Have a cup of coffee first."

As she sat him down, there was a knock on the door. "Room service."

THE RESPONSE to his text was immediate: *$50,000. I want it fast. No excuses.* A second message provided the wire transfer instructions. They wanted the money sent to a bank in the Cayman Islands.

Fifty thousand was a lot, but Cory was making good money. He called his manager.

"Lew, I need you to arrange a wire for me, ASAP."

"All right, you have the bank information?"

"Yeah, I'll text it to you."

"Good. How much is it for?"

"Fifty thousand."

"That's a considerable sum. You buying something?"

"Uh, no, a friend of mine is in a jam."

"You can't help everybody, kid. People will be coming out of the woodwork if it gets around."

"It's for an old buddy. He's down on his luck."

"Okay, just be careful with this type of stuff."

"Okay, Daddy."

Cory sent the information in a text and immediately felt better. He checked the time; it was 10:20 a.m. It was a bit early to start drinking, but it was time to celebrate. Everything was going to be okay; his secret was safe.

He took a sip. As the heat traveled down his throat, the phone rang. "Yeah, Lew. What's up?"

"That bank you want the money going to, it's in the Cayman Islands."

"Yeah, I saw that. Was that a problem?"

"No, but it's unusual. People use offshore accounts for privacy."

"I didn't know that. So, if we wanted to trace who the bank account belonged to, we couldn't?"

"It'd be very difficult, if not impossible. The banking laws in those countries protect privacy."

"Makes sense."

"What do you mean?"

"Nothing, just that, uh, some people need privacy."

"You want to check with your friend to make sure before we send it out?"

"Good idea. I'll get back to you."

Cory hadn't thought of using the banking information to track down who it was, but a foreign bank made sense. These people knew what they were doing. Cory wanted them to go away, but his confidence that they would started to melt.

He waited five minutes before giving Lew the go-ahead to send the money.

CORY KEPT CHECKING his phone as they walked the downtown area of Phoenix. Lew said he sent the money, but did they get it yet? Would they send an acknowledgment? He didn't want to ask; he just wanted to know.

The sun was out and the mountainous backdrop pretty.

Cory cleared his throat as they entered Talking Stick Arena. Tracy said, "You got to make sure you drink enough water. The air out here is bone dry."

"I can feel it in my throat."

"We'll have plenty of water on stage. Drink between songs and whenever Joanne takes a solo. They're long enough."

"Her playing is so sweet."

"Uhm, don't take this the wrong way, it's none of my business, but whatever is going on between you two, I'd suggest keeping it private."

"What are you talking about?"

"Come on, Cory. Did you forget that last week I had to kill a story you two were an item?"

"Don't worry about it. I got it handled."

"I'm not judging, but you're married with two kids, and one of them is a newborn."

"You're jealous. Besides, what does that have to do with anything? I'm just having some fun."

"I want to keep the focus on the music, not your personal life."

"Let's see the dressing room before we start."

As Tracy checked how the room was outfitted, Cory grabbed two bottles of Evian. He spilled half the contents out of them, replacing it with bourbon. Cory took a long sip. He winced and topped it off with more booze.

Tracy said, "You're not going to fool anybody."

"I don't care."

"Okay, but alcohol is a diuretic, it's exactly the opposite of what you should be drinking."

"Don't worry so much. I'll drink extra water. Okay?"

"Just don't overdo it. You look tired."

"I'm not tired, just a little uptight. Do me a favor and go get Joanne."

Tracy left, and Cory took pictures of his dressing room. He sent them to Ava and sat down.

A quick knock on the door and Joanne stuck her head in. "Hey, how's it going?"

Cory eyed his piano player. "A lot better since you showed up. Get over here."

Joanne kissed him, and Cory pulled her onto his lap. "I could use a line, how about you?"

"I can't do more than one; my hands get too jittery on the keyboard."

Cory slid his hand under her shirt. "It's just a soundcheck, man."

"You're right."

Joanne took her coke kit out and spooned some out of the vial. Cory took a hit up each nostril. "That's good stuff."

"I know, but it's expensive."

"I don't care how much it costs. I'll pay for it. Give me another hit."

She handed him the kit. "I got to put some music on."

Cory took a double dose and rubbed cocaine on his gums. "This is super good shit."

Joanne started dancing, and Cory's face erupted into a smile. As she writhed, his desire for her increased. She was perfect. He had wanted her since the day they first met, and now he had her.

It had been easy since he'd hit the charts. Not that he had tried anything before the album, but he knew she would have blown him off before.

Someone knocked on the door. Cory said, "Come in."

It was Bob Zepher, the band's road manager. "Sorry to disturb you, Mr. Loop, but Tracy asked me to come and let you know the band is onstage. They're ready whenever you are."

"Okay, we'll be right there."

Cory thought about how everything had changed. People who'd treated him like crap were concerned if he had everything he needed. It was like being surrounded by high-end concierges who were ready to tend to any of his needs, real or imagined.

Everything was easy now, and it felt good.

23

———

After seeing the mess in Cory's suite, Tracy switched the location of the interview to the W Hotel's rooftop lounge. In the ride up the elevator, she reminded him to keep it real and low-key. As they approached the reporter, Tracy whispered, "Be as humble as you can."

Cory shook hands with the *Rolling Stone* journalist and sat on a red velvet couch.

The journalist took out a recording device. "Ready?"

Cory nodded, and the reporter clicked the record button.

"It's nice to finally be able to chat with you."

"I'm glad to be here."

"You've had a meteoric rise to the top of the charts. How's the ride been?"

"To be honest, I haven't had much time to think about it. Just yesterday, some of the changes began to come into focus."

"Such as?"

"Well, I mean it's silly, but my dressing room has enough food to feed a family. It's quite wasteful. And you know, now

I stay in a suite instead of the Red Roof Inn. It's all nice, but I've been thinking about whether it's necessary or not."

"You sound like you're grounded."

"I hope so. I came from humble beginnings."

"Do you believe it helped you navigate the overnight success you've had?"

"Well, the reality is, and I don't want to sound ungrateful, but I've been around a long time. I've been on thirty-something recordings and writing since I was a teenager, so I don't consider it overnight."

"But you have to admit that your success with the public has been almost unprecedented."

"That's true, and I'm super thankful."

"Do you believe some of it fills the void that people have since Jay Bird's passing?"

"Uhm, I knew Jay and played on all his recordings. I can't say why people do what they do."

"But you'd agree that your music, the style, is similar to what Jay Bird did."

"Every artist has their own voice. Trying to be someone else never works."

"So, the rumor that you didn't compose the material on *Loop Around* is unfounded?"

"Yeah, of course."

"I'd like to circle back to your early days. I understand your father, Martin Lupinski, was an accountant."

"Yeah, he had his own little practice."

"He wasn't supportive of your pursuit of music as a career, was he?"

"To him, music was a hobby, not a career. He didn't approve of it. He was a practical man, you know, get-a-real-job type of guy."

"Good thing you didn't listen to him."

"Luckily, things worked out."

"You wish he were around to see it?"

"Boy, you got that right."

"Sounds like we hit a nerve there."

"Look, he gave me a hard time when I'd have to borrow money to take care of my family, but he wanted the best for me. Just like I want for my family."

"You and your wife have a newborn son and a seven-year-old daughter. How has this newfound fame impacted your relationships?"

"Uh, I miss them all and can't wait to get home."

"Life on the road, especially, it seems, for musicians, is difficult. Many get into trouble when they travel. Separation is difficult and there's no shortage of shiny objects and ways to numb yourself. What's your experience been?"

"It's been fine."

"There was a report about an incident where a hotel manager had to use a master key to get into your room."

"Oh, that? It was nothing. I hadn't been sleeping and took a pill. I had a prescription for it."

"No alcohol or other substances were involved?"

"No."

"There were reports that you were drinking heavily at the backstage party that night."

"Heavily? That's not was it was. Nothing happened, I was in a deep sleep."

"Tell me about the band. How did the core of the ensemble come about?"

"I'm lucky to get on stage with such an accomplished set of players. We'd played together on various recordings, and they're the ones I wanted. Donny and me go way back, to the third grade."

"Tell me about Joanne Claymore. She's the only woman in the group."

"Joanne's an amazing player. She plays a different solo every night. I don't know where she gets her ideas from."

"Any truth to the rumor you're romantically involved with her?"

"No. I'm happily married."

"Let's get back to the music. Where do you get ideas for songs?"

"I don't know. Just from living. The world around me, is like, a big well. Things hit me and I play around with them."

"You make it sound easy."

"Trust me, it's not. But it's something I do, every day."

"You must have enough material ready for a follow-up album."

"I have some material ready."

"The record label told us that you're going back into the studio after the tour ends."

"We'll see about that. I'd like some time off."

"At the moment, the formula is to strike while the iron is hot. You know, to build upon the success you already have."

"I keep hearing fans will forget you if you don't produce quickly, but I don't buy it."

"You can't deny the cycle is much shorter these days. It makes it hard to enjoy the success you have now."

"I'm doing my best."

"Thank you, Cory, it's been a pleasure."

Cory said goodbye to the reporter and went up to Tracy. "And this guy is a friend of yours?"

"It wasn't that bad."

"The reason I can't enjoy the success is because of people like him. How the hell did he find out about the hotel and

Joanne? This is gonna be a disaster if you can't keep that stuff out."

As he stormed away, a text came in. It was the blackmailer. What the hell did he want now?

24

———

Cory stared at the message. His mind churned like a washing machine. He'd just sent the bastard fifty thousand. How could he have the nerve to ask for more?

Cory felt they were trying to see how far they could push him. He knew that if he sent more money so soon, it would spin out of control. He couldn't allow that to ruin everything. As he thought about what to do, his phone rang. It was his wife.

"How could you?"

"What? What's the matter?"

"Don't you play dumb with me. What do you think, I'm some kind of fool? I'm here raising your kids, and you're screwing that bitch?"

"It's not true. I didn't do anything."

"Don't give me that bullshit. You're disgusting, you know that?"

"I swear, Linda, the press is making it up. There's nothing to it."

"How can you lie like that? There's a picture in the *Post* of the two of you. You make me sick."

"But it isn't what it looks like."

"Are you kidding me? At least be a man about it and admit it."

"I'm sorry."

"You better find a new place to live. I don't want you near me or the kids."

"Ah, come—" She hung up on him.

Cory called back but it went to voice mail. He tried again but she wouldn't answer. He punched in another number.

"Tracy, we got to do something. Linda found out about Joanne. There was a story in a New York paper. The damn press is looking to bring me down."

"I told you, you have to be discreet. There's no shortage of reporters looking for celebrity stories."

"I know, but what am I going to do? She's freaked out, doesn't want me coming back to the apartment. I gotta see my kids."

"Let me make some calls. I'll reserve the suite at the Mandarin and check on short-term rentals if you can't patch it up quickly."

"That's too far uptown. I want to be closer to my kids."

"Trust me on this. What Linda needs right now is space. Plus, the hotel is right across the street from Central Park. You can take the kids there."

"All right. Look, is there anything we can do about Joanne?"

"You want to replace her?"

"No. I wasn't thinking that, but maybe that's an idea."

"Don't rush into anything. She's an important piece of the band."

"I know but . . ."

"Let me think this over a little. Maybe I'll talk to Joanne and plant a story about her and a longtime boyfriend."

"Oh, that would be a lifesaver, thanks."

"But you still have to work on it with Linda."

"I will."

"Just please remember, the press likes to build people up, but they really enjoy tearing them down."

Cory flopped onto the couch. If the media ever found out about the stolen music, he'd be destroyed. He had to find a solution, but first he had to repair the damage he'd done to his family.

He hit redial. "Tracy, I need you to get some toys sent over to the apartment for the kids."

"I've never had kids, but I think it might be better to pick up a couple of things here and give them to the kids when you see them."

"But with everything going on, I figured—"

"I doubt that Linda said anything to the kids. Just be yourself with them."

"She better not have."

"Don't worry, you have one more show. That'll give her some time to cool off a little. And when you're back in two days, you'll have to patch things up."

"Okay. Send her two dozen roses. Make sure they're red."

CORY FELT it was a slog at times, but the final show went well. He poured himself a bourbon. "This time tomorrow, I'll be back in the city. I don't want to be away from my kids this many days again."

Tracy said, "This wasn't a long tour. You do Europe and you'll be away a lot longer."

"I won't do it."

"You may have to. The European circuit is very lucrative. But you can take your family with you."

"That's an idea. I'm beat. I'm going to sleep the whole flight home."

"I have to check on tomorrow's arrangements. I'll be back."

Cory thought about seeing his kids as he put ice cubes in his glass. He couldn't wait to see them. He tipped the Pappy Van Winkle bottle, but only poured half a glass. He didn't want to be hungover tomorrow.

Finishing his drink, he reclined on the sofa and closed his eyes. He tried to imagine how much Tommy might have changed in three weeks. Pictures only provided a snapshot of a moment; seeing and playing with his son would reveal how much he developed.

Wondering what his children would do for a living, his phone signaled a text. He reached for his phone.

It was the blackmailer: *Don't fuck with me. That was stupid and it's going to cost you. Now I want thirty grand. By tomorrow.*

THE PLANE BEGAN ITS DESCENT. The coffee wasn't working. He dug into his backpack and pulled out a bottle of Adderall. He took two of the stimulants and watched the city come into view.

As soon as Cory landed at Newark Airport, he called Linda. "Hey, I just got off the plane. I want to see you and the kids."

"You can see the kids, but I'm nowhere near ready."

"Aw, come on, Linda."

"You hurt me, Cory. I need time to get over this, if I ever do."

"You don't understand. Nothing happened."

"Please don't say that, it insults my intelligence. Give me an hour and I'll have the kids ready."

He hung up and said to Tracy, "She won't see me. We're gonna have to pick up the kids."

"Did she say anything about the hotel last night?"

"No."

"Be prepared, it'll get out."

"I hope not."

Cory put the privacy screen up in the SUV. They were parked in front of an apartment building, his eyes on the door. He took a vial of coke out and snorted four hits. It felt good. Watching the entrance, he slipped the small bottle into his pocket.

The doorman held the door as Tracy, holding Ava's hand, and the nanny, rolling a stroller, emerged.

He bounded out. "Hey, guys."

Ava ran toward him. "Daddy!"

Cory scooped her up. "I missed you so much."

"Me too!"

He set her down and knelt by the carriage. "Hey, little man, how you doing?"

Someone yelled out, "Hey, look, it's Cory Loop."

As a small crowd formed, Tracy said, "We better get in the car."

25

———

THEY DOUBLE-PARKED IN FRONT OF A GLASS BUILDING. A chorus of beeping horns sounded, almost drowning out Ava. "Do we have to go, Daddy?"

"Yes, Mommy is waiting for you."

"Why can't you come home with us?"

"I have to work very late the next week or two. I'm working on the new album."

"Can I come and watch?"

"Absolutely. I promise that as soon as possible, you can come to the studio and watch."

"When?"

"I'll let you know."

"Can I bring Mary with me?"

"Sure. Let's get your new toys together."

After seeing the kids off, Cory was dropped off at his hotel. Up in his suite, Tracy said, "Good to see you smiling again."

"It went so much better than I expected. Ava is something, isn't she?"

"A special little lady."

"Be honest with me, Tommy seems tiny, doesn't he?"

"He's only a couple of months old. Kids grow at different rates. He'll probably have a growth spurt."

"I gotta ask Linda what the pediatrician says. He was in something likethe eightieth percentile last time."

"I'm sure he'll be okay."

Cory's phone pinged with a text: *Where is my money?*

His fingers tapped back: *It was sent. Let me check on it.*

Cory dialed the phone as he retreated to the bathroom. "Lew, what happened with the wire I told you to send?"

"Oh, sorry, I forgot about it."

"Are you shitting me?"

"Take it easy, Cory. I'll get it out in the morning."

"No! I want it out now."

"I'll see what I can do."

"Don't see what you can do. Just fucking do it!"

Cory told the blackmailer it had been sent and did two lines of coke. When he came back into the living area, Tracy was on the phone. He poured a glass of bourbon and put the TV on.

Tracy hung up. "That was the general manager of the hotel."

"Yeah. What do they want?"

"They'd like us to leave."

"Why?"

"The Mandarin is part of the same company that owns the one in Dallas. Corporate office told them after what happened there, we're not welcome."

"That's bullshit. How can they kick me out?"

She sat next to him. "Cory, that suite was really trashed."

"So? I'll pay for whatever happened. What's the big frigging deal?"

"Money can't fix everything. We'll have to move fast; they want us out in two days."

"Screw them. I hate this frigging place anyway."

"I'll see what's available. If you think the situation with Linda is going to persist for a while, perhaps we should look at a short-term lease on an apartment."

"Do it. Make sure it's got bedrooms for the kids. I'm gonna hop in the shower. Tommy drooled down my back."

Cory went into the bathroom. Undressing, he noticed a trickle of blood coming out a nostril. He wiped it away and tilted his head back.

TRACY BROUGHT her laptop to Cory. "Here are the places I think are suitable for you. They're all three bedrooms, except the one in Hudson Yards, it's a four-bedroom place, and furnished. I'm only showing it to you because it happens to have a studio with a baby grand piano in it. It's not short-term, and at twenty-eight thousand a month, it's steep."

"I like it."

"Take your time. The others are nice, and the one on West Thirtieth has a large terrace space."

"How much is it?"

"Twenty thousand a month on a short-term basis."

"Okay."

"You tell me which ones you want to see, and I'll set it up."

"Just take the one with the studio."

"You don't want to see it first?"

"In the pictures it looks super. I dig the studio, and with the piano, maybe I can get some writing done."

"But it's a full-year lease."

"I know, but after the crap came out about the hotel, Linda is demanding we go to marriage counseling."

"It might be a good idea."

"It's bullshit. But we start tomorrow. I'm frigging dreading it."

"Just be open about it, and it'll work out fine."

DONNY STEPPED out of the elevator into Cory's apartment. "Hey, it's good to see you."

"Yeah, been too long. You want a hit?" Cory extended a joint.

"Nah. What's with the new place? I thought you said you were going stay at a hotel until you patched things up with Linda."

"She insisted we go for counseling."

"Oh. How's that going?"

"This woman doctor is tough. She's always breaking my balls."

"She's taking sides?"

"A little, but the other day she said what we needed was to find a place we can get away from everything and have some family time."

"Sounds like a plan."

"Yeah, she said to maybe find a place out of the city, away from all the distractions. I got Tracy looking at properties in Connecticut."

"Connecticut?"

"Yeah, Linda doesn't want it to be in a high-profile place like the Hamptons."

"She's got a point."

Cory took a drag as he went to the bar. "You want a drink?"

"Uh, no. It's kind of early, isn't it?"

"It's two o'clock."

"It's not good to be partying so much, bro."

"Lighten up, man."

"Can I say something without you flipping?"

"Of course, we're brothers."

"I'm worried about you."

"Me?"

"Yeah, I know you're under a lot of stress with everything coming at you a hundred miles an hour, but it's changing you, man."

"Bullshit. I'm still me."

"The old Cory wouldn't be drinking and popping pills like you're doing."

"Just trying to relax a little—"

"It's way past that, man. You're losing control."

"That's bullshit!"

"Yeah, what about you screwing around on Linda? The sad thing is, you're not even being cool about it."

"I fucked up. I know it, and I'm working to fix it. I know what I'm doing."

"Yeah? How do explain trashing the hotel? How could you let things get so out of control?"

"It was a mistake. I went overboard a little."

"Do yourself a favor and stop with the partying. Now."

"I can stop anytime I want."

"Well do it. Because you don't want to end up like Jay Bird."

Cory got up and poured his drink down the drain. "You happy now?"

"I'm just calling it like I see it."

"Well, let me tell you something, okay? You aren't seeing it right."

"I just want the best for you, man."

"I know. Look, I got to get ready for a meeting with the suits."

Cory thought about what his friend had said. He'd drank and anesthetized himself from the stress of being blackmailed, but he could handle it. As far as women were concerned, there was no doubt he'd been reckless. But it was the first time he got to be like a kid alone in an ice cream store.

Though women like Joanne were hard to resist, he had to smooth things out with Linda. Cory loved her and especially his kids and didn't want to hurt them. Maybe Donny was right. He'd slipped up, but he'd fix things.

First thing he had to do was finish writing the tunes for the next album. He went into the studio and sat at the piano. He couldn't focus. What if they didn't like what he wrote? They never liked his stuff before. Why did he think they would now?

Cory had one song left from what he'd stolen. It felt like another winner. He'd used pieces of the partial songs and weaved them into two songs, but they needed work. Three other originals were pretty good, but they were like the stuff he'd always written. He needed help. But who could he reach out to?

Cory got up and poured himself a drink. As he sipped the bourbon, it came to him. He pulled out his phone and made a call.

26

———

The phone woke Cory up. He grabbed it off the nightstand. "Hello?"

"Don't tell me you're still sleeping."

"Yeah. I was up late. I was writing all night."

"Hurry up, Linda and I are waiting in the car for you."

"Oh shit! I forgot we're going to Connecticut. Uh, don't come up. Go get coffee for me. I'll be right down."

"Okay. See you in a bit."

Cory hopped out of bed. Joanne said, "What's the matter?"

"I gotta get going. Tracy is waiting on me. We're heading to the country."

"Cool. Can I come?"

"Not this time. Where's your purse?"

"In the living room. Why?"

"My ass is dragging. I need a hit before I jump in the shower."

CORY HOPPED in the front seat of the SUV. "Sorry, guys. I was up till three composing." He blew a kiss to Linda, saying, "You look super nice today."

"Thanks. Uh, you could use a shave."

"I know. Tell you the truth, I just got out of bed and jumped into the shower. I didn't want to keep you waiting."

Tracy said, "I was showing Linda the properties we're going to see. Which one did you like, Cory?"

"Uh, I . . . I think Linda and me need to see them. Make sure they're good for us and the kids."

Linda said, "I'm impressed. The whole time we've been talking to Dr. Bruno, I thought you weren't listening."

Cory smiled. "She's growing on me."

The gate to the second property swung open, and they drove up a long, winding driveway. When it ended, Linda said, "Look at that view! You can see Long Island Sound from here."

Tracy said, "It's a special estate. Twenty-two acres, with a main house, a guest cottage, and a barn outfitted for entertaining. It'd be a great space for the kids. But at eighteen million, it's the most expensive of them all."

Cory said, "Isn't that always the case?"

"Usually. I'm not selling you on it, but the size of this place gives you the privacy and security you need."

The Realtor showed them the entire property, then left Linda and Cory by the pool to talk alone. Linda said, "This place is incredible. Look at this pool area and the tennis courts. I always wanted my kids to play."

"They will. You like this place, don't you?"

"Who wouldn't? It's amazing, but it's too much house and way too expensive."

"We can swing it."

"No, it's a crazy amount of money."

"It'd be great for us, for the family. We'd have our own getaway compound. That'd be super cool."

"I know. We could spend the summers and weekends out here. Who knows? Maybe we could send the kids to school here."

"I never thought of that."

"But we can't afford it."

"I think we can. Let me check with Lew."

"Are you sure?"

"I don't want to see another one, unless you do."

"Lew, we just saw a place in Connecticut that we'd like to buy."

"Tracy told me about it, but it's just out of reach, kid."

"Why? The tour brought in almost ten million."

"Yes, but there are expenses, and the property is eighteen million."

"Get a mortgage or something. Figure it out. I need to have this place."

"You can stretch for it, kid, but you'd be taking on too much risk. If the next album doesn't make it or your popularity cools, the payments could get difficult for you."

"We'll be okay."

"With this price tag, you're going to have to put down at least a million. The monthly cost would be about seventy grand. And that's without the taxes and upkeep. It'll be a good hundred K a month. And we're talking after-tax money here."

"It's all right. I can handle it."

"Isn't there something a bit more reasonable?"

"No. This is the one I want."

"I have to advise you, as your manager, I think you're making a mistake."

"Noted. Get in touch with Tracy. She has the contact details for the seller. Get a hold of them and try to do better on the price."

"I'll see what room there is, but it's not going to change the economics of it."

"And get them to do a short-term lease or something. We want to get in there immediately. I don't want to wait to close on it."

"Are you sure about all of this? You're moving too fast. You have to think these types of things through."

"I did. Now just get it done. Text me after you speak with them."

Cory hung up and called to Linda, "Guess what?"

"You spoke to Lew?"

"Sure did."

"What did he say about the house?"

"We're going to get it."

"What? He didn't say anything about how much it was?"

"Said we can handle it, no problem."

"Oh my God, I can't believe it."

"It's going to be great. The kids are going to love it. And it'd be good for your mom."

"It's a dream house. Ava is going to go crazy when she sees it."

"Don't tell her. Let's do it together, you know, keep it a family thing."

"Sure."

"Can I come over later? We can show her pictures of it on the iPad."

Linda agreed. Cory felt he'd turned a corner in their relationship. He thought about Dr. Bruno. He'd only agreed to go for marriage counseling to get his family back together. He was skeptical but had a newfound appreciation for the doctor.

He envisioned flopping around in the pool with Ava. Maybe they'd get a boat. He wondered how much the one he saw in San Diego was. It was huge and had to be expensive. Lew's warning rang in his ear. But this was important to him. He needed to get things back where they were.

Cory's concern eased when he thought about moving back in with Linda. He could probably sublet the apartment he'd taken, saving money. Things would be fine.

A text sounded. Cory palmed his phone, anxious to see the deal that Lew had struck. It wasn't his manager. He read the message. Cory threw the phone aside and made himself a drink. A tall one.

27

———

Cory checked the clock on Dr. Bruno's credenza as Linda beat the trust drum. How could there still be ten minutes left? When Linda came up for air, Dr. Bruno said, "Trust is the basis for every relationship. In a marriage, partners must be able to rely on each other, to have a certain predictability regarding their mate's behavior. That confidence is even more important when children are involved. Do you understand why Linda is upset over what happened yesterday?"

"Uhm, yeah. I get it. It was a one-off thing."

Linda rolled her eyes but remained quiet.

"It would be reassuring to her if you could state your intention not to repeat it."

"I'm sorry. I was celebrating that we got the house and, I guess, got a little carried away."

"A little? You almost dropped Tommy."

"I didn't, but I don't want to argue about it. I admit I was drunk, and I'm sorry."

"Linda? Do you accept Cory's apology?"

"Yes, but this has to end."

"Cory, do you understand the commitment that Linda is asking of you?"

"Yeah, I got it. We're all good."

"Excellent. Well, time's up. We'll see each other next week."

On the way to the door, Dr. Bruno said, "Cory, may I speak with you?"

She closed the door. "Sit down a moment."

"Is everything all right?"

"Yes. You're aware that I rarely do marriage counseling."

"Yeah, I know you did Linda a favor. We appreciate it."

"My practice and passion is employing psychotherapy to help people overcome their reaction to situations, to reframe them in a way that makes it possible to deal with them."

Folding his arms over his chest, Cory said, "I don't know much about that stuff."

"It's very effective."

"Good."

"I wanted to discuss your drinking."

"It's not a problem, Doc."

"We've talked about the importance of honesty in your relationship with Linda. But equally important is being true to yourself. It's a fact, both the easiest and hardest person to lie to is ourselves."

"I guess so."

"In an attempt to hide from the truth, we tell ourselves stories that we want to hear." She paused, then said, "Truthfully, are you drinking too much?"

"Not really, it's mostly just social drinking. You know, the music business and all."

"Yesterday you were drunk in the middle of the afternoon. That's not social."

"Like I said earlier, it was a one-off thing."

"Cory, I read the papers, and some of the stories, even if exaggerated, appear to be signs of trouble. There's usually an underlying reason why people turn to drugs and alcohol. They offer temporary relief, but the benefit is short-lived and ultimately self-destructive."

Cory shifted in his chair. "I guess I got too much on my mind."

"Why don't we talk about that? Naturally, it would be confidential. I believe it would not only help you, but it would further the work we're doing with Linda. Psychotherapists are just like lawyers, when you tell us something, we're bound by law to keep it between us."

Cory shrugged.

"How about next Monday?"

CORY COULDN'T CONCENTRATE. His mind was focused on the new demand for money that arrived just before a writing session. He wondered how he was going to explain the new wiring instructions to Lew.

This time they wanted the money to go to a bank in the Isle of Man. He had to Google the place. It was more evidence that whoever was behind it was sophisticated. Cory tried to think of a reasonable explanation. Maybe he could use the excuse it was for medical costs for his mother-in-law.

Using health as a reason would provide privacy, but he'd have to be careful it wouldn't slip out to Linda in a harmless conversation. Why did everything have to be so complicated? Resolving to tell Lew to do what he wanted if he started asking questions, a pair of hands rubbed his shoulders.

Joanne said, "Boy, you're so tense. What's going on?"

"I guess it's the pressure to get more songs ready."

"Don't worry, we'll get it done." She went to the piano. "How do you like this chord progression?"

"It's dark. Where would we use it?"

"If we alter the melody in the bridge on 'Tropical Storm,' we can use it to heighten the feel moving into the final sixteen bars."

"All right. Let me sing it up a third. One, two, one, two, three four."

After Cory sang it, Joanne said, "Yeah, that works. It could be way-out cool if you hung on 'rain' as long as you could."

Cory sang it as suggested. Joanne said, "That's it. But bend it, like this." She sang it, bringing the note down and then back in tune.

"I like that."

They ran it a couple of times and Joanne said, "It could be one of those lines everybody is going to sing along with."

"You think so?"

"Relax, have some fun with it. You're too self-conscious or something. Why don't you have a drink or something?"

"I just got a lot on my mind." Cory took the guitar off his shoulder. "You want a drink?"

"Sure, I'm gonna have a hit." She held up a vial. "You want some?"

"Definitely."

Cory took a sip of bourbon. He had a second gulp, relishing the comfort it spread. "You sure you don't want some Pappy V? It's the best."

"Nah, I'm good. Here." She held out a spoonful and Cory snorted it. After the fourth hit he shook his head. "Yeah, that's nice."

"Feeling loose now?"

"Yeah, let's get something done and then, you know, have some fun."

28

They turned onto Franklin Street, stopping in front of a five-story brick building. Tracy said, "Cory, wait in the car for a few minutes. Joanne, go on in."

Joanne closed the door of the SUV. Tracy said, "You're going to blow it with Linda if you keep this up."

"She was helping me last night. It just got really late and she stayed over."

Tracy didn't say anything.

"You have to see what we did with a couple of the tunes. I'm telling you, they're a lot better."

"That's good, but besides your wife, you have to think about how it looks to the band. You have a good thing going. Don't screw it up by being careless."

"Don't worry. I got it handled."

"I hope so." She dug into her purse. "Here, take one of these." She handed him a mint.

Popping the freshener in his mouth, Cory wondered how badly he reeked of alcohol and walked into the recording session.

Cory stayed in the studio, talking with the players as they packed up. He wasn't anxious to go in the sound booth and review the tracks they'd laid down. He stole a glance through the window. Iggy, the producer, was shaking his head as he talked with Cory's agent and the sound engineer.

"Cory, come on up."

It was Dave. He signaled his agent and said goodbye to Donny.

"Hey, how'd it sound in here?"

Iggy said, "Everybody liked track two, 'Circles,' but the rest—it doesn't have the energy of the last recording."

"Circles" was the last song Cory had stolen.

"Really? What about 'Tropical Storm'? I thought it hit all the emotional bells."

Dave said, "Yeah, it was good. You said you liked it, Iggy."

"I think I can fix it in the mix. We'll record new horn lines, ones with more feeling, and it should come together."

"Is there anything else you can do to pump up the others?"

"Look, I'm not saying they won't work, but we're aiming at the pop genre with this. That's your audience. You want to go in a different direction, it's your artistic license, man. Just it ain't what the suits are expecting."

"I have some other material I'm working on. A couple of them are coming along."

Dave said, "We don't have time. The label wants a single out now. They want it to chart before they put out the album, to get some momentum."

Iggy said, "It's gotta be 'Circles.' At this point, nothing else has a shot."

"You'll need a couple of days to add horns and to mix it, right? I'll see what I can do with what's almost done."

"I'll get the horns to lay some shit down tomorrow. You got two days, max."

"All right."

Dave followed Cory out of the booth and pulled him aside. "Is everything all right?"

Cory shrugged.

"I'm only saying this to offer constructive criticism, but most of the material was, uh, very different from what's on *Loop Around*. If you're moving in a different creative direction, it might be better to make the mix a little more even."

"Like what?"

"Say, half the songs like 'Circles,' that's what the fans expect. The other half you can do whatever you want. If the fans like where you are going, you'll be fine. If they don't respond, we go back to what works."

"We? I didn't see you in the damn studio."

"Take it easy, Cory, I didn't mean anything by it."

"Yeah, well, leave me alone."

"Come on, I'm just trying to make suggestions, that's all."

"You want to help? Then you write the fucking songs."

"I'm sorry if I offended your artistry. Look, I overstepped, I get it, but I was only trying to prevent the label from giving us any pushback."

"Yeah, right." Cory walked away.

CORY NEEDED ANOTHER DRINK. He went to the bar. The bottle on it had nothing in it. He opened the cabinet, taking a new one out. Unscrewing the cap, he caught a glimpse of the trash can behind the bar. It had another empty bottle of bourbon in it. He paused before pouring another glass. Remembering he was going to get help from Dr. Bruno, he filled the glass and sipped away.

Cory thought over what to tell the therapist when they met. He wondered if telling Linda that he was going would help get them back together. Knowing he was seeking help could go two ways: either it was a good sign he was looking to correct his ways, or it confirmed an unsolvable addiction.

The confidentiality comment on not divulging what was said between a client and attorney got him thinking. Maybe there was a way out of the turmoil he was feeling. He considered his options. There were no painless paths, but one idea kept surfacing.

The plan he concocted would not only end the blackmailing but would enable him to come clean. Though it would be tough to put his family through the embarrassment that would come by revealing he'd stolen the music, if he could hold on to some of the money he'd made, they'd be miles better off.

Reaching for his glass, Cory misjudged, knocking it off the table. He couldn't live like this any longer; he had to take the risk. Cory cleaned up the booze and put a pod of coffee in the machine. He'd straighten up before making the call that could change everything.

29

———

THE WALL BEHIND CARMINE PISONI'S DESK WAS FILLED WITH framed diplomas. Cory figured he charged a thousand an hour to pay off his school loans. In a dark blue suit and red tie, Pisoni circled his desk, easing into his chair.

The silver-haired lawyer said, "What brings you here today?"

"I, uh, wanted to talk about something that's confidential, but I want to be sure what I'm going to say doesn't leave this room."

"Our discussions are protected under a statute known as attorney-client privilege. Whatever you tell me and the counsel I may give cannot be revealed to anyone."

"I read something on the web that a client had to actually pay a lawyer's bill, otherwise it wouldn't be protected."

"That's not accurate. For example, when we do pro bono work, where the lawyer provides legal representation for free, conversations between the parties are also protected."

Cory took a wad of cash out of his pocket. "Here's a thousand. Just to be certain."

"It's really not necessary, Mr. Lupinski."

"Can you write out a receipt?"

"If you insist." Pisoni wrote a receipt and handed it to Cory.

"Thanks." Cory took a deep breath. "I don't know how much you know about me."

"I familiarize myself before meeting a new client, and when I saw that your stage name was Loop, it hit me." He smiled. "We have two teenage daughters, and they're fans. I must say, your music is catchy."

"Thanks. I'm not new to the scene. I've played in scores of recordings but never as a leader. Anyway, what I want to know is, I've been doing good now from the album sales and mostly from touring, but what would happen if, say, the music on the album wasn't really written by me?"

"Presently, you're credited with composing the songs?"

"Yes."

"Do you have the consent of the person who wrote them?"

"That's the thing. The guy died."

"If he didn't give you the right to the songs, then his estate would have a claim on the royalties a songwriter is entitled to. It's somewhere in the neighborhood of nine cents per song."

"So, any money I made from, say, sales and downloads would have to be given back?"

"Without seeing the contract, I believe the songwriting royalties would be subject to a clawback."

"Okay, but what about the other money? Would I have to give back the money from touring?"

"No. Let me rephrase that. I'm not well versed in entertainment law, but the way I understand it is, it's the venue's responsibility to obtain public performance licenses and pay any required license fees. As you can imagine, it would be impossible for an arena to know what arrangement an artist had made on the songs they perform during a show. Therefore, to cover themselves, venues affiliate themselves with performing rights organizations who ensure songwriters are compensated."

"So, I can keep the money from touring?"

"I believe so."

"I thought so."

"You may want to consider trying to strike an agreement with the estate."

"He had no family. Nothing at all. He was abandoned as an infant in Brooklyn and never married or had kids."

"If that's the case, you'd be up against the State of New York."

"Since they're broke, I guess they'd come after me."

"Eventually. Maybe there's a deal that could be struck, some middle ground. I'm talking out loud here, but given the hole in the state budget, a payment upfront would likely be welcome, and who knows, maybe you perform a free concert or two."

"Really?"

"Just throwing out ideas. How did you obtain the material? Were you collaborating?"

"Yeah, kind of. We were in the studio writing that night, and he died suddenly. I took the sheet music with me."

"Why not just come out and explain the cooperative nature of the relationship? You could give co-credit to the individual. That would solve the issue and at half the possible cost."

"It's not that easy. You see, this artist was very successful, and he never worked with anybody. Or so he said. Everybody in the industry knew he didn't compose with other musicians."

"It might require a publicity campaign to educate the public on the circumstances."

Cory frowned and Pisoni said, "I get it." He smiled. "Today, the press is even less respected than lawyers are. The thing is, they'll make a big deal over it, but in a day or two they'll move on."

"Yeah, but that's after they destroy you. Thanks for the advice. I'll think over what you said."

CORY SAT AT THE PIANO, but nothing was coming out. He played a simple melody line over a major chord. He jotted down the notes to the cheery sound it created. Unable to develop the line further, he repeated the four-bar phrase.

Stuck, he moved to exploring lyrics but kept drifting back to what the lawyer had said. He paced the apartment thinking through the possible outcomes. He made a drink and halfway through it, made his mind up.

As soon as the new album was done, he'd talk to Lew and make sure he had enough money to last if his career cratered. Cory topped off his drink. He felt good and returned to the piano. Cory was good at singing harmonies, and he started stacking notes in different inversions.

The sounds were too heavy for pop music, but one progression reminded him of the one that Joanne had used during their writing session. He pulled his phone out.

"Hey Jo, what are you doing?"

"I'm out. What's up?"

"I need some help writing. I'm really jammed up. I could use your help getting unfrozen."

"No can do, I'm out."

"Aw, come on, man!"

"Take it easy, Cory. I can't do it now."

"What about later?"

"Maybe tomorrow."

"I need the fucking tunes by tomorrow."

"I'm sorry our schedules don't sync up. I gotta run."

Cory pounded the keyboard with his fist. "That bitch." He got up thinking about what she had said. Her schedule didn't sync up. What the hell did that mean? Was she out with another guy? He didn't care about her being with someone else; he needed help.

He made another drink, muttering, "Sync up, my ass," when an idea hit him.

30

Cory's phone was ringing. Again. He reached for it. "Hello?"

"Mr. Lupinski, It's Johnny. I've been waiting downstairs. I haveto take you downtown, to Platinum Studios."

Cory dragged himself out of bed and into the bathroom. He popped two Advils and took a leak Turning the shower on, he returned to his bedroom. Cory grabbed the bottle of Adderall. Spilling out two pills, he dry swallowed them and showered.

Dave was standing outside the studio. "Hey Cory, how are you doing today?"

"Good. Is the band here?"

"Oh yeah. Everyone's ready to roll."

"Me too. I wrote something last night. I think it's gonna work."

"Really? You were pretty much in the tank when you called."

Cory held out a piece of sheet music. "Make copies for everyone."

"'You Need to Come Home.' I like the title."

"Let's get going."

Cory addressed the band. "On this tune, we need a deep groove going. Donny, I want it way behind the beat, but make sure you don't slow the tempo. It can breathe a little, but it's got to move."

"You want background vocals on the bridge?"

"No. I want it clean for the moment. Let Iggy do what he knows how to do with it later."

Joanne said, "You want fills in the vocal spaces?"

"Uh-huh, but keep it simple and don't step on me."

"No worries. You want an intro?"

"Play the last eight bars at the moment. I'm thinking maybe a vamp upfront, but I'll let Iggy make the call. Everybody ready?"

Cory counted off the tempo, and Joanne led the band into the top of the tune.

When the song ended, Cory said, "Good, good. What did you think?"

Riley said, "Man, that sounds familiar, but I like it. You know a vamp at the end, with you chanting, 'You Need to Come Home,' would be cool."

Joanne said, "Yeah, it reminds me of something from when I was a kid."

Cory said, "Really? A lot of stuff sounds the same. Let's run it again and add the vamp. Do the vamp in G minor."

They ran it four times, and Cory ended the session. Donny hung back as the musicians filed out of the studio. Cory said, "That went pretty good, didn't it?"

He shook his head. "I heard what you did."

"What are you talking about?"

"Come on, bro, that was an old NSYNC song, 'I Want You Back.' All you did was write new lyrics over it. The melody is almost exactly the same. You just changed a couple of the quarter notes into eighths."

"No, man. That's not it."

"Come on, Cory. We wore out that record when we were kids."

"But, there's no harmonies and—"

"You're going to get sued, bro. It's going to be a mess. You're inviting trouble. I don't know, man, between the drinking, screwing around, and now this, you looking to self-destruct or something?"

"I didn't realize. It just came out, I swear."

"After all the bullshit that you took from the Jay Bird rumors, you do this? What were you thinking, man?"

"Uh, I guess I didn't give it much thought."

"Exactly, use your head, or you're going to regret it."

"Should I just kill it, then?"

"I'm not saying you shouldn't do it, but you'd need the rights to it, otherwise it's reckless, at best."

"You're right. Thanks."

"Look, I've told you before, but you better back off with all the partying you're doing."

"You don't know what you're talking about. It's not what you think it is."

"Oh yeah? Every frigging day we were on the road, you were hammered. It's not good, man."

"Just having a little fun, that's all."

"Bullshit, Cory. All I'm saying is if you want things to get back to normal with Linda and the kids, you better end it, and fast."

Tracy stuck her head in the studio. "Cory, we got to move it. You have an appointment with the hairstylist before the photo shoot."

Cory put his earbuds in and searched Spotify for

NSYNC's "I Want You Back." As it played, Cory shook his head. Though there was no doubt about the plagiarism, he didn't remember copying the tune beat for beat. He'd have to cool it with the partying, especially when he was composing.

DR. BRUNO SAID, "Please, make yourself comfortable."

Cory surveyed the dimly lit room. Though it wasn't the same one he and Linda had used, it didn't contain any pictures or personal items. He sank into a corduroy chair. "Okay, I'm here. You happy now?"

"It's your happiness I'm concerned about."

Cory shrugged.

"You appear tired. Did you sleep well last night?"

"Haven't had a good night's rest in a long time."

"What prevents you from getting rest?"

"I fall asleep pretty fast, but I wake up, and then it's hard to get back to sleep."

"Because your mind is busy?"

"Yeah."

"What kind of things do you contemplate?"

"Everything, the situation with my wife and kids, the new album, and trying to handle everything that's been going on since the first record came out."

"Do you feel like at times it's too much to handle?"

"Yeah, sometimes."

"I understand the need to find a way to relax, to escape the pressure you're under with such a high-profile career. It's not easy."

"You said it."

"What I'm concerned about is using alcohol and drugs as a place of refuge. In the short term, they provide a measure of escapism, but the evidence is solid they contribute to psychological distress, fatigue, and paranoia. Eventually they make the situation worse, much worse."

"I can see that."

"Do you feel you're indulging in them too much?"

"Maybe. Sometimes."

"If we can identify the triggers that stress you to a point you seek relief, we can find ways to reframe them, preventing a repeat of the situations you've found yourself in. Does that sound reasonable?"

"I guess. There's a lot of pressure on me, from every place."

"What about your family? Do you feel any pressure being exerted on you?"

"By my wife and kids?"

"Yes, unless there is another member of the family causing stress."

"No, my wife and kids are good. My father, he's the one who thought I'd never make it. He considered me a failure. Nothing I did was good enough."

"Did he get to see any of your success?"

"No. He was gone already, but . . ."

"He's still haunting you?"

"A little."

"Oftentimes, when someone is under stress, they lose control of their emotions. The feelings they have drive them back to a painful place. In your case, that could be feelings of insecurity. Have you been experiencing anything like that?"

"Yeah, I mean, there's pressure that I'm not going to duplicate the success I had with the first album."

"But on an intellectual level, you realize that the chances of two megahits in a row are pretty remote. Don't you?"

"Oh definitely. I mean, not many people have done it, not even Jay Bird."

"So, what is causing you anxiety?"

"Nothing really."

"Remember what I said about being honest with yourself? You can't expect to address a problem until you define it. Tell me, I'm here to help."

"I . . . I can't . . . right now."

"That's okay, I understand. Possibly next week we can talk about it."

"I have a plan to deal with it."

"That's good. In the meantime, I'd recommend you engage in some form of physical exercise. It will help your body deal with the stress."

31

Seeing his manager made Cory's heart race. He didn't know how he was going to start the conversation. "Hey, Lew, I got to use the bathroom."

"You know where it is. I'll be in my office."

Cory ducked into a stall and took out his flask. He took a gulp. Before the burn dissipated, he took a long pull and capped the container. Cory flushed the toilet, washed his hands, and popped a Halls cough drop in his mouth.

He walked to Lew's office telling himself he could do it.

"You redecorate or something?"

"A little bit. The furniture needed upgrading, and the carpet had some stains."

"Looks good."

"I know you're concerned about the new album and all, but you shouldn't be. Everything is set. The single is going to get monster airplay. I'm predicting it'll be number one faster than anything anyone has released."

"That would be nice. What about the new deal? You said I would get a higher split of the royalties."

"Don't worry, kid. You take care of the music, and I've got the finances under control."

"I want to know."

"Okay. They fought me on it, but I pushed them like crazy, and we're getting an extra dollar for every album sold."

"What about the singles?"

"They wouldn't budge, said the costs for delivery were too high."

"Are you kidding me? You got to go back to them. I need the money."

"You'll do fine. The money is in the touring anyway."

"How much money do I have?"

"Uh, it's always changing."

"How much do I have, right this second?"

"Is something the matter, kid? You can tell me."

"It's a simple question, Lew. How much do I have sitting in the bank right now?"

"Uh, I'd have to check, but I'd say three hundred thousand—"

"That's it?"

"I can be off. I haven't checked in a couple—"

"How much did we net from the tour? Three million?"

"More like two point six."

"And the single and album sales and downloads?"

"I'd estimate about seven hundred thousand."

"Is there a lot still coming in?"

"No, I mean the sales and downloads take three months to settle, but it's not that much."

"Where the fuck is my money?"

"Take it easy, Cory. I could be off, but don't forget the expenses. You're paying for a couple of apartments and the house in Connecticut—"

"How much is that every month?"

"Uh, I have to look at the numbers again, but the mortgage in Connecticut is sixty thousand a month, and the two apartments around another thirty. And the taxes and upkeep. Plus, you've been helping your mother-in-law and friends out. It's a lot, but I'll put it to paper if you want."

Cory was terrible at math, but he rounded the housing costs to a hundred thousand a month. Even at six months, it was only about a half a million, plus the two hundred thousand he'd paid to the blackmailer.

"I want to see the numbers for myself."

"Of course, I'll email them to you, okay?"

AVA CAME out of her room. "Mom, I'm thirsty."

Cory jumped up and took care of her. When she was back in bed, he came back into the living room. Linda said, "Ava never settles down when you come over."

"She just wants to see me. If you let me move back in . . ."

Linda said, "I'm not ready for that."

"But we're together when we're in Connecticut."

"We have separate bedrooms there. Don't start this now. We had a good day, let's keep it there."

"Can't blame me for trying."

She silently shook her head.

"You have any more wine?"

"That's enough, Cory."

"Okay, okay. Just so you know, I've cut back a lot on the drinking."

"I hope so."

"You don't notice it?"

"Not really, you're actually pretty jittery tonight."

"The new single is coming out tomorrow."

"I really like it. It's going to do great."

"I hope so. We could use the money."

"What do you mean?"

"Lew was saying that most of the money was gone."

"Don't you know?"

"You know I hate all things accounting."

"You can't keep using what your father did for a living as an excuse not to pay attention to money."

"I just don't like doing it."

"Well, then you should find someone you trust, then."

"That's what Lew is for."

"After what he pulled with our old landlord? He told you he was going to take care of him, but he never did."

"He said he forgot, that's all."

"And you believe him?"

"What are you saying?"

"You need to get someone who understands numbers to verify all this. If you want, I can call Marilyn. She's with a big accounting firm in the city."

CORY HOPPED IN THE SUV. Tracy handed him a pork pie hat.

"Baby blue?"

"It's Ellen DeGeneres's favorite color. She'll get a kick out of it."

"It's not like we need to soften her up, do we?"

"No, she's a fan."

"Good. I could use some good coverage."

"You know, the press can be tough, but you can control some of it. I'm not telling you how to live your life, but if you feel the need to blow off steam and party, don't do it in public."

"They blew it out of proportion."

Tracy's phone rang. She had a brief talk and hung up smiling. "'Circles' just hit the Billboard chart at number five."

"All right. Now we're talking."

"After the media blitz we have arranged, it'll climb to number one, and then we'll follow with 'Tropical Storm.'"

"What do you think of 'Tropical Storm'?"

"I don't know much about music."

"You don't have to know anything, it's whether you like it or not."

"It's pretty good."

"You don't like it."

"Yes, I do."

A text hit Cory's phone. He read it and said, "Goddamn it! Why can't I get to enjoy anything?"

"What's the matter?"

"Nothing."

"Come on, Cory, you can tell me. Get it off your chest."

"I can't."

"Sure, you can. You can trust me. It's not only my job, but I want to help you."

"Not with this you can't."

"Is it about Linda?"

"No."

"Tell me."

He took his AirPods out. "Leave me alone."

32

***

THE DOWNER CORY HAD TAKEN BEFORE APPEARING ON THE *Ellen DeGeneres Show* began to really kick in as he walked off the set. Even though his face hurt from trying not to yawn, he wondered if it was the drugs or Ellen's disarming personality that made the interview fun.

Cory needed to tell Lew to get the wire sent. He retreated to an empty set in the next studio.

"Hey, how did the appearance go?"

"Good, real good. She's funny as hell."

"Yeah, I like her. What's going on?"

"I'm sending over another wire request."

"Okay . . . how much we have to send?"

"A hundred."

"Thousand?"

"Yep."

"I don't know."

"You said I had six hundred-plus in the bank. What the problem?"

"Okay, it's your money, but are you in trouble or something, kid?"

"No."

"Oh, I get it. You're splitting up with Linda and shifting some assets out of her reach."

"Kind of."

"Don't worry about me, kid. I can keep a secret. I'll get it going for you."

"Thanks."

"Oh, I got a call from some woman who said she was going to audit your finances."

"Yeah, it's probably from my wife's lawyer."

"If you give them access, they're going to see the wires."

"At this point, I almost don't care anymore."

"But you're not making sense, kid. You want me to send a wire out and then let them see the books?"

"Just do it. If they find it, they find it."

"But—"

"Get it out. Now."

Cory was nodding out in the SUV when Tracy said, "Look at this story. It's like a spy movie or something." She pointed to an article in the newspaper. The headline said, "Vigilante Killer Strikes Again."

Cory couldn't focus his vision on the text. "I'm too tired to read. Just tell me what it's about."

"There's this man out there, the police think it's the same guy. He's killed three people who were acquitted of murder even though everybody thinks they did it. Remember the man in Brooklyn, who was accused of killing his fiancée? He was all over TV saying he was out fishing when she was killed."

"Yeah, the guy with the granny glasses."

"Yep, that's him. Remember he changed his story when the video came out that showed his boat never left the dock?"

"Yeah."

"Well, he got off, but this vigilante killer, he took him out yesterday and got away without a trace."

"They'll catch him. Nobody gets away with it."

"Are you kidding me? The article just said forty percent of murders are never solved."

"That's crazy."

"I know, that's what I thought when I read it. Even if it's off by half, that's still one out of every five killers that gets away."

"How many in the city?"

Tracy typed the question into Google. "Since 1985, almost ten thousand unsolved murders in New York City."

"Geez. How many is that a year?"

She put the numbers into the calculator app. "Two hundred and sixty."

"That's super dangerous. Maybe I should move the family out to Connecticut."

"You still going up there next week?"

BACK IN HIS APARTMENT, Cory lit a joint and poured himself a bourbon. He finished the joint and flopped onto the couch. Cory grabbed his drink, took a sip, and closed his eyes. The skin on his face felt dry. He had to wash off the makeup they'd put on. His mind drifted.

Heart racing, Cory bolted upright. He looked around. He'd been dreaming. In the dream, Cory had hired Ellen's cameraman to kill Damien, an up-and-coming singer whom he was battling for supremacy on the Billboard charts.

Cory reached for his drink, wondering how the mind combined bits of information into something believable. His phone chimed a text. Cory hesitated before looking. He exhaled. It was from Linda. But it wasn't all good.

She wanted to know why he wasn't at Ava's dance rehearsal. Cory gulped the rest of the drink down and opened the Uber app.

As a line of girls in red and white costumes took the stage, Cory slid into a seat next to Linda. He whispered, "Sorry, I—"

"Save it, I don't want to hear it."

"When is Ava coming on?"

"She just got off the stage."

"Oh, come on, really?"

"Yeah, really Cory. You missed it."

"Don't tell her I didn't see it. What color outfit did they have on?"

"Look, you want to lie to your daughter, I don't like it, but it's your call. Just don't ask me to cover for you."

A parent behind them said, "Shush."

Cory leaned in, "It's not a lie, I just got stuck on the TV show."

Linda's eyes bored into him. "You've been drinking. What did I tell you about being around the children when you're drunk?"

"I'm not drunk, I had one drink."

"I want you to leave."

"Aw, come on."

"Goodbye, Cory."

"We're supposed to have dinner together."

"Not in your condition. You better leave, or you'll make things worse than they already are."

As soon as Cory got in an Uber, he called Tracy. "How come you didn't remind me about Ava's recital?"

"What are you talking about? I told you on the way back from the *Ellen* show."

"No, you didn't."

"I certainly did. Don't tell me you missed it."

"Yeah, I blew it. I forgot about it."

"How did you do that? Were you writing?"

"Uh, yeah. I lost track of time. Do me a favor and send roses to Ava and Linda."

"Will do. Listen, you better start taking care of yourself. Did you call Dylan, the trainer I told you about?"

"Yeah, he's coming Thursday."

"That's tomorrow."

"Oh, right."

"I know you said no, but I'm going to get Barbara to send you prepared meals when you're in town."

"I don't need that. I have a million places around me, and they all deliver."

"You have to start eating healthier. Pizza doesn't cut it."

A text chimed in. "I got to go. I think Linda is texting me."

Cory went to his messages. It was the blackmailer, and he was pissed.

33

WHAT DO YOU THINK, WE GOT A DAMN LAYAWAY PLAN? SEND ME the rest of the fucking money or you'll regret it.

Cory recounted his conversation with Lew. He'd been buzzed. Had he made a mistake with the amount when he sent the wiring instructions? He scrolled through his texts. The amount was correct. He punched in his manager's number. It went straight to voice mail.

Was he avoiding him? He waited five minutes and redialed. No luck. He called the office but was told Lew was out and not expected back. Pouring himself a drink, he heard a text arrive. He figured it was Lew. It wasn't:

Where's the rest of the money?

I'm checking on it.

Don't fuck with me.

I'm not. I told my manager to send it. I'm trying to get a hold of him.

Cory called Tracy and asked her to track down Lew. He made another drink, but before he could take a sip his cell rang. He didn't recognize the number and hesitated. Figuring it was Lew calling from another location, he answered.

"Mr. Lupinski?"

"Yes? Who is this?"

"Wendy Wilcox, the accountant."

"Oh. Hi. What's going on?"

"Well, I started to audit the books, and found something concerning."

"Wires to my friends?"

"No. This concerns a series of transfers. You see, in an audit, we verify what appears on the books. We go a level deeper to make sure what shows on the surface is actually where the money goes and—"

"Tell me what you found."

"Well, there are a dozen transfers, in varying amounts, that went into Mr. Stein's account."

"What? Are you sure?"

"Yes, I always start with transfers and wires, focusing on big round numbers. I like to vet those first. Right away, I noticed a transfer for fifty thousand dollars in the check register. According to the paperwork, it went to a company called the Promotion Pros. But, following where the money actually went, it didn't go there, it went to Lewis Stein."

"I can't believe this. Are you sure it isn't some kind of paperwork mistake?"

"Unfortunately, it appears orchestrated. After uncovering the first inconsistency, I searched the books for others and found eleven other transfers, each of them to Lewis Stein."

"The bastard is stealing from me?"

"It's preliminary, but that's how it appears."

"How much money in total?"

"Five hundred and sixty thousand dollars."

"I swear, I'll kill the bastard."

"Please calm down, Mr. Lupinski. It's possible Mr. Stein has an explanation."

"What can you send me as proof about what you uncovered?"

"I can send you copies of the transfers detailing where the money went."

"Text them to me. Now."

Realizing the reason the blackmailer only got half the money, Cory gulped his drink. He was broke, he thought, as the documentation hit his phone. He opened three. There didn't seem to be any doubt that his manager got the money. Why? Was Lew involved in the blackmailing scheme as well?

It couldn't be, otherwise he'd know the money wasn't there. But was that just a cover to make him think he wasn't involved? He bounced between believing it was a ruse, to thinking it was impossible. He couldn't think straight.

Cory downed his drink and ordered an Uber car. He put a jacket on, hammering the elevator button like a morphine pump. When the elevator sounded, he ran into the kitchen. Grabbing a steak knife, he shoved it in a pocket and hopped into the elevator.

34

———

AS CORY COLLAPSED ONTO THE COUCH, DR. BRUNO SAID, "I'm pleased you reached out."

"I lost it and guess I got scared."

"It would be helpful to talk about it, if you're comfortable sharing it."

"Well, I found out that Lew had been stealing my money. I mean, he had this whole scheme to cover his tracks, but a friend uncovered it." Cory exhaled. "And I went a little crazy and wanted to confront him. So, I went to his house. I didn't really want to hurt him, but I took a knife from the kitchen in case, you know, he had a weapon."

"Did he?"

Cory shook his head. "No, but I was just trying to scare him, to get my money back. Then his wife came home and freaked out. She called the cops, and they came, and it was a frigging mess."

"Fortunately, it didn't escalate further."

"I can't believe the whole thing even happened."

"I understand how upsetting the revelation must have been."

"You got no idea."

"Do you believe you overreacted?"

"He stole more than half a million. I got nothing left. I had to do something."

"There are ways other than going after him with a knife to obtain justice."

"I know, I know. It was a mistake going after him."

"You trusted your manager?"

"Yeah, or else I wouldn't have given him control of my money."

"How was that trust built?"

"What are you talking about?"

"Did you know him before you became successful?"

"No. He was recommended by my agent."

"Are you angry with your agent?"

"Hey, this isn't about me, the bastard stole from me, from my family. Now I'm in deep shit."

"I understand, but I'm trying to understand if some of your anger is rooted in the recognition you may be responsible for what happened and—"

"Me? You're not making any sense."

"Allow me to clarify. Based upon a recommendation, you hired a manager to handle your finances. Would you agree that is a large responsibility?"

"Of course."

"But other than taking someone's advice, you did nothing to vet the manager?"

"So, it's my fault he's a degenerate gambler?"

"No, but perhaps you lost control because you're disappointed in your failure to ensure he was trustworthy."

"That's totally wrong. I'm not good with numbers, and Lew's been around for ages. How the hell was I supposed to know he has a gambling addiction?"

"Do you believe it was the loss of money that triggered your outburst?"

"Of course it was."

"I'm not making light of the sum. It's more money than I've ever had. But speaking frankly, I'm sure you've made several multiples of the loss, and even if you never recover the money from him, you'll earn more than enough to offset it."

"Maybe."

"Are you worried about the durability of your career?"

"A little. But I'm broke now. That's what worries me."

"Okay. Let's talk about that. Can you see that it is likely a short-term situation?"

Cory shrugged. "I need money. Now."

"I'm sure you can arrange a loan against your future earnings. It couldn't take more than a week or two."

"That's too long."

"Tell me what makes this so pressing?"

"I don't want to talk about it."

"That's unfortunate."

Cory remained silent, and Bruno said, "Let me use an analogy. Say you're trying to sleep, and someone is playing music so loud it keeps you awake. In order to ask that person to tone it down, you first have to identify them. Does that make sense?"

"I can't talk about it."

"Whenever you're ready, I'm here for you. Keep in mind, our conversations are strictly confidential."

On the ride back to his apartment, Cory went over the session. He wanted to confide in someone and get help, but it was too shaming. He thought about what she said. Recalling what Bruno said about identifying the person keeping him up with their loud music struck a chord.

If he could find out who was behind the blackmailing, maybe he could so something. Negotiate an end to it somehow. They were pressuring him for the balance. The story that came out in the press mentioned the theft but not that he was broke.

The publicist didn't want to release that information, and Cory was afraid to put it in a text. If he could explain what happened with his manager to him, he'd have to understand. He had no other choice.

Cory called Tracy. "Hey, I have someone, an old friend of mine, I want to track down, but it's got to be done super discreetly."

"You want a private investigator?"

"Yes. Who do you know?"

"Tell me what it's about."

"I can't. Just give me a couple of names that can be trusted."

"Does this concern Linda?"

"No."

"I'll get right back to you, but please be careful."

<hr>

THE MAN who stepped off the elevator didn't look anything like an investigator. His hair was on the long side, and he wore jeans and a leather jacket.

He offered his hand. "Good to meet you, sir."

Cory said, "I'm hoping you can help me. And your name is?"

"Refer to me as Mr. Black."

"That's not your real name?"

"No. What can I do for you?"

"If you recall, someone was spreading a rumor that I hadn't composed certain songs on my album."

Mr. Black's expression didn't change. "And you want to know who it was."

"Exactly. That's what I want to find out."

"You think it might be someone close to you?"

"Possibly. Whoever it is can't be trusted, and I need to know who it is."

"I understand."

"Can you do something like that?"

Black smiled. "No problem."

"How quickly?"

"It depends. If you have anything to work with, it'll speed things up."

"I have cell numbers that I believe might be mirror numbers."

"I'll check them out. Anything else?"

"Yes. I think whoever took these pictures is the person." Cory showed him the pictures of Jay Bird and the sheet music.

"When and where was this?"

"Mirrortone Studios. I think it was taken around a week or two before Jay Bird died."

"Excellent. I'm sure they have video."

"Not in the studios themselves."

"That's okay. I'll narrow it down."

"Good."

"After we determine who it is, do you want me to make contact? Put a scare in them?"

"How would you do that?"

Black smiled. "We have our methods, and they're very effective."

"Not now. I'd like to know who it is first before doing anything about it."

"Fair enough. Anything else?"

"This has to be kept between the two of us. Is that clear?"

"I didn't build my business helping public figures by being undisciplined."

"I didn't mean you, but anyone you work with."

"The only person who will know you're the client is me. If anyone needs to be brought in, you'll be an unknown, female client in her sixties."

"I understand, but the less people the better. How long will this take?"

"A week, two maximum."

35

Cory checked the time. Tracy was on the way over. He was dreading the Zoom call. He lit a joint and inhaled deeply. The last thing he needed was a problem with the law. He was glad the label and their team of lawyers were involved. It was proof he was worth something to them, but also that he was in trouble.

Cory replayed the encounter. Stein was surprised by Cory's visit, stumbling over himself as he let Cory in.

Cory didn't have a plan, and his anger surfaced. He pulled the knife out, screaming at Stein to give him back his money. His manager backed down the hallway as Cory threatened him. Stein's wife came down the stairs and started yelling for help.

If she hadn't been home, what would have happened? Would he have stabbed Stein? He shook his head; it was surreal. He had felt like a spectator, not a participant. While he didn't think he would have hurt Stein, he was grateful Stein's wife interfered.

Cory took a toke, thinking that things were bad but could

have been much worse. Tracy stepped off the elevator, scrunching her nose. "How are you?"

"Okay."

Tracy slid the terrace doors open. "Smoke that over here. I don't want my clothes to smell."

Cory smiled. "You want a hit?"

"Not now. This call is too important."

Tracy set the laptop on the kitchen table. "It's just about seven. Sit down."

"I hope they can fix this."

"These guys are good. Here we go."

Tracy answered the call, and a man in a white shirt and red tie appeared on the screen. "Good evening, Mr. Lupinski, Ms. Burnett. My name is John Doolan. I'm chief counsel for the label and will be directing the response to the episode."

Cory said, "So, I don't need a lawyer?"

"Not unless you're uncomfortable with our representation."

"Well, it was one of your agents, Dave Bee, that got me involved with that thief Stein. How do I know this is going to work out for me?"

"We're aware of the introduction, but the label wasn't a party to the contract between you and Mr. Stein and accepts no responsibility."

"Figures."

"Now, though this is a serious matter, we believe there is a path free of criminal charges."

"I hope so."

"We've been in touch with the DA and Mr. Stein. The state has limited interest in prosecuting an assault—"

"I didn't assault anybody."

"It may come across as legal semantics, but threatening bodily harm, in a convincing way, is considered an assault.

You may be thinking of assault and battery, battery being the physical contact part."

"I was just trying to scare him."

"Now, we believe we can argue successfully that no real threat existed. We can convince the DA to drop any charges as long as Mr. Stein doesn't file a complaint."

"I'm the one who should be filing a complaint. He stole from me."

"We had a preliminary discussion with Mr. Stein and his wife. If you're prepared not to seek restitution, they will not file a complaint."

"So, I never get my money back?"

"If you want to be assured that no criminal charges will be filed, I'm afraid so."

Tracy said, "Would Cory have to make a court appearance or anything like that?"

"No. We'll handle what is necessary."

"I'll think about it."

Tracy ended the call. "I'd say that's a good way to put this to bed."

"But I need my money back."

"I understand, but Stein doesn't have the money. He lost it all. He's in hock up to his neck already, and he's going to lose whatever clients he has left."

Cory went to the bar. "All right. Tell them to make this go away."

After Tracy made the call and left, Cory flopped on the couch. One problem was gone, but he wasn't happy. He needed cheering up and made a call.

"Ava, it's Daddy. How are you?"

"Good, Dad. What are you doing?"

"Just finished a writing session. How was school?"

"Boring. We're doing division and multiplication. Uh, it's

so hard. I don't like it."

"You have to be good at math."

"Why? I'm never going to use it."

"Oh, you will. Every day. You'll see. Anytime you have to buy something, it involves math. You have to keep track of your money. I didn't do a good job, and I regret it."

"It's okay, Daddy. You do great."

"Promise me you'll be the best in your math class."

"I will, don't worry."

"Great. How's Tommy?"

"He's crawling all over the place. We have to run after him all the time."

"Oh, I remember chasing after you."

Cory heard Linda say, "Who are you talking to?"

"Daddy."

"You have to get off the phone and get ready for bed."

"Can't I have five more—"

"Now."

"I gotta go, Dad. Bye."

The line went dead. He understood that Linda was pissed at him for going at his manager with a knife, but rushing Ava off the phone was unfair. He wanted to call back, but Bruno said when someone was mad not to push it. He'd wait until she calmed down.

Cory scrolled through pictures of his kids on his phone. He wanted to find one of Ava crawling around like Tommy was and send it to her.

He found one of her in the bedroom. Cory couldn't believe how small the room was. He paged through photos, not looking at Ava but at the apartment they'd lived in. It was old and cramped.

Cory had to figure a way out of the mess he was in because there was no way he was going back to his old life.

36

———————

Between the lighting, traditional furniture, and barely audible speech, the place reminded Cory of a funeral parlor. Cory took comfort in knowing Joe Baffa needed a sparkler in his hand to get noticed.

The sixtyish Baffa said, "We've only had one other client in the entertainment sector. We normally shy away from clients with visible profiles, but given what you've experienced in your previous relationship, we're willing to assist."

"I appreciate that. You've been around a long time, right?"

"Since 1925. My grandfather built this business servicing the needs of families who owned successful businesses. He guided many prominent families through the Great Depression and made a name for the firm. Our philosophy is conservative; we don't swing for the fences. We'll take the singles and doubles while avoiding risk. It's not sexy, but it allowed generations of families to protect and grow their assets. Does that strategy suit your objectives, Mr. Lupinski?"

"Yes. I don't know any other way to say this, but I make

music. Math isn't my bag. How can I be sure I won't get robbed again?"

"We're not the custodians of your assets. They'll be held in your name at Bank of America. We'll set an amount on payments, say five thousand dollars, that will require your sign-off. For recurring payments, such as mortgages or rents, you'll sign an authorization allowing those to be paid without your permission."

"So, nobody can send money out without checking with me?"

"You can allow payments to be made up to whatever limit you are comfortable with. Anything above it will require Bank of America to have your concurrence."

"Sounds good. Let's do it."

"We appreciate the trust you place in us. The first order of business will be a transfer of the financial records and accounts. We'll have an authorization drafted to move the assets to Bank of America. Now, Mr. Lupinski, what are your financial goals?"

"To not have to worry about money. Right now, I've taken a bad hit, and I got expenses, a family to take care of."

Cory liked the way Baffa talked about financial security. He left the meeting feeling that the new manager was the right one, especially with Bank of America in the middle. It was the first thing Cory felt good about in a while.

CORY EXITED HIS BUILDING, heading toward a waiting Navigator. Tracy was on the sidewalk, holding the door open. A man in a suit stepped in front of Cory. "Mr. Lupinski?"

"Yeah?"

He handed Cory a document. "You've been served."

Cory's eyes moved from the man to the paperwork. "What the fuck?"

Tracy grabbed Cory's arm. "Jump in. We'll deal with this."

Cory climbed in the SUV. "Linda wants a divorce."

"We'll handle it."

"We? What the fuck does that mean? My family's being destroyed!"

"I know it's difficult, but I'm sure there's a way to reconcile the—"

"Stop the car! I said stop the fucking car!"

The driver pulled over. Cory opened the door.

"Where are you going?"

"Back to my apartment."

"But they're waiting at the studio. You have to shoot the video today."

"I'm not doing it."

"You have to."

"Don't tell me what to do! I'm sick of everybody running my goddamn life for me." Cory got out and slammed the door.

Walking to the apartment, he called Linda. "What the hell is going on? Now you want a divorce?"

"Calm down, Cory."

"Don't you think you should have talked to me about it?"

"I made a decision."

"How could you?"

"How could I? It wasn't me who attacked someone with a knife. I'm not the one high all the time—"

"That's bullshit, and you know it."

"What I know is that I don't feel the children are safe around you."

"That's bullshit! You think I'd harm my own kids? You're

fucking sick, you know that?"

"You have anything to say, you're going to have to go through my lawyer."

"Fuck the lawyers! We got to work this out—" Cory realized she had hung up. "Goddamn it!"

Shoving the phone in his pocket, Cory realized a handful of people were recording his outburst with their cell phones. "Get the fuck out of my way."

Back in his apartment, Cory fumed as he made a drink. How could she divorce me? That crap about him being violent was nothing more than a setup to take his kids away from him. He took a sip wondering how anyone could believe he was dangerous. It was bullshit. Her lawyer was going to use it to suck money out of him.

His cell rang. It was Tracy. He swiped the call away. A second later the intercom sounded.

"Hello?"

"Mr. Lupinski, it's Spencer, from the front desk. Ms. Tracy is here. Shall I let her up?"

"No! If you do, I'll make sure you get fired."

CORY SQUINTED at the sunlight streaming into the living room. His head pounded as he got off the couch. He picked up the empty bottle of bourbon that lay on the floor and closed the curtains.

Cory checked his phone. Ten missed calls from Tracy and a voice mail from a number he didn't recognize. He listened to the message: "Uh. Hi, Mr. Loop, this is Terry Gimlet from the *New York Post*. I'd like to get your side of the story on your, uh, the way you lost it yesterday outside your apartment. You can reach me at—"

37

Cory sank into the couch. Dr. Bruno said, "How are you feeling?"

He shrugged. "How am I supposed to feel? My wife filed for divorce."

"I'm sorry."

"She didn't even have the nerve to talk to me about it. I mean, we were doing good, pretty well, anyway. It's not a straight line, right?"

"All relationships have their ups and downs. How the low periods are resolved is key to maintaining a healthy connection to each other."

"She got bent out of shape about the whole Lew thing. Said some bullshit about the kids not being safe around me. What kind of frigging nonsense is that?"

"I realize your manager stealing from you was a frustrating experience, but your reaction was uncommon. Can you see how she might have concerns regarding it?"

"No. We've been together too long. I'll bet you it's her damn lawyer. Frigging scumbag just wants to run up the bill."

"It might be helpful to see it from her perspective."

"And she should see it through my eyes. I mean, the bastard stole from not just me, but from our family. What did she want me to do, sit on my fucking hands?"

"It may be her viewpoint isn't solely shaped by the manager incident. Linda is aware you've been drinking too much."

"That has nothing to fucking do with anything."

"Using alcohol or drugs removes the filter we develop. Under normal circumstances, when a situation is stressful, we're usually able to keep it in check. But when our guard is down, for example, when we're under the influence of alcohol, our judgment is off. We go outside the bounds of acceptable behavior. Basically, our anger gets the best of us."

Cory shrugged.

"Do you believe that you could have handled the situation better?"

"Yeah, I guess so. I was so damn mad at the bastard that I lost it."

"I understand. Anger is the go-to emotion for many people. However, oftentimes, the expression of anger toward others is nothing more than an attempt to blame someone else for a problem. The reality is, though there may be some culpability, below the surface of someone's anger is fear or a sense of hopelessness."

"Of course, I'm afraid. Afraid of losing money, and now my wife and kids. I can't lose my kids. No way. I swear, I'll kill her if she takes them away from me."

"It's not helpful to speak in a violent—"

"It's an expression, that's all."

"It sounds angry and aggressive. Language can contribute to an escalation—"

"All right already. I get it.

"I'd like to return to your fear of losing money. Let's go

back to before you had any money to lose. Did you feel you were happy then?"

"Definitely. I mean, it wasn't easy in a one-bedroom apartment with a kid, but we did all right. Everything was good."

"Is it the inability to deal with money or fame that bothers you?"

"Look, I've experienced both, and I can tell you, having money is a heck of a lot better than being broke."

"What about becoming famous? You've mentioned your father never believed you would make it. Was obtaining the success you achieved a validation of some kind? Does it feel good, or are feelings of inadequacy still there?"

Cory shifted positions. "Like I'm not good enough? And don't deserve it or something?"

"A common feeling among successful people is something we call the impostor syndrome. It's a thought pattern where someone doubts their success is real and fears being exposed as a fraud."

"We're almost out of time, and I got an appointment I can't be late for."

Cory rushed out of the office and turned his phone on. Two voice messages. He listened to Tracy's appeal to call her. He made a mental note to make her wait another couple of hours and deleted the voice mail.

He clicked the next message and froze as he heard a familiar voice. "This is Mr. Black. Get back to me as soon as possible. We've identified the party in question."

Cory leaned against the wall as blood pounded in his ears. He was about to find out who it was, but now he wasn't sure he wanted to know. He told himself there could be an easy way to end the blackmailing. He called back Mr. Black, asking him to meet at his apartment in thirty minutes.

38

His nerves calmed by a joint and a glass of bourbon, Cory and Mr. Black settled into a pair of white club chairs. Cory said, "So, you found who it is?"

"Yes." He opened a manila envelope and handed Cory a photo. "It's Joseph Bonner."

"Joe Bonner?"

"You know him?"

"He seems familiar, but I can't place him."

"I did a background investigation on him."

"You did? What did you find?" He was afraid Black found out what he'd done and held his breath.

"Bonner teaches piano—"

"Jay Bird was taking lessons?"

"No. Bonner taught Jay Bird as a kid. He tunes pianos on the side. He was at the studio to tune theirs and ran into Jay Bird."

"So, that's why he was there. What else were you able to find out?"

"That's about it. He lives in Sheepshead Bay. Takes the occasional tae kwon do class and is divorced."

"How old is he? And is he a big guy?"

"Bonner is in his early sixties. Five feet eight, about one hundred fifty or so. What do you want to do?"

"I'm not sure."

"If he's a threat, you need to take precautions. He knows some martial arts. My recommendation would be bodyguards on a twenty-four by seven basis. We can make the arrangements."

"I don't want any more people around me than I already have."

"Our men won't interfere in your life; they're virtually invisible."

"Thanks, but I'll pass for now."

"Well, then you should be prepared to defend yourself."

Cory leaned forward. "And how would I do that?"

"With a firearm."

"A gun?"

"Unfortunately, public figures are targets for the lunatics out there."

"I don't know."

"I understand your hesitancy, but the failure to prepare could have dire consequences."

Cory got up. "I need a drink. Can I get you a bourbon or something?"

"No, I don't let anything interfere with my reaction time or judgment."

"I need something to calm my nerves."

"The optimal way to take care of your problem is elimination."

"Elimination?"

"Yes. Proactively confront the threat and extinguish it."

Cory's hand shook as he set his drink down. "Does that mean what I think it does?"

Black's eyes narrowed as he nodded.

"How would you do something like that?"

"We have our ways."

Cory liked that Black was tight-lipped, but hiring someone to deal with the blackmailer was something he never considered.

"This is all crazy to me. I can't even think straight."

"My job is to present options."

Cory poured a glass of bourbon and took a sip. "What about just scaring the person?"

"In some rare cases it's an effective strategy, but we've learned in the majority of cases it inflames a situation. You have to remember these individuals are mentally unstable."

"I don't think this Bonner guy is going to go crazy."

"That's a chance I'd be unwilling to take."

"I really appreciate the concern, and I'll think about it, but I can't, you know, do something like that."

"Give it some thought. If you're not going to deploy bodyguards, then you really should be armed."

"I'm not comfortable carrying a gun."

"At the least, you should have one here. Someone breaks in, you'll be able to defend yourself."

"This building is very secure. We have a front desk."

Black smiled. "My definition of secure is very different from yours, Mr. Lupinski. To size up the threat, I entered the building through a service door. Unfortunately, no one challenged me."

"I'm super surprised to hear that."

"Being surprised is something I work hard at preventing. You ever handle a firearm?"

"Years ago. My uncle took me to the range every Saturday when I was fifteen or so."

"Good. I'll have someone bring you a small-caliber pistol,

one with a laser guide. Just keep it in the safe I'll send with it."

"Don't I need a permit or something?"

"Technically you do. But make sure you keep it in the apartment. If you ever have to use it on someone breaking in or threatening you, you'll be in the right."

"I don't know."

Black stood. "Trust me on this, Mr. Lupinski."

"Okay."

Cory poured another drink, replaying the meeting. He stared at the picture of Joe Bonner. He was being blackmailed by a piano teacher? Was this how someone who had to resort to tuning pianos to pay the bills would strike back at someone who had made it?

Bonner was getting old. Maybe his plan was to get enough money to finance his retirement and disappear. It was an idea, but the problem was greed. Cory knew most people could never have enough money. When they reached a financial target, an insecurity would make it insufficient. Bonner wasn't going to go easily.

He wondered exactly how Mr. Black would eliminate Bonner. Would they really kill him? It couldn't be. They'd probably give him a beating, maybe break an arm or something to scare Bonner off. Black had said that scaring someone usually didn't work, but Cory warmed to the idea of seeing his nemesis suffer.

Bonner was a piano tuner, not a construction worker. Tae kwon do aside, he'd probably run for the hills if he got his ass kicked.

If he could stop the blackmailing, everything would be good. He'd get back on track and convince Linda to get back together somehow. Cory knew Bonner wouldn't be scared off by verbal threats. What Cory needed to find was the kind of pushback that couldn't be denied.

39

———

As the Uber came out of the Brooklyn–Battery Tunnel, Cory started thinking he should ask the driver to turn around. Coming here was a mistake, he thought. What if someone saw him? He put his collar up. He was becoming more recognizable by the day. Maybe someone would put things together.

Traveling east on the Belt Parkway, the driver put the turn signal on. They got off the exit for Sheepshead Bay. Cory saw they were heading to the water. The car slowed as it turned onto Avenue Y.

"Are we almost there?"

"Yep, here we are." The driver pulled over.

Heart racing, Cory slumped down, looking at the two-story brick home. "Hey, I just got a text. I gotta go back to the city."

"You're not getting out?"

"No, take me back. I'll pay you in cash if you want."

"Sure thing."

The driver made a U-turn, and Cory kept his eyes on the house until it faded from sight.

TRACY PICKED up the glasses and pizza box littering the coffee table. She said, "Come on, Cory. Coffee's ready."

Barefoot, Cory came out of the bedroom. "I didn't sleep at all last night."

"What's bothering you?"

"How about my wife is trying to take the kids away from me?"

Tracy handed him a mug of coffee and opened the drapes. "What does your attorney say?"

"He's a fucking moron. Said there was no hearing regarding custody and that I'd get normal visitation. He thinks I'm being paranoid."

"He could be right."

Cory sipped his cup. "No way. I know Linda. That's what she's planning. I can feel it."

"How's the coffee?"

"Okay."

"Dave said the label wants you to do a series of appearances to boost the new material."

"Where are the singles?"

"'Circles' dropped a little."

"Where is it?

"Number sixteen."

"What? It never got higher than five. What about 'Tropical Storm'?"

"Didn't make it on yet."

"What the hell?"

"Don't worry. It's early. You do a couple of the late-night shows, and everything will be all right."

"I'm worried. 'Circles' is a killer tune."

"It is, but maybe releasing 'Tropical' wasn't the right call. It didn't give it the boost you'd normally expect."

"This is a disaster."

"Hold on, Cory. 'Circles' is still on the charts, and lots of songs fall off and come back stronger."

"That's bullshit."

"No, it's not. Take the Britney Spears album *Oops, I Did it Again*. It debuted at number two, then fell off quickly. But almost half a year later it was back in the top twenty and stayed there for a long time."

"That was way back when. It's a totally different game now."

"What are you doing?"

"A little hair of the dog. My head is killing me."

"It's ten thirty, and we have a full day ahead."

"I only put a tiny taste in, so stop hassling me, will you?"

"Look, I've worked with a lot of people in this business. I know how tough it is to stay on top, and I've seen a lot of stars screw their careers up with drinking. This is a little bump in the road and—"

"Yeah, yeah, yeah. What does the frigging day look like?"

"First up is the marketing meeting at the label."

"Why do I have to go to that?"

"Like I told you before, it shows you're connected. You want them working as hard as possible to make this launch a success. They love it when an artist takes the time and interest to see what they're doing."

"All right."

"Then we'll hit a couple of radio stations for five-minute chats. We have WKTU at one, Z100 at two, and AT40 at two forty-five."

Cory frowned. "You're going to kill me with all this."

"Come on, if you want the songs to do well, we have to

promote them, especially with the . . . anyway, you need to shower."

"What's with the especially crap?"

"Nothing."

"Tell me what the hell is going on? Is the label gonna drop me?"

"No. Of course not."

"What is it, then?"

"Bosco reviewed the album in the *New York Times*."

"How the hell did they get it?"

"Come on, you know the label sends advance copies to the press."

"He hates me. What did that bastard say?"

"It wasn't that it was bad, it just wasn't that good."

"Read it to me."

"You're not supposed to read these. You have to ignore what the critics say. It's the fans that count."

"Tell me what he said!"

Tracy tapped her phone: "'Cory Loop's new album, *Tropical Storm*, is the follow-up to his wildly successful debut album, *Loop Around*. While the title tune and "Circles," a catchy ditty with a funky bass line are mildly memorable, the balance of the songs left me wondering if Mr. Loop was lost at sea.

'The lack of a consistent theme throughout the recording had me feeling that Mr. Loop had tacked toward a new style of expression. This critic is uncertain whether the change will work or whether Mr. Loop will join the cadre of one-hit wonders.'"

"Great. He thinks I'm finished."

"No, he doesn't. It doesn't matter anyway. That's the opinion of one critic."

"He thinks I'm going to end up like Carl Douglas."

"Who's that?"

"You see? You didn't know Douglas did 'Kung Fu Fighting.' It was his one and only hit."

"You're not a one-hit wonder. You forget you wrote five that charted?"

"The bastard's screwing me. I'm doomed."

"Don't get down about it. It's one review. We have the radio spots to do, and then we have . . ."

As Tracy rattled off the rest of the schedule, Cory retreated to the bedroom. He popped three Adderall pills and swallowed them with his bourbon-laced coffee.

40

Feeling good after snorting two lines of coke, Cory stepped into the offices of Flat 13 Records. The receptionist always reminded him of his mother.

"Nice to see you, Mr. Loop."

"Hiya, Diane. They treating you okay around here?"

"Oh yes, sir."

"Maybe you can tell me what the secret is, then."

She held out a tissue. "Uh, your nose is bleeding."

He took it and dabbed his nose. "It's nothing. I had a cold."

"Can I get you anything?"

"No, thanks." Coming down the hall was his friend Donny and his agent, Dave. Cory said, "What's he doing here?"

"I'm not sure, but he had an appointment."

"When did he make it?"

"Uh, I'll have to look that up."

As they came into the reception area, Cory said, "Forget it."

Dave said, "Hey, Cory. How are you?"

Donny said, "I didn't know you were coming up."

"You would've changed your appointment?"

Donny laughed. "No, it's always good to see you, my man."

"What are you doing here?"

Dave said, "Nothing, just shooting the shit."

"About me?"

"What?"

"It's a simple question, are you talking about me?"

"No."

"That's bullshit."

"Come on, Cory, lighten up. We're not talking about you."

"Yeah, right."

Donny said, "I don't know what gave you that idea. But you're way wrong, man."

"I remember you took piano lessons as a kid, didn't you?"

"Piano? What are you talking about?"

"You used to go to a piano teacher."

"Oh man, that was a long time ago. I didn't last long and switched to bass right away."

"Who was the teacher?"

"Geez, I can't remember his name."

"Was it Joe Bonner?"

"Bonner? Maybe, it sounds familiar."

Dave said, "I hate to break up the reminiscing party, but Cory and I have to get to a meeting."

Donny walked away. "Have a good day, guys."

Dave said, "We're in conference room B."

"What was he doing up here?"

"Exploring his options."

"What options?"

"Playing options, what else?"

"What did he say about me?"

"Nothing."

"Tell me the truth."

"I am. Other than talking about your next tour."

"What about it? Is there something you gotta tell me?"

He stopped before opening the door. "Take it easy, Cory. Nothing is going on. Let's get this meeting going."

After the introductions, Cory and Dave sat at the far end of the walnut table. Cory couldn't get his mind off Donny knowing Bonner. Could his friend be behind the blackmailing?

As a presenter explained the marketing plan, Cory leaned over and whispered, "Are you sure Donny didn't say anything about me?"

"Absolutely. How do you like the marketing plan? I like the idea of tweeting out lyric lines."

"I never heard of that."

"And the video teasers, it's not new, but they work."

"Did you hear that?"

"What? About the ad campaign?"

"No. Somebody said something about me being a one-hit wonder."

"You're imagining things."

"No, I'm not, I heard it."

"Nobody said anything like that. Now, listen up, they're talking about the release party."

Cory's mind drifted back to Donny and Bonner. He was going to call Mr. Black as soon as this was over and have him find the connection. But what would he do when he found out they were working together? It was a betrayal even Hollywood couldn't imagine.

"Cory, we're thinking of holding the release party at One Oak. How does that sound to you?"

"Cory?"

Dave elbowed Cory. "You on board with One Oak for the party?"

"Sure."

"We'd really like to do a FB Live from the party. Is that something you're okay doing?"

"Yeah, I'm good with that."

"Excellent."

Cory leaned into Dave. "That guy keeps staring at me. Who is he?"

"That's Bryan. He's not staring."

"He is so."

"I'm sitting next to you, and I didn't see anything like that. You're too sensitive."

"Sensitive?"

"Keep it down."

As the discussion turned to the type of incentives to increase airplay, Cory turned to Dave. "I got a bad headache. Can I go now?"

Dave stood. "Thanks, guys. This is really exciting. As you know, Cory has a series of radio show appearances today and needs to get going."

Cory thanked the group and slipped out the door. Dave was right behind him. "Hold on a sec."

Cory turned around. "What's up?"

"Where's Tracy?"

"Why? You need somebody to keep an eye on me?"

"No, that's not it at all. I just wanted to know—"

"That's bullshit. The label wants to keep tabs on me."

"Oh, come on, Cory, you're making too much of a simple comment."

"Tell it to me straight, they want to dump me, don't they?"

"Who?"

"The label."

"No. Where did you get that idea?"

"I saw the way everybody was looking at me today."

"I don't know what to say. Are you feeling okay?"

"I'm outta here."

CORY POURED himself a drink as soon as he got back in the apartment. The box the doorman had left was on the foyer floor. He was surprised by its weight. Cory opened it. Seeing the fingerprint reader, he knew it was the firearm safe.

Cory pulled the safe out. Three boxes of bullets lined the bottom of the carton. He unlocked the safe with the key attached to it, pausing before lifting the lid.

A handwritten note lay on top of a gleaming black pistol: "I've taken the liberty of loading the revolver. The safety lock is on. The red button activates the laser. Always use it. You have experience with firearms, but I recommend you go to a range and practice. I have several contacts that will make it easy for you. At the very least, watch a couple of YouTube videos to refresh your memory. I'll be in touch."

Cory stared at the pistol. He gulped the rest of his drink down and picked the gun up. It was cold but fit his hand. He held it out with one arm, then used two hands like he'd seen on TV. He clicked the red button, and the laser came on.

Cory pointed the laser at different spots. He smiled. Using the red dot as a guide made things super easy. He put the gun down and followed the instructions to program the safe with his fingerprint.

He opened the second drawer in his nightstand and shoved the socks aside. Placing the safe in the space, Cory smiled at the thought that if anyone fucked with him now, he'd deal with them. Fast.

41

Cory jumped into the back of an Uber and called Mr. Black. It went to voice mail: "This is Cory. Call me as soon as possible. It's an emergency."

Then he called Tracy. "Meet me at the apartment."

"The apartment? What about the meeting?"

"It was all bullshit. Dave said it was okay to leave."

"But—"

"Look, I made an appearance like you wanted. Meet me there."

"Wait there, we'll pick you up at the station."

"No. I forgot something at the apartment."

Cory poured himself a drink and gulped half of it. He went to the bedroom and grabbed a bottle of Adderall off the nightstand. On the way back to the living room, he saw the manila envelope Mr. Black had given him.

Cory sat down and took the picture of Bonner out. He stared at it, cursing the blackmailer. This was the man responsible for ruining his life, he thought. Cory shook two pills out and washed them down with bourbon.

Thinking over Bonner's connection with Donny, Cory

replayed the last couple of times he was with someone he had considered his best friend. He remembered what Donny had said about being true to himself as an artist. Was he trying to signal that he knew about the stolen songs?

He went back to the making of the demo at Van Gelder Studios. On the drive to Englewood Cliffs, Donny was himself. His friend was unusually quiet when they played the demo, but Cory had chalked it up as not wanting to get in the way.

As Cory thought about the ride back, detecting a certain distance, the front desk announced Tracy's arrival.

CORY WAS GIVEN a thumbs-up by an engineer and stepped into the radio studio. The DJ said, "Cory Loop is in the house. He just stepped into the booth. Here, put these on."

Cory was handed a pair of headphones and sat across from the DJ. His phone rang. He looked at the number and got up. "I have to get this."

Tracy was behind the glass waving her arms as the DJ said, "Hey, where you going? Well, folks, this is a first for KTU, Cory Loop just took a phone call, live on the air. Cory's signaling he'll be right back, so let's play his latest release, 'Tropical Storm,' as he takes care of business."

Tracy said, "Are you crazy? You were on the air."

Cory turned his back, putting a finger in his ear. He whispered into the phone, "Thanks for calling me back. Look, I need you to find out if there is a connection between Donny Blake, he's the bass player in my band, and Bonner. I think something is going on between them, and I want to know what."

"Give me a day or so."

"Keep it quiet, because I'm pretty sure Donny knows I'm onto him and Bonner."

"No worries. I'll be in touch."

As soon as Cory hung up, Tracy said, "Hurry, get back in there."

Cory entered the studio, and the DJ motion muted his mic. "Everything okay?"

"Yeah, sorry. Family emergency, but it's under control."

"Good. Okay, the song is ending. We're going live in five seconds."

"Cory Loop is back in the studio. Welcome to WKTU."

"It's good to be here."

"Really?"

"Why? You don't want me here?"

"No, I was referring to you taking a phone call in the booth."

"What of it?"

"It was unusual."

"Why is everyone on my back? I can't do anything without a comment."

"I'm sorry. Let's start over. Shall we? WKTU is excited that Cory Loop is in the house. Tell us about the new album."

"It's coming out Friday, just a few days away, and we're having a giant party to celebrate at uh, uh, damn, I can't remember right now, but you're all invited."

"I think it's at One Oak. That sound right?"

"Yeah, that's it. We're going to have a lot of goodies to give away, so come on out."

"Can you tell the audience what they can expect from the rest of the album?"

"I think fans will like it. We worked hard on it, and I'm hoping it does well."

"We wish you luck with it. Are you going on tour?"

"Yeah, even though I'd like to stay put for a while. They want me to get out on the road."

"You don't enjoy playing live?"

"No, no, I do. I love meeting fans, but I'm a little tired, and living out of a suitcase is not as much fun as it looks like. Nobody really likes it."

"Rumors are you might be replacing a couple of the players. Is that because they don't want to go on the road?"

"Who told you that? Was it Dave?" He pointed at Tracy. "Was it you?"

"Just a rumor. How about we play the other single from the album, 'Circles'?"

The DJ muted the mic and ripped his headphones off. "Hey, man, I don't know what's going on. I'm just trying to get a little scoop for my listeners."

Cory stood. "Where did you hear that?"

"When I told somebody you were coming in, he told me he heard it."

Tracy opened the door. "Cory, come on, we have to get a move on."

Cory walked out, and Tracy said, "I'm sorry, he's under a lot of pressure," she lowered her voice, "family problems."

As they drove to the next appointment, Tracy said, "You've got to calm things down. It's like you're ready to jump down everybody's throat."

"I'm not jumping on anyone; everybody is attacking me."

"Were you drinking?"

"No."

"Take anything?"

"No."

"Are you sure? because you're slurring your words."

"Leave me alone."

"I just want this next one to go well. You know Z100 plays your music more than anyone else, especially Artie—"

"He was close to Jay Bird."

"I didn't know that."

"I'm not going on his show, am I?"

"No. He goes off the air just before you go on."

CORY AND TRACY checked in and went into a small reception area. A young woman sitting said, "Are you Cory Loop?"

"Yep."

She got up and extended her hand. "I'm Rosie Garland. I'm a reporter with the *Daily News*."

Tracy said, "Sorry, but we can't do an interview."

"Okay, but this is so exciting. Are you going on the air?"

"Yeah. Got to push the new album. It's out on Friday."

"I loved the first one."

"Thanks." Cory's phone chimed and he pulled it out. "Shit."

"What's the matter?"

"Nothing."

Cory turned his back and read the text: *Fifty thousand. Send it now.*

"Motherfucker."

Tracy said, "Shush. What's the matter?"

"Leave me alone." He dug out the bottle of Adderall and dropped it. The bottle rolled away, and the reporter bent down, picking it up.

She looked at the label before handing it to Cory. "Here you go."

Artie, the DJ, came into the room. "Hey there, Rosie. Hanging with the stars, are we?" After the introductions,

Artie said, "You should come back. I'd love to have you on my show."

Tracy said, "Sure. I'll contact the office and throw out some dates."

"Perfect. You know, I used to play piano back in the day."

Cory said, "Super. You don't play anymore?"

"Actually, I started playing again about a year ago."

Cory said, "You taking lessons?"

"No, don't have the time, but I still have my books from when I took them as a kid."

"Who was your teacher?"

"Oh, I don't remember the guy's name."

"I'll bet it was Joe Bonner."

"I don't know."

"Oh, yeah you do. You and him, it makes sense. You know Donny Blake?"

"Who?"

"Don't play fucking dumb with me."

42

———

Tracy and Dave arrived just before 7 p.m. The front desk announced their presence to Cory. Head pounding, Cory wanted to tell them he wasn't feeling well. He felt like shit, but he knew he'd have to deal with them sooner or later and gave the go-ahead.

Cory ran his hands through his hair as he tidied the place up. The elevator pinged, and the visitors entered the apartment.

Tracy said, "How are you, Cory?"

"All right."

Dave said, "We've got some damage control to do."

"I know, but I'm warning you, if you start with the I-told-you-so bullshit, you're out of here."

Dave said, "You won't hear it from me. But that doesn't mean we don't have to get out in front of this. Where's the remote?"

Cory pointed, and Dave pulled his tablet out. "Sit down. You need to see this."

The theme song to *Entertainment Tonight* played, and the host of the show said, "Welcome to *ET*. Our lead story this evening is one that's unfortunately become too familiar to viewers."

A montage of images of Cory Loop, none flattering, replaced the show's anchor, as the voice-over announced: "We have a confidential source that pop star Cory Loop is heading into rehab. The Grammy-winning artist is seeking treatment for drug abuse. It's believed to be an addiction to Adderall as reported in the Page Six column of today's *Daily News*.

"This latest development follows Cory Loop's bizarre appearance on Z100, a New York radio station.

"Last year's new artist of the year slurred his speech and at times was incoherent during an interview on Z100. Just before going on the show, Mr. Loop had an altercation with DJ Artie, the station's most popular disc jockey.

"We wish him well and look forward to his next musical project."

"Rehab? I ain't going, and I don't need that bullshit."

Dave said, "I hope you give consideration to going. Success is a tough thing for most people to deal with."

Tracy said, "Dave's right. There's no stigma to seeking help."

"You two think you're cute, don't you?"

"What are you talking about?"

"Coming together, ganging up on me with this rehab crap."

"We want the best for you, Cory. We're concerned about your health."

"Who put you up to it? The label?"

Tracy sat next to Cory. "You may not realize it, but you have a problem. If you deal with it now, it'll be easier to overcome."

"I can handle it myself. I'm not going to one of those places."

"There are a couple of facilities, small ones, that cater to people like you—"

"People like me? What the fuck is that supposed to mean?"

"Take it easy. I was referring to successful people who need privacy."

Dave said, "If you're getting help, the public will forgive incidents like this. We'll release a statement, and you'll get the space you need to recover, and it will fade away."

"I told you I'm not going, so forget it."

"Think it over some. If you don't change your mind, we're going to have to address it. I don't want to remind you the label has an out in the contract—"

"What out?"

"A morals clause. I not a lawyer, but if they feel an artist is dragging them into a scandal, it could damage their reputation."

"Scandal? Now I'm a fucking scandal?"

"Geez, I didn't mean it like that. Look, my job is to do what's best for you. We're not the enemy."

Cory resisted the urge to make a drink. He grabbed the remote and put the TV on.

Tracy said, "There's no problem with canceling what we have on the calendar. We'll just push any commitments back until you're ready."

"The album is coming out. I got to support it."

Tracy said, "Maybe we can delay it."

Dave said, "I, uh, don't think that's an option at this point. The wheels are in motion, media buys have been made . . ."

"If you're not going to get help, then we're going to need a plan to address the negative publicity. Parents aren't going to give their kids money to buy the album if they think you're out of control."

"Tell me what you want me to do."

Dave said, "We'll do a series of appearances, but you got to be sober. There's no other way."

"Don't worry about me. Set it up."

Tracy said, "We need to do something charitable. It will give the media something to focus on. Something that would benefit children, maybe a sizable donation to a cancer hospital that cares for sick kids."

"I like the idea, but what's sizable?"

"Half a million."

"Five hundred thousand? That's a ton of money. Money I don't have right now."

"Exactly. That's why it will work. It's a large amount, and you're doing it despite the fact your manager stole from you."

"But I don't have the money."

"Don't worry, we'll work out the timing of the donation. The important thing is to make the announcement and get the press. You won't have to make good on it for six months."

Cory's phone rang. It was Mr. Black. "I got to take this." Cory closed the bedroom door behind him and answered the call.

43

———————

Cory mulled the blackmail request that came in when he landed. He had to get it off his mind and sent a message to his new manager to wire the funds. It was hard to believe that Bonner was working alone. Mr. Black had said he couldn't find a connection between Bonner and Donny, but that didn't stop Cory from going off on his friend.

Cory had exploded when Donny told him he was heading for the same ending as Jay Bird had. Donny had no idea what he was talking about.

He turned to Tracy. "Do me a favor and tell Donny to watch this tonight."

She smiled. "Sure."

The door to the green room opened, and a young woman poked her head in. "It's time for you to go on."

Tracy walked Cory out, saying, "Keep it cool out there. You do well, and we'll get all this behind us."

"I know."

"You got this."

Cory stood just offstage as Conan O'Brien said, "Our

next guest has taken the music industry by storm. Let's give it up for the best new artist of the year, Cory Loop."

A pair of cameras followed Cory as polite applause broke out. He waved to the middle-aged audience, who made up the core of the talk show's fans.

Cory shook Conan's hand and sat down. "Welcome to the show."

"It's good to be here."

"Well, I guess it is. Reports had it you were going to be somewhere else for a while."

Cory smiled. "That's why they're called rumors."

"You're doing okay, then?"

"All's good. As most people know, I had an incident on a radio station, but like a lot of things in my life these days, it got blown out of proportion. My nutritionist has me taking a bunch of supplements, and one of them interacted with an allergy medicine my doctor prescribed."

"I know what you mean. My hair used to be black before I started taking vitamins."

The audience broke out in laughter and Conan said, "The new album is coming out tomorrow, right?"

"Yes."

"Your first one is a tough act to follow. If it doesn't do as well, will it bother you?"

"I'm okay with whatever happens. I mean, I'd love for it to do well. I certainly worked hard trying to make it the best it could be, but I'm just so grateful to be able to do what I love doing. I can't complain."

"Let me see if I can help you with the complaining part of that. You must have been upset to learn your manager was allegedly stealing from you."

"It wasn't alleged, he did steal, and it was a significant

amount of money. I was hurt by the way he broke the trust I had in him, but I'm over it."

"My kids are older than yours, but I remember coming up, doing shows in a different town every night. It was hard to maintain the right balance between work and family."

"No doubt it's been tough. My wife and I are struggling with it, but I make sure to see them when I'm in town and to talk with them just about every day."

"It's worth the effort."

"Definitely."

"We have a special treat tonight. Cory is going to do an acoustical version of 'Circles,' off the new album."

Cory played the guitar and sang the single live. The audience loved it, and he walked offstage to a standing ovation.

Tracy said, "That was wonderful."

"You think so?"

"Absolutely. You seemed to have a little chemistry thing going with Conan."

"I met him once backstage. He took his daughter to the Staples Center show we did."

"It's good neither of you mentioned it. How do you feel?"

"Good."

"You sure?"

"Yeah."

"Okay. If you still want to do it, before we head to the airport, we'll go to Cedar Sinai hospital and stop in the children's wing. Say hello, sign some autographs and cheer some kids up."

"That'll be fun."

Tracy called the hospital to set up the visit and the *Los Angeles Times* to make sure they would be there to cover it.

As the SUV drove down Beverly Boulevard, Cory's

phone rang. It was his financial manager, Joe Baffa. "Mr. Lupinski, we need to talk."

"I'm in Los Angeles right now. What's up?"

"I arranged the wire, but there's nothing left. You're running a deficit. We need to cut expenses, and quickly, or you'll be insolvent."

"The new album is going to start bringing money in."

"That may be the reality, but there is a significant time lag between the sales and receipt of royalty payments. Anywhere between ninety and a hundred and eighty days."

"That sounds about right."

"You'll be in arrears. The bank may start foreclosure proceedings on your Connecticut home."

"I can't lose the house. We'll have to borrow time somehow. I'm going to tour soon, and that's where the money is."

"I'm aware, but ticket vendors don't pay any faster."

"Can't we get a loan to tide me over?"

"It's possible, but a lender is going to be diligent—"

Pulling in front of the hospital, Cory said, "With all due respect, can't you handle this? Get working on a loan or something to get us some time?"

"I'll begin the process, but it is my recommendation that you consider selling the home and pare back your spending. If something would happen to you or some event were to transpire, preventing or limiting the ability to tour, you'd be in dire financial straits. I'm asking you to seriously consider the advice I'm giving you."

"I will. I gotta go."

Cory pocketed his phone. "Every day it's something else."

Tracy said, "Managing the money is a challenge for most artists. It starts coming in and they spend more than they realize and—"

"You think I don't fucking realize that? What's wrong with you?"

"I'm just saying it's a common problem. It might make sense to get out of the Connecticut place, especially with what's going on with Linda."

"No fucking way I'm doing that."

"Are you going to be okay with doing this?"

"Yeah, I'm just fucking great."

"Let's get this over with, and when we get back to New York we'll work on fixing things. Take a few minutes to cool down."

"I gotta take a piss, let's go."

Cory hit the men's room and snorted three hits up each nostril. Washing his hands, a drop of blood hit the back of his hand. He looked in the mirror. Blood was leaking from his nose. He bent his head back, wiping the blood with a paper towel.

***

CORY AND TRACY stepped off the elevator into the hospital's lobby.

Tracy said, "That was perfect. Great job with the kids."

Cory threw up his hands. "Would you look at this place."

"What do you mean? We saw it on the way in."

"The ceilings are fifty feet high. All this glass must have cost millions. And they got a grand piano? Come on, man, it looks like a high-end hotel."

"I think it's nice."

"It's a waste of money. They're cashing in on those poor kids."

"All the hospitals have the same setup."

"Of course, they do. It's nothing but a money-making machine."

"They're taking care of a lot of sick people."

"Well, they should be finding cures."

44

____

"Hey, Linda, how's it going?"

"Okay."

"How are the kids?"

"They're good."

"Did you see Conan last night?"

"No."

"I was on the show, and it went really well. You should check it out on demand. He's a good guy."

"What did you call for?"

"Just to say hello, that's all."

"I've got to go."

"Hold on. I wanted to tell you we stopped off at this hospital in LA. It was fun. The kids were really pumped. Man, I couldn't believe how sick some of them were. We're super lucky the kids are healthy, you know."

"I know. Look, I'm happy things went well for you, but I have to go."

"You know, a lot of the stuff that's been said about me isn't true. You know that, don't you?"

"I know what I've seen with my own eyes."

"I'm changing, working on things."

"I'm glad for you."

"I'd really like to see you."

"No."

"Why don't we go back to Dr. Bruno?"

"It's too late for that."

"What are you talking about? We can fix things."

"Forget it, Cory. I'm hanging up."

"Fuck you! Okay? Fuck you!"

Linda hung up and Cory flung his phone, cracking the glass on a piece of artwork. He poured himself a drink. He was mad at her and pissed at himself that he'd lost it with her. She was slipping away, and it was all because of the pressure he was under.

Lew had made things worse by stealing from him, but if it wasn't for the bullshit Bonner weighed him down with, he'd be with his family enjoying the good life. The idea to hire Mr. Black to eliminate Bonner popped into his head. He got up and picked up his phone.

Trying to decide whether to call him, his phone rang. It was Tracy.

"Yeah?"

"Are you okay?"

"Yeah, why?"

"Linda called me."

"She called you?"

"Yes. Said you had an argument and you starting cursing at her."

"She's pushing me away."

"It's not helpful to—"

"You think I don't know that?"

"I know it's difficult, but you have to find a way to keep

cool, otherwise you'll make it impossible to work things out with her."

"Thanks for stating the obvious."

"Perhaps you should consider talking to someone about it. Therapists are trained in helping people control their emotions."

"I'll think about it."

"This might be a good time to write. Channel the emotions you're experiencing into music."

"I don't feel like it."

"You haven't been writing, have you?"

"No, look, I got to go."

He hung up and made a call.

"YOU LOOK like some kind of business executive."

Dr. Bruno glanced at her blue pants suit. "Do you feel the way I'm dressed is too impersonal?"

"I don't know. Yeah, maybe."

She kicked off her shoes. "Better?"

Cory smiled. "It is. How do you do that?"

Bruno smiled. "Let's talk about what brought you here today. On the phone you said it was about Linda."

Cory told her about the phone call, finishing with, "The whole thing got me so mad, I didn't know what to do."

"I'm pleased you reached out. It displays maturity."

Cory shrugged.

"I'm wondering whether seeking to discuss the encounter is driven by your concern over the relationship or by the origins of your outburst."

"Outburst? I want to get back with my wife and kids."

"I understand that. But do you believe cursing at her, even when frustrated, is helpful?"

Cory wagged his head.

"Intellectually, we realize certain urges, in this case anger, have to be suppressed, but emotions override clear thinking. Does that make sense?"

"Yeah."

"Often, anger surfaces when people are under pressure. We've discussed the falseness of seeking a retreat through things like alcohol or drugs. Now is a good time to chat about the origins. A public profile brings its own set of pressures. What do you think are the things that apply pressure, generating stress?"

"How much time you got? No, seriously, like, right now, I have this new album and there's a ton of pressure."

"External or internal?"

"What do you mean?"

"Is it the record company pushing, or are you worried it won't do well?"

"The label hasn't really been bad about it. I guess I just want it to do well."

"In order to validate your success?"

"To be honest about it, there's some of that."

"I previously mentioned the impostor syndrome. It's a common feeling successful people have. They worry that they're not good enough and the world will find out. Are you afraid your success will be short-lived?"

"Yeah, I think about it, but I need the money too. And I don't even want to think about if the divorce goes through how much it's going to cost me."

"Did you find a trustworthy manager?"

Cory filled her in on Baffa and his conservative style.

"He might be the perfect person to manage your affairs and alleviate your concerns about money."

"I thought so, but he's pressing me to sell the Connecticut home."

"Why is that?"

"Can't afford it."

"Well, if that's the case, it might be a good idea."

"But that was supposed to be our family place."

"Sometimes things change. It's better to accept the new reality rather than holding on and creating a larger problem."

"The press will have another picnic at my expense if I have to sell it."

"You can't worry about what anyone says if you want to be happy. You have to be comfortable in how you lead your life and the decisions you make."

"I guess so, but how do you fix past problems?"

"With honesty. Take responsibility for your mistakes and attempt to fix them."

"Easier said than done."

"Nothing worthwhile is easy. We're going to have to wrap this up. I have another client right after this session."

45

Back in his apartment, Cory thought about what Dr. Bruno said. It sounded like she thought there was no chance to get back with Linda. He didn't want to lose her. Cory called his wife.

"Hi, Daddy."

"Oh, Ava. How are you?"

"Okay, Mommy can't talk now."

"Is she's all right?"

"Yes, but please don't make her cry anymore."

"I won't, I mean, I didn't make her cry, she must have—"

Linda's voice was in the background. "Hang up the phone, Ava. Tell your father you'll talk to him tomorrow."

"Sorry, Daddy, I have to go now. We can talk tomorrow. Bye."

"Hold on."

"Here's Mommy."

The phone went dead. Cory redialed, but it went to voice mail. He sent a text, telling Linda he just wanted to talk. He felt anger moving from his gut to his head and didn't know what to do.

Cory paced the room and stopped by the bar to pour himself a bourbon. He thought of Dr. Bruno and the need to stay calm.

He took his drink into the studio and strapped on his guitar. He strummed away, launching into 'Circles.' When he got to the bridge he stopped. Why was he playing a Jay Bird song? He tried to think of something else to play but took his guitar off and grabbed his phone.

As they barreled their way down West Street, Cory's phone rang. It was Dave.

"Where are you?"

"We're almost there."

"Hurry up, you're an hour late."

"We're only two minutes away."

"Is Joanne with you?"

"Yeah. See you in a few."

The SUV pulled up to the Stanton Street building that housed Rivertone Studios. Dave met them just outside the rehearsal space. "The two of you okay?"

Cory lowered his hat. "Yeah, just a late night, that's all."

He handed him a bottle of Visine. "Put a couple of drops in before you go in."

They did as he said and entered the studio. "Hey guys, sorry. The traffic getting crosstown was nuts."

Joanne slid behind the piano and warmed up. Cory said, "Where's my guitar?"

Dave said, "You were supposed to bring it."

"I was?"

Donny said, "Oh come on, man. If your axe is in your apartment, it's up to you to bring it, right?"

"Uh, yeah. Sorry. Dave, can you get it for me? I'll do a couple of tunes, just with vocals, until you get back."

Dave left, and Cory sang "Tropical Storm." The band played the introduction, and Cory came in late. "Sorry, guys. Let's try again. One, two, ah, one, two."

The band launched into the tune, and Cory missed his entrance again. "Sorry, man. My ass is dragging a little. You guys play it, I got to hit the bathroom."

Cory went into a stall and pulled a vial of coke out. He took two hits up each nostril and went back to the rehearsal.

As the players filed out after the practice session, Donny said, "Cory, hang on a second."

Cory told Joanne to wait in the car and said, "What's up?"

"The question is what's up with you?"

"What do you mean?"

"How about I start with, you look like shit, you forgot your axe, and you're still screwing around with Joanne?"

"That's none of your fucking business."

"Come on, man, I saw Linda, she said you went nuts on her."

"You saw Linda?"

"Yeah."

"Where?"

"I ran into her at Whole Foods."

"You screwing my wife?"

"What?"

"Answer me."

"Of course not. You're frigging nuts, you know that?"

"You better watch yourself."

"Me? You better watch yourself and stop the drugs and drinking."

"Don't worry about me."

"You're out of control."

"No, I'm not."

"You came late. You forgot your guitar for God's sake, and you played sloppy as hell."

"That's why it's called a rehearsal. I'll tighten things."

"The music is bullshit; you're playing with your life."

"Yeah? Well, mind your own business and don't ever embarrass me in front of the band."

Cory climbed into the SUV and said, "I'm thinking of replacing Donny. What do you think?"

"Donny? But you guys are friends."

"He's not cutting it anymore."

"I thought he held it down pretty nice today."

"He wasn't locked in with the drums."

"Who you thinking of?"

"Kenshaw lays down a nice groove."

"Yeah, he's got great time. If he's available, he'd be an amazing addition."

Cory dug his phone out. "Tracy, check on Kenshaw Cooper. See if he's available to do the tour. I want to replace Donny."

"Are you sure about that?"

"Yes. Just do it."

"All right. If that's what you want."

"That's what I want."

"Okay, hey, you left your Amex card at the club last night. I'll have it sent to the apartment."

46

Cory led Tracy down a hallway filled with kids waiting outside their rooms. Tracy took a stuffed toy off the cart and handed it to Cory. He gave it to a girl in a wheelchair. "How it's going today, sunshine?"

"This is so cool. Can we take a picture?"

Cory knelt beside the girl, and Tracy took pictures with the girl's phone. "We have a lot of toys to give out. I got to get going."

"Don't forget Meghan." The kid pointed inside her room. "She's too weak to get out of bed."

"No way. Hey, Megan, here we come."

Cory grabbed a dinosaur and stepped into the darkened room. "Hi Megan, I'm Cory. Here's a stuffed animal."

The little girl's eyes were half open. She smiled, but she didn't reach for the toy. Cory nuzzled the animal by her neck and the kid smiled. "This guy needs a name, doesn't he? Or is it a she?"

"It's a girl, 'cause it's pink."

"Oh yeah. So, what do you think? Suzie? Carmen? Mary?"

"She looks like a Candice."

"You're right, she does. All right, Candice, you sit right here and keep Megan happy." He placed the dinosaur on her stomach.

Megan moaned.

Cory swiped the toy off her. "Are you okay?"

Her eyes teared. "My stomach hurts."

"Tracy, get help for her."

A nurse came in and Cory said, "I'll be back in a couple of minutes, feel better."

In the hallway he asked Tracy, "This poor kid, what's she got?"

"Pancreatic cancer. The nurse said she doesn't have much time."

"Oh my God. She's the same age as Ava."

"It's so sad."

"Isn't there anything they can do for her?"

"They can't do much with pancreatic cancer."

"That's crazy, no kid should be robbed of their life. They got to find something to help people with it, especially children."

"Just being here is helping."

"That's bullshit. You know what, let's do the press thing in her room. It'll get the message out there."

"I don't know, Cory. Sloan set it up in their media room."

"If they want the half a million donation, they'll do it where I say."

CORY OPENED up the first of four video files Tracy sent. It was a video clip from NBC. A reporter said, "We're here at

New York's Sloan Kettering Hospital, in the children's cancer unit. Grammy-winning artist Cory Loop is here, bringing cheer to the kids and money to help find a cure for cancer."

Cory's heart ached at the sight of Megan propped up in her bed as he raised a giant-sized check. "It's my hope that this donation will begin to raise awareness of the children hit by cancer. We need to find cures. We need to help kids, like my new friend Megan. We need everybody to pitch in. Even the smallest amount helps."

The video cut to Cory walking next to the reporter. "It's obvious that you care for the children here. What makes this issue important to you?"

"I have two kids of my own, and they're healthy, thank God. Seeing so many children suffer from cancer is heartbreaking. They're innocent and should be out playing, not getting an armful of drugs that make them sick."

"Are you suggesting alternative means of treatment?"

"I don't know anything about it. All I know is, there's a lot of money being spent, and we got to find a cure, and fast."

The reporter ended the piece with, "If you'd like to join Cory Loop in his effort to help children with cancer, call the number below or visit the website and make a donation."

He watched another video that began with an overview of the numbers of children afflicted with cancer. Cory shook his head; he had no idea there were so many kids and families dealing with the disease.

Shoving the possibility of Ava or Tommy getting cancer aside, he knew he had to do something. He couldn't just sit around while poor kids like Megan wasted away. How much could he do? There were billions of dollars being spent treating those afflicted.

Whatever money he would earn from music wouldn't

make a dent. The five hundred thousand he didn't have but was on the hook for was nothing but a rounding error in the battle against cancer. Anger and pity swirled through his head.

Cory grabbed a bottle of bourbon and retreated to the studio. He was hopeful the emotions coursing through him would help him write something that would resonate.

He was drawn to the dark sounds of minor chords. It fit the mood he was in. Cory pecked out a simple melody going down minor thirds. It triggered the memory of a nursery rhyme that scared him as a child.

Cory wanted something to cheer kids up. He crossed out what he'd written down and began playing with major chords. The joyful sounds made him feel good. He played with a melody using fifths. He forced himself from using the interval too often, as in his mind's ear he heard "My Favorite Things."

Cory's excitement rose. He was on the right track. Humming a series of notes, a text came in. Seeing a preview of the message, Cory hesitated before opening it.

Lying is going to cost you. I want 200,000 thousand and I want it fast.

Cory typed back: *What lie? I didn't lie and I don't have that kind of money.*

Bullshit. You gave a half a million to a hospital.

I didn't actually give them the money. I got six months to pay it.

I don't do installment plans. You find the money and fast or you'll regret it.

I can't get the money. I'm going on tour and then I'll make some. You'll have to wait.

You play with fire, you get burned.

What's that supposed to mean?
If you don't send the money, you'll find out.
I told you I need time.
No more time. Send the money. NOW!

47

TRACY CAME OFF THE ELEVATOR WITH A SHOPPING BAG FROM Nobu. "Hope you're hungry. I got a great assortment of sushi."

"I'm starving, thanks."

She set the contents on the table. "You know, we've been getting calls all day about having you appear on the talk show circuit. Doing this cancer thing was a stroke of genius."

"I gotta be honest with you, I know it was a public relations kind of thing, but I really feel like I have to do something."

"Okay, when you get back from the tour, we'll get you on some shows and you can talk about it. You know what would be fabulous? Hooking up with the Make-A-Wish Foundation."

"I don't know. Being around kids that are dying? That's depressing."

"But it makes them happy."

"I get it, but maybe working as a spokesman or something. An ambassador. You know, cheering kids up and shaming people with money to pony up for a cure."

"A lot of people believe the medical industry doesn't want a cure. There's too much money in keeping things like they are."

Cory picked up a pair of chopsticks. "Are you saying there's a conspiracy? Let kids suffer and die so they can make money off them?"

"Just in America, the National Cancer Institute spends six billion a year on research. And they're only one organization. That's a lot, but one hundred and fifty billion is spent treating it around the world."

"This is all fucked up."

"It's a huge problem. Don't get all down about it. Do what you can and leave it at that."

"I got to do more. Right now, I have some name value. Where could we leverage it while we can? And not just making kids forget for a second they're going to die."

"What about St. Jude's? They have a research hospital for kids with cancer."

"Really? That sounds like a cool fit. Call them, see what we can do."

THE SOUND of a tune Cory had written for Linda startled Cory. It was his phone. He couldn't remember changing the ringtone. Tracy was calling.

"Hi Cory, I just wanted to let you know it's done. Kenshaw is on board, and Donny is out."

"Really?"

"It's what you wanted, isn't it?"

"Yeah, I just, you know, we go back a long way."

"I know, that's why I wanted you to be sure."

"Can't we, uh, reverse it?"

"It's done already."

"How'd he take it?"

"Well, he was surprised and couldn't believe it. He wanted to know if you were the one behind it."

"What did you tell him?"

"What was I supposed to say?"

"He say anything else?"

"Wanted to know who was replacing him, and I said it was Kenshaw. He said he couldn't believe it."

Cory's phone vibrated. Another call was coming in. It was Donny. He swiped it away. "That was him."

"Talk to him, you've been friends a long time."

"You think I don't know that?"

"Sorry."

A voice mail hit his box. "I got to go."

Cory looked at the voice message. His finger hovered over delete but hit play instead. His shoulders sank when he heard Donny's voice: "Tracy just told me I'm being replaced. I don't know what to . . . I just can't believe it. I mean, you can do what you want, but at least have the balls to tell me yourself. I don't know what's going on with you. You know what? Actually, I do. You changed, man. You're not the same Cory I knew my whole life. All the drugs and drinking are fucking you up, man. Open your eyes before it's too late. I'm telling you, you better wise up. I'll see you around."

Cory sighed at Donny's last words. He knew he wouldn't see him, and if he did, the relationship would never be the same. But whose fault was it? Twisting the cap off a fresh bottle of Pappy Van Winkle, he pushed a growing feeling of guilt aside.

Sipping the bourbon, Cory's stomach churned. Yeah, Donny was his best friend, but this was his band. He could do what he wanted. Donny was probably jealous. And what was that bullshit he happened to run into Linda? Was he trying to take advantage of their separation?

It hit Cory that Linda would find out. He had to make sure she knew it was about the music. Kenshaw had been on the road with the best, and he could solo. That was it. The band needed another world-class soloist, and Kenshaw was the one.

It made sense, and she didn't know anything about music anyway. Cory went into the bedroom, spilled two Adderall pills out, and washed them down with bourbon. He dialed his phone.

"Hey, Linda, how you doing?"

"Fine, Cory. What do you want?"

"How are the kids?"

"They're fine."

"Fine? Is that the word of the week?"

"Have you been drinking?"

"No."

"What do you want?"

"I wanted to tell you something about Donny."

"Donny? What about him?"

"You saw him recently?"

"Yeah, at Whole Foods, what about it?"

"And that was it?"

"What was it?"

"You saw him and that was it?"

"We talked for a couple of minutes, that's all. What are you trying to say?"

"Nothing, just that Donny is out of the band."

"He left?"

"No, I replaced him with Kenshaw."

"Why?"

"We needed someone who can solo, and Kenshaw is a monster."

"How could you do that to him?"

"I didn't do anything, it's what the music needed."

"You're pushing everybody away. I hope you're happy, goodbye."

"Wait—" She hung up. Cory hit redial and it went to voice mail. "That bitch!"

Cory went into the kitchen and added ice to his drink. He opened the fridge door to grab an Evian and dropped his drink on the floor. "Fuck!" He kicked the shards of glass aside and filled another glass with ice and bourbon.

Cory plopped on the couch and drained his drink. He put the TV on and poured another drink. He cycled through a hundred channels before shutting it off. Cory went into the bathroom and popped a handful of Tums into his mouth. He chewed them and put his mouth under the faucet to wash away the chalky taste.

The movement made him dizzy. He shuffled to the couch, kicking off his shoes. The room was spinning and Cory closed his eyes. His stomach heaved, spraying bile up his throat. He swallowed it down, but a wave forced him up.

Cory ran to the kitchen sink and puked. He stepped back. "Ouch! What the fuck?" He looked at the blood pouring from his foot and threw up again.

48

———————

"Tracy, I need help. I cut my foot. It's real bad."

"How bad?"

"Bleeding like crazy. I can't stop it."

"You're drunk, aren't you?"

"What does that have to do with anything? My fucking foot is sliced open!"

"Call 911. I'll be right over."

"911? I need help."

"I'm not a doctor and I'm twenty minutes away. Call 911, I'll be there as soon as possible."

Cory dialed 911 and wrapped a towel around his foot. Ten minutes later a pair of medics with EMT jackets on trampled into the apartment. A police officer came in behind them.

On the floor, Cory had his foot propped against a kitchen drawer. "What happened, sir?"

"I cut my foot on some glass. I, I dropped a glass and went to clean it up and I stepped right on it."

The medic unwrapped the towel. "You've lost a lot of blood. This looks like it needs to be stitched. We'll have to take you to the hospital."

"No. Can't you do it?"

"I'm a paramedic and can suture, but I'd need a doctor's authorization."

"Please get it. You know who I am, right?"

"Yes."

"Well, if I go to the hospital, the press will be all over it, and, you know, it won't be good. They'll say all kinds of shit about me. I'd really appreciate it if we handle this here."

"Let me make a call."

The police officer stepped forward. "You've been drinking."

"I had a couple of drinks."

"By the looks of the vomit, I'd say you exceeded your limits."

Cory shrugged. "I'm in the privacy of my own home."

The officer turned to the medics. "You need me?"

They shook their heads. "Okay, I'm done with babysitting a drunk."

"What'd he say?"

The medic said, "That he's leaving."

"He fucking better."

"Sir, if you don't calm down, we're going to have to do this at the hospital."

After stitching up Cory, the medics left. Adjusting the pillow under his leg, Tracy said, "Dr. Boren is on the way. He wants to take a look at this and wants you on antibiotics. He wants to make sure you don't get an infection."

"All right. It feels pretty good right now."

Tracy went into the kitchen. "I hope this doesn't interfere with the tour."

"No way, I got to tour. I'll be okay in a day or two."

Picking up pieces of glass with a towel, she said, "I hope so, but it looked like a really deep cut."

Cory shrugged.

"You want to tell me what happened?"

"Nothing, I dropped a glass, and trying to clean it up, I stepped on it."

"There's vomit all over the place."

"My stomach was bothering me, and when I cut myself, I just upchucked."

"You were drinking bourbon on an upset stomach?"

"I was putting the glass in the sink."

Tracy picked up the glass of bourbon on the coffee table. She looked at Cory, who closed his eyes.

CANE IN HAND, Cory limped into his manager's office and settled into a chair as Baffa asked him how his foot was. After being assured the injury was nothing to be concerned with, Baffa changed gears and the pleasantries vanished.

"We take our role seriously, Mr. Lupinski. It's impossible for us to meet our fiduciary responsibilities if clients aren't forthright. We understand you make the decisions regarding the music you create, but authorizing a sizable bonus to replace a player is something we need to know about. Before, not after it happens."

Cory shrunk in his chair, feeling as if he was being scolded by the grammar school principal.

"In order for this relationship to be effective, we need to know about all financial transactions, in particular, outflows. Especially large donations, such as the St. Jude's one."

"But we didn't pay them yet."

"And it's a good thing, as the funds aren't available. But even so, that commitment sits on your balance sheet as a liability. It affects your cash flow and the ability to borrow."

"Sorry, I guess I should've asked first."

"We support the philanthropic efforts of our clients. In fact, we encourage it, but not at the expense of solvency. We've modeled revenues and expenses." Baffa slid a graph across the desk. "We've adjusted for the higher salary cost for the new player and reduced projected revenues from album sales and touring—'

"Why?"

"Given the negative publicity surrounding the, uh, accident in your apartment, we believe it's prudent to revise it downward. This graph displays a healthy trajectory by cutting two outflows." Baffa passed a document covered in green to his client. "The Connecticut home needs to be sold, and the support to your friends needs to be seriously curtailed. Assisting loved ones is noble, but you can't afford to do fifty thousand dollars at a time."

"I don't want to sell Connecticut."

"I'm afraid you don't have a choice. You don't have much equity in it, but the mortgage and upkeep represent substantial outflows. What I'd suggest is putting it on the market. Estates of this magnitude take a long time to sell. The pool of buyers is limited by the price. If the financial picture significantly brightens, you can remove the listing."

"How much money can I get out of it?"

"That would depend on the sales price less expenses. I'd estimate less than a hundred thousand."

"That's it?"

"I'm afraid so."

"I'll think about it."

"Okay, meanwhile, I took the liberty of asking Sotheby's to conduct a market analysis."

"How much cash do I have?"

"Essentially, nothing. We're expecting streaming royalties

to come in, but they're highly unpredictable and are slated to cover a portion of your housing expenses."

"The tour will get things back to normal."

"In preparing the financial models, we spoke with the label to get an estimate of the numbers, and there seemed to be a bit of concern over ticket sales."

"What are you talking about?"

"I understand the previous tour was entirely sold out, but this one is lagging behind."

49

Cory couldn't believe he was sitting in another office. He was glad he'd chosen music over a nine-to-five gig in a stuffy office filled with people wearing suits and fake smiles.

His divorce attorney, Larry Gold, was rambling on about the weather. Cory wondered if he would be paying the thousand-dollar-an-hour rate or whether the clock would start when the small talk ended.

"So, it's good to finally meet you in person, Mr. Lupinski."

"I just wish it weren't over a divorce."

"My job is to help you through the process and defend your rights as a father."

"Okay, you said we had to talk about the children. What exactly did you mean?"

Gold clasped his hands. "Your wife has filed a motion to deny you visitation rights during the separation."

"How can she do that?"

He lifted up a multi-page document. "The motion's legal argument is you're a danger to the children."

"What? That's crazy. I would never do anything to hurt my kids. I love them. They mean everything to me."

"Demonstrating your devotion to the court shouldn't be challenging, but we'll have to address your, uhm, erratic behavior."

"What?"

"They're claiming recent episodes are evidence of instability. They reference suspected substance abuse, and in a call with opposing counsel, they made it clear they would use the knife incident as proof you can be violent when under the influence."

"This is bullshit. Yeah, okay, I lost it when my manager stole my money, our money. But I mean, come on, the judge would understand something like that."

"The circumstances may be mitigating, but it's a damaging event that the judge will have to consider."

"But—"

"They also referenced a recent radio appearance when you appeared intoxicated, a hotel suite that you allegedly trashed, and several incidents where you were reportedly inebriated."

"Just a little partying after a show."

"Would you consider going into rehab?"

"Would it help?"

"It may. I'd have to weigh the admission of an addiction against seeking help for a problem. It could go either way, but most likely, you'd be unable to see them until you completed the program."

"I'm not doing that."

"Another way to ensure visitation during the time a divorce agreement is negotiated would be to agree to supervised visits."

"Supervised?"

"A monitor would be present during visits."

"They think I need a fucking babysitter? This is bullshit!"

"Please, Mr. Lupinski. Exploring options is part of the process. Family courts generally favor mothers in custody battles. I've represented entertainers and public figures, usually their high profile is an advantage. In this case, though, we'll have to find an effective way to rebut the danger argument, or there's a high probability the judge will not allow unmonitored visits."

Fingering the bottle of Adderall in his pocket, Cory said, "Please, you have to find a way to help me."

"I'll do my best. It's critically important that you keep things on an even keel until the hearing. Another incident would seriously damage whatever chances we have."

THE DRIVER SAID, "Mr. Lupinski? We're in front of your building."

"Uh, yeah, thanks."

Cory nodded to the doorman and kept his head down as he hustled inside. He kept replaying the closing words his attorney had said: 'whatever chances we have' His father had always said that lawyers overstated your chances of success in the early stages and would flip to trying to settle things as the case neared a conclusion.

Stepping off the elevator, Cory wondered if that was what Gold was doing. Though Cory never met him before, the initial conversations were always a reassurance that a court would never deny him joint custody. Now, with a hearing looming, Gold was backpedaling like an Olympian medalist.

Cory made a beeline for the bar, trying to figure out why he had lied to him. Gold had let him down, joining a long list of people he'd turned his life over to. Everybody just wanted money from him. He drained his drink thinking they were no better than Bonner the blackmailer.

If he lost custody, there was no turning back. His relationship would be permanently damaged, especially with Ava. She was too old to disguise the reality if a court agreed with her mother and considered him a threat.

Cory poured another drink and wondered how Linda could even make a statement like that. Was she in it for the money too? He punched a number into his phone.

"Linda, we got to talk."

"Let the attorneys work it out."

"Don't hang up. Hear me out."

"What?"

"You know I'd never hurt the kids, don't you?"

"I have no idea what you'd do. I don't even know who you are anymore."

"Aw, come on. Nobody knows me better than you."

"Really? Well, I'd never figured you'd betray me and the children. Maybe I was stupid thinking you wouldn't cheat, but in public? You made us look like fools."

"I made a mistake. You know I love you."

"You have a weird way of showing it."

"I'll work on it, you'll see. I know it will take time, but I'll prove it to you."

"It's over, Cory."

"No, I won't accept that. And I won't accept having my kids taken from me. Can't you see it my way?"

"I'd ask you to see it through my eyes. You've done some crazy things, and it scares me and the children."

"But—"

"You're out of control, Cory. I can't take chances with the kids."

"You're going to deny me the right to see them?"

"I didn't do anything, you did it to yourself."

"That's bullshit and you know it."

"Goodbye, Cory."

Cory started redialing when a text came in. It was brief: *Tick Tock. Time is running out.*

50

Cory's manager returned his call.

"Hello, Mr. Lupinski. What can I do for you?"

"I wanted to tell you to go ahead and sell the Connecticut house."

"Certainly. May I ask why the sudden change of heart?"

"It looks like I'm not going to be able to patch things up with my wife, so I figured to take your advice and sell it to get whatever I can out of it. I'd also like to see if we can get out of the lease for her apartment and get something less expensive."

"I see. We're going to need her consent to sell the house—"

"Why? It's my house."

"I'm not an attorney, but it's considered joint property under marital law. And if she refuses, you'd have to go to court."

"Are you kidding me?"

"No. Generally, courts will mandate that you keep her in the style and manner she has become accustomed to."

"But you said I need to cut expenses."

"Yes, but we'd have to go to court and prove financial duress. We could probably do that, but it would become public."

"Can't anything go my fucking way?"

"Please. Language like that is unhelpful."

"What? You're going to jump on me too?"

CORY SMILED at the roomful of sick children as a frail-looking kid sat next to him. Cory was at ease for the first time in weeks.

"Put your hand over here." Cory moved the boy's hand up the fretboard. "Put your first finger here. These little boxes are called frets." He maneuvered the kid's fingers and said, "Okay. This is called the first position. Now, use your other hand and strum the strings."

The kid stroked downward, and Cory said, "Good. This time, make sure you don't lift your fingers off the strings."

The kid tried again. "Super! That was really nice. You produced a great sound."

"Really? I did?"

"Yep. Very sweet. Let me show you how to finger a C chord. Hundreds of songs are in the key of C, so learning this and two or three more chords will get you through a ton of tunes."

After helping the child play the popular chord, Cory said, "All right, who wants to go next?"

Tracy slipped out of the room as every one of the twenty kids raised their hands. "Don't worry, guys. I'm not leaving until each one of you gets a chance. Let's start with you." Cory pointed to one of the younger girls in the room.

Cory's stomach turned when he saw the blotchy bruises

on her arms. Cory showed her the first position and said, "Pay attention, guys. I'm going to show you how to make a G chord now." He moved the kid's fingers. "Okay. Let's hear what it sounds like." The girl swept upward.

"Nice. You bring up something worth mentioning. Did everyone see that she strummed up rather than down?"

Half the heads in the room nodded.

"Okay. Do it down, this time." The kid did, and Cory said, "Did anyone notice the difference in sound?"

Seeing the bewildered look on their faces, Cory grabbed his guitar and played slowly, first down, then up. "It's the same chord, but we're starting on a different note. Does that make sense?"

As the kids nodded, Cory said, "You guys are so good that I got a surprise for you. You like surprises?"

When the chorus of yeahs died down, Cory said, "I'm going to get each and every one of you your own guitar."

The room exploded into cheers. Cory was showing the last kid a chord when Tracy came into the room with a man. They watched him put a smile on the kid's face as Cory went through the fundamentals.

When the brief lesson was over, Cory said, "All right, guys, you did fantastic today. I'm going to get you the guitars, and I'll be back in a day or so. I'll see you soon."

As the kids filed out, Tracy said, "Cory, this is George Cooper from the *New York Post*."

"Nice to meet you."

"I gotta say, you really have a soft touch with the kids."

"It's nothing."

"No, you have something special."

"Just trying to help them focus on something that brings joy. Being in a place like this, dealing with cancer, I don't know how they even deal with it."

"It's generous of you to spend so much time with them."

"They need to learn, experience, and grow. It will help them decide what they want to do when they're adults."

"You realize that some of these children are so sick they won't make it, don't you?"

"We can save these kids, every child, if we really wanted to."

"I don't think it's a matter of will, it's—"

"You're right, it's not will, it's money."

"No doubt, researching a cure is expensive."

"They don't want a cure; there's too much money being made treating cancer."

"You really believe that?"

"Look at this place. There are hundreds of them like it. It's big business, that's what it is."

"Are you saying there's a conspiracy in the medical community to keep things as they currently are, rather than cure cancer because of money?"

"It's impossible to think otherwise. Everything is about money. It makes the world go round, doesn't it?"

51

"ANSWER THE PHONE, GODDAMN IT!" CORY HIT REDIAL. IT went to voice mail again. He sent a text: *I need to talk to you. About the house.*

A text chimed in: *Whatever you have to say, tell it to your lawyer.*

He called his divorce lawyer. "Mr. Gold, it's Cory."

"Good afternoon. What can I do for you?"

"My wife won't talk to me. I called her, but she won't pick up. I even tried texting her, but she still won't respond. She said to call my lawyer."

"Frankly, not a good sign that she wants communications to go through counsel. What did you want to convey to her?"

"I need to sell the Connecticut house. It's expensive as hell, and I need to cut expenses. I haven't even been there in ages."

"The home is a joint asset, so you'd need written authorization to sell it, and the proceeds would likely be held in escrow until the divorce agreement is finalized."

"There isn't much, if any, money in the house. The mortgage is huge, and the payments are too much for me."

"If she doesn't agree, we could approach the court and ask for a hardship waiver. Let me call the other side and see where they are on this."

"OH, THIS ONE IS AMAZING." Joanne made the music louder.

Over the booming pulse of a bass line, Cory said, "Hey, Jo, you have any more blow?" Cory held up a vial.

"I brought three over."

"They're empty."

"All of them?"

"Yeah."

"You kidding me? That was an eight ball. I only had a couple of hits."

"We got to get more. Call your guy up."

"No, forget it. It's too late anyway."

"Come on, just a little more. Call him."

Joanne shook her booty. "Come here. Dance with me."

"Call him first."

"You're gonna crash."

"Call him!"

"Okay, okay."

CORY ELBOWED JOANNE. "YOU HEAR THAT?"

"What?"

He put his finger to his lips. "Shush." He nodded. "Someone's in the apartment."

"Oh my God."

Reaching into his nightstand, Cory whispered, "Don't worry." He grabbed the gun and slid out of bed.

"Don't. I'm calling 911."

"No. I know who it is."

"Who is it?"

Cory tiptoed out of the bedroom. Mimicking what he'd seen on TV, he held the gun under his chin and kept his back to the wall as he went room to room. No one was in the apartment.

"It's all clear! He left."

"Who?"

"Forget it."

"How did they get in and out?"

"We left the terrace sliders open."

"But we're on the twenty-eighth floor. How could they have gotten in?"

"They have their ways."

"Come back to bed."

"I got to get moving, it's almost twelve."

"Really? Ugh, I got to go. I'm getting my hair colored at two."

"Where'd you leave the vials?"

"You better lay off that stuff. You're getting paranoid."

"Where is it?"

"They're on the kitchen counter."

Cory did two lines and put a pod of coffee in. "You want a cup?"

"No, I'll grab a Dunkin'." She kissed him. "I'll see you later."

Cory's phone rang. It was Gold. "Mr. Lupinski, I spoke with your wife's lawyer, and they will not agree to selling the Connecticut home or to move into a less expensive apartment."

"Why not?"

"They don't believe money is an issue. They seem to be playing hardball."

"I can't afford it."

"We can make a hardship appeal to the judge. They'll want your financial records to verify the situation."

"All my records?"

"Absolutely, they want to be sure you can't afford to keep them until the divorce is finalized. They'll also look them over to be sure assets haven't been moved out of your name."

"I, I can't do that."

"Why not?"

"Uhm, I don't want the public to know any more than they do. I'm sick of having my life torn apart."

"I understand the privacy aspect, but if you want to proceed with a hardship petition, there is no other way."

"Forget it, then."

"Are you sure?"

"Yeah, I gotta go, I'm getting another call."

Cory swiped to Tracy's call. "What?"

"You okay?"

"Yeah, just fucking dandy. What's up?" Cory grabbed the bottle of bourbon and put it to his lips.

"I, uh, just heard from the PR woman at St. Jude's. They're not going to go ahead with the spokesperson role we talked about."

He wiped his mouth with the back of his hand. "Why?"

"The *New York Post* story. They feel your views don't align with the hospital's mission. They're worried it will be a distraction."

"What bullshit! They can go screw themselves. You know what? I don't give a damn about them and being a spokesperson, I just care about the kids. As long as I give them a break by going there, teaching a little guitar, I'm good."

"Well, about that. They don't want you on the campus any longer. They said the statements you made were insulting to the men and women who dedicate their lives to finding a cure."

"They're a fucking joke. You know that? Fuck them."

"Calm down. There'll be other opportunities that come along. I'll put feelers out. Just relax and keep cool. We got the tour right in front of us."

"Yeah, I know. I'll talk to you later."

Cory took a long pull from the bottle and called his wife. She wouldn't pick up. He sent a text telling her he wanted to talk to his daughter. Cory got up and did three lines of coke. A text sounded.

He was hoping his wife wouldn't give him a hard time. But it wasn't from his wife. It was Bonner, the blackmailer:

You're about to start a tour. Aren't you?

Yes. I told you I'd make the money then.

No good. Time's just about up. If the money doesn't come by end of the day. I'm going public about the stolen songs and fuck up your tour.

Hold on. I just need a little more time.

No.

Cory collapsed on the couch. He was screwed. His reputation would be trashed, and his kids would lose respect for him. It was over. There was no way out.

He got up, drained the rest of the bourbon, and went to his bedroom. The pistol was sitting on the nightstand. Cory knew what he had to do. He picked the gun up.

52

Cory's hands shook. Could he do it? He had to. There just was no other option. He tugged his Yankees hat as low as it would go.

Cory kept his head down as he climbed the steps to the door. He rang the bell. When the door cracked open, Cory rammed his shoulder into the door. Bonner stumbled backward.

The color drained from Bonner's face when he saw the gun. "Hey, take it easy now."

Cory pointed the pistol at him, holding it with both hands to control the shaking. "Why did you have to do this? You kept pushing and pushing. It was never enough for you."

"Put the gun down. We can work this out."

"Now you want to talk?"

"What are you going to do? Shoot me? Look at you, you're shaking all over."

"Shut up!"

"Calm down. We'll work everything out. I'll give you the pictures. Okay?"

"How do I know I'd get all of them?"

"Put the gun down and I'll show you."

Cory lowered the revolver, and Bonner rushed him. Cory pulled the trigger.

Bang.

Cory's ears were ringing, and Bonner's voice was muffled. "Ah! I'm shot! Help!"

Bonner seemed to be falling in slow motion. Blood soaked the thigh area of his pants. Cory looked at the gun, then at Bonner. He pointed the gun at Bonner.

Bonner crawled away. "No, please. Don't shoot. Please."

A tear dripped off Cory's chin.

"I won't say anything. I'll give you back the money. All of it."

"Why did you have to do it?"

"I'm sorry."

"You kept pushing and pushing."

"You'll get it all back."

Cory blinked rapidly to clear the tears and aimed the pistol.

"No! Please. I'm begging for mercy."

53

Cory shoved the gun in his jacket as he went outside. He looked both ways. It was clear. He skipped down the steps and got in his Tesla. He drove out three blocks and pulled over at an empty corner.

Cory got out of the car and looked around. Bending down, he took the gun out of his pocket and tossed it into a storm drain. Back behind the wheel, Cory made a call.

"I need help. I did something."

Mr. Black said, "Tell me what's going on."

"I know you said not to go there, but I . . . went to Bonner's house to try and scare him, but I shot him."

"Is he alive?"

"Yes, the bullet hit his leg, in the thigh. I don't know what to do. I didn't mean to shoot him, but he tried to get the gun from me—"

"Sounds like self-defense."

"Can you help me out?"

"Depends, tell me what you need."

"I don't know what to do. Can you fix this?"

"I'm not sure elimination at this point is possible."

"No, no, don't kill him. Is there any way you can get me out of this?"

"This happened at his house?"

"Yes, just a few minutes ago."

"Did you wear a disguise?"

"No."

"He's probably already called 911. If he survives, which sounds likely with a leg wound, he'll identify you as the shooter. I'd say the only option is self-defense."

"There has to be something else to make it go away. Isn't there?"

"Not at this point. I'll text you the name of an excellent criminal attorney, Barney Tower. He's the go-to guy for incidents like this. He's the lawyer the mob guys use and is very effective."

"The mafia?"

"Not just them. Who do you think the governor used when his mistress was found dead in his bed?"

"Okay."

"Look, you want a record that it was self-defense, so call 911 and report the shooting immediately."

BY THE TIME Cory crossed into Manhattan, he still had an hour to kill before his appointment with Tower. He was afraid to go back to his apartment. What had he done? He wanted to die and regretted throwing the gun away.

He got off the FDR Drive and drove north on Second Avenue. He swiped the second call from Tracy away. How was he going to explain to her what happened? To the record label? He couldn't even think of his kids. Would they ever understand?

Cory pulled to the curb. He didn't clear the fire hydrant, but he left the car there and headed to Murphy's. The fire-engine-red exterior gave him pause, but when he stepped inside the dark bar, his anxiety eased a bit.

He took a stool at the far end of the bar where he could watch the door. The bartender had an Irish accent. "What can I get you?"

"What's the best bourbon you have?"

"Wild Turkey, but it's twenty a glass."

"Bring me the bottle."

Cory had four drinks. It was time to go. He put a hundred dollars on the bar and started walking to his car before flagging down a yellow cab.

JET-BLACK HAIR GREASED BACK, Barney Tower wore a shiny silk suit. Cory recognized the lawyer as one he'd seen on TV. He put a fat cigar in an ashtray and extended his hand. "Nice to meet you."

Cory almost wiped his hand after shaking Tower's.

The lawyer cleared a stack of files off the corner of his desk. "Sorry about the mess, we're preparing for a trial."

Cory nodded.

"You look like you could use some coffee."

"No. Got anything harder?"

"Sorry. I don't drink, never have. You said you were in trouble. Why don't you tell me about it?"

As Tower positioned a yellow pad in front of him, Cory said, "If I tell you everything, will it be kept private?"

"Yes, our conversations are protected by law. However, I usually recommend that if a client killed someone, not to tell me. So, it's okay to—"

"I shot Joe Bonner, but he's not dead."

"Is he getting help?"

"I called 911. I didn't mean to shoot him. I only wanted to scare him, but he tried to take the gun and it went off."

"It sounds like a possible self-defense situation. What precipitated the incident?"

"I'd rather not say."

"I understand your reluctance, but the information may help explain the circumstances and bolster a self-defense claim."

"But my reputation . . ."

"If we can keep it or parts of it confidential, we will. If it's vital to a defense, we'll reframe it."

Cory stood. "Okay, uhm. Bonner was blackmailing me." As Cory paced the room, he told Tower about stealing the music and the demands from Bonner that led to the confrontation.

"How much money have you paid him?"

"I lost count, but over half a million."

"That's substantial. What made you decide to confront him?"

"I was having money problems. My manager stole from me, and then Bonner. I asked him to wait as I was going on tour and would make a lot of money to pay him, but he kept pushing . . ."

"How much will the tour generate for you?"

"I don't know now, but last time we took in over five million, and I just started, so we should have done better this tour, but now . . ."

"I see. Is there anything else?"

"No, but my family. It's a mess. My wife is divorcing me, and she wants to take the kids away from me and—"

"You're concerned about how this will affect that situation?"

"Definitely, my divorce lawyer is going to go crazy when he hears."

"I'll handle him. Who is it?"

Cory told Tower, who said, "Based upon what you've told me, I have a strategy in mind, but I need to work through it. There's a strong likelihood Mr. Bonner will tell the police you shot him, and they'll arrest you."

"Are you kidding me?"

"Mr. Lupinski, you shot a man. Even under the most extenuating circumstance, the police would bring you in."

Cory shrugged.

"At this point, you can't go home. I have a contact at the New Yorker Hotel on Eighth Avenue. I'll book you a room under my name. They won't ask questions. Don't leave the room. Order room service. Do you understand?"

"Yes."

"You do what I say, and you're going to be okay."

Tower picked up the phone and asked an assistant to get a black car to take Cory to the hotel.

"A car will be here in five. Brenda will escort you there."

"Thanks."

"Try not to worry too much. Don't tell anyone why you went to see Bonner or about the blackmailing. It may hurt the case. Keep quiet and let me handle things."

"Trust me, I don't want anybody to know but . . ."

"You better get going. I'll be in touch."

54

Tower's assistant opened the hotel door and handed him the key card. "If you need anything, call us." She gave Cory a card and left.

Cory went straight to the minibar. He unscrewed the cap off the two Dewar's bottles and downed them. He closed the drapes and put the TV on. Cory cycled through channels, looking for news on the shooting. There was none.

His cell rang. It was Tracy. He had to tell her. He took a deep breath and answered. "Where are you?"

"I can't say."

"What's going on?"

"I . . . I shot someone."

"You did what?"

"I know it's crazy, but I shot someone."

"Oh my God, is he . . . dead?"

"No, he was hit in the leg."

"Was it an accident?"

"Not exactly. My lawyer says it's self-defense."

"Who's your lawyer?"

"Barney Tower."

"Tower? He's a mob lawyer. Where did you get him?"

"A friend in the security business. He's supposed to be good."

"He is, but . . . Okay, what did he say is next?"

"I don't know. He's working things out."

"I hope this isn't going to interfere with the tour. Will it?"

"I don't know. I don't know what to do."

"Let me come and stay with you. I can help you deal with this."

"I can't. My lawyer doesn't want me doing anything but stay in my room, alone."

"You're in a hotel?"

Cory went back to the minibar. "Yeah." The only booze was a small bottle of wine. He flipped through the menu.

"But—"

"Let me call you back, my lawyer's calling."

Cory hung up and called room service. He ordered a burger and bottle of Koval bourbon.

He ate and poured another drink. Cory swiped the third call from his agent away and shut the lights. He was about to sit when Tracy called.

"Hey, sorry, I was about to call you back."

"It's all over the news. It's not good, Cory. They're saying you drove to Brooklyn and shot a man. Did you?"

"Yeah, it's true, but I didn't mean to shoot him, he came at me."

"But where did you get a gun?"

Another call was coming in. He stared at the screen. It was Donny. He let it go to voice mail. "I had one to protect myself."

"They said you didn't have a permit for one. Don't tell me you didn't have one."

"I didn't."

"Oh, Cory, what the heck is going on?"

"I need to talk to Linda. I have to explain this somehow. She's going to think I lost it. How is Ava going to understand this? Can you call Linda for me? Tell her—"

"I talked to her, she called me."

"What did she say?"

"Obviously, she's upset and couldn't believe it. She wanted to know if you were hurt."

"She did?"

"Yes, I told her you were okay and we were waiting to see what the lawyers were going to suggest."

"I need to talk to her."

"She doesn't want to speak with you. At this point, she's angry, and you're better off not speaking to her."

"But—"

"Uh-oh. Are you watching the news?"

"No. Why?"

"They just reported that an arrest warrant for you has been issued."

"What? I got to go and call my lawyer."

Cory put the TV on and called his lawyer. "Mr. Tower, it's Cory Lupinski. The news said I'm going to be arrested. I can't go to jail."

"Just take a deep breath, Mr. Lupinski. We're in the early stages at this point."

"But I'm going on tour. What can you do?"

"I've advised the Manhattan DA's office that we're representing you in this matter."

"So, I'm not going to be arrested?"

"We're discussing the matter."

"What are they saying?"

"At this point, we're negotiating with all parties."

"Negotiating what?"

"Various aspects of the charges. Look, your concerns are justified, but try and take it easy. Allow me to do what I do here."

"But what's going to happen to me?"

"Speculation at this point isn't helpful."

"When will I know what's going on?

"I expect to have an understanding worked out by tomorrow morning, if not tonight. Try and get some sleep."

The talk with Tower did nothing to alleviate Cory's fear of being arrested. The attorney seemed to be holding back information. He couldn't go to jail for this, could he? He guzzled a quarter of the bottle of bourbon and paced the room.

When he saw the breaking news banner roll across the screen, Cory guzzled another quarter of the bottle. Watching the broadcast made him dizzy. He shut the TV off and propped himself up on the bed. Cory took another gulp of booze and closed his eyes.

SOMEONE WAS BANGING on the hotel door. Cory woke up. He swung his feet off the bed and froze when the banging restarted. Was it the police? He crept up to the door and looked through the peephole.

It was Brenda, Tower's assistant. He opened the door. Brenda stepped in, pulling her head back. "Uh, why don't you shower? Give me the key to your place, and I'll pick up some fresh clothes."

"Where are we going?"

"Mr. Tower didn't say. He just wanted me to make sure you were presentable."

"You have aspirin?"

She dug in her pocketbook and handed him a packet of Advil. "Here. I'll be back in twenty minutes."

Cory swallowed the pills and took a shower. Trying to relieve the headache, he pinched between his eyes and wrapped a towel around his waist. He sat on the bed and saw the bottle of bourbon sitting on the desk. There was an inch left.

He put the bottle to his lips and drained it. He hoped the warmth going down would be enough to offset the pounding in his head. Where was he going? To Tower's office?

55

—————

Two black SUVs, turned onto Fifty-First Street, stopping in front of a building whose lower level was covered in black marble. It looked more like an office building than the home of NYPD's Precinct Seventeen.

Four men in dark suits and sunglasses jumped out of the lead vehicle. They stood by the Escalade carrying criminal attorney Barney Tower and his client Cory Loop.

Tower pocketed his phone. "They're waiting for us. You ready?"

Cory nodded. "You're coming with me, right?"

"Yes, but when they process you, I'm unable to accompany you."

"Okay."

"You don't have anything on you, such as jewelry or money?"

"No, I left everything at home, like you said to."

"Good. Remember, don't say a word and stay right behind me."

"All right."

Tower grabbed the door handle. "Here we go."

Cory pulled a denim jacket over his head and followed his lawyer out of the SUV. A throng of reporters surged forward. Cory put his hands on Tower's hips as the security force pushed the media back. Tower repeated, "No comment," as they made their way to the glass doors.

A pair of police officers and two assistant DA's were waiting in the narrow lobby. One of the officers stepped forward with a pair of handcuffs. Tower said, "Is that really necessary?"

"Standard procedure."

Tower motioned to the crowd outside. "Can we do this out of sight, please?"

"Sorry, sir."

He grabbed Cory's wrist and slapped a cuff on, spinning him around to cuff his other arm behind his back. Tower said, "It's going to be all right. I'll get you out after you're arraigned."

"When's that going to be?"

"Should be this evening."

"It better be."

"Don't talk to anybody about more than the weather. You understand?"

"Yes, but hurry and get me out."

CORY WAS CURLED up on the cement bench that hung off the cell's wall. He wanted a drink almost as much as he wanted to get out of jail.

A buzzer went off. Someone was coming in. Cory leapt up. It had to be Tower. He grabbed the bars and put his head as far out as possible.

It wasn't his lawyer. It was a woman officer. "Excuse me, ma'am. What time is it?"

"Midnight."

"Is the court still open?"

"Just for another hour, honey."

"I'm supposed to be arraigned and released."

The officer smiled and walked away.

Cory realized he'd spend the night in prison. He got back on the bench, getting into the fetal position on the cold, hard surface. How had he gone from the plushest suites to this?

He worried that Tower would forget about him or not care enough to do what was necessary to get him released. Why should Tower give a damn about him? He was just in it for the money, like most of the people around him.

Cory missed Tracy. She could be tough on him, but she really seemed to care. But most of all he missed his wife and kids. Would he ever see them again? What if he was sent to prison for a long time? Would Linda visit? If she did, she'd never bring the kids.

Ava was eight. He'd have to wait ten years before she could come on her own. Would she even remember him? And then there was his son. He was only a year old. Forget about teaching him to ride a bike like he taught Ava, they'd never even know each other.

Cory wiped a tear off his cheek and pounded the bench with his hand. He wished he'd never taken the music. He wondered if coming clean about what he'd done would help fix things. Bruno said it was the only way, but would Linda and the kids think even worse of him? They were the most important people to him, but he also had a professional career. He'd be mocked by people he respected.

And then there was Donny. Growing up, they dreamed of success but had sworn to stay true to the creative process.

Donny would be so disappointed in him. Why had he treated him so badly? He doubted he'd ever find a way to repair the damage he'd done. Cory wished he'd turned the gun on himself and drifted off to sleep.

Cory bolted upright, disoriented. Where was he? Realizing he was in a jail cell, he felt relief. He'd had a dream, a bad one.

Cory was in a wheelchair being rolled down a dark hallway. He was just a kid, around six years old. Pushed into a room, a woman in a lab coat had her back to him. When she turned around, it was his wife. He tried to talk but couldn't.

Linda opened his shirt, exposing a port. She said, "Your cancer has spread."

A door opened and his children came in holding IV bags. Unsmiling, they handed them to their mother.

As she connected the bags to the port, Cory saw a skull and crossbones on them.

CORY HOPED Linda would be there. Tower had called her, asking her to appear as a show of support. She was noncommittal. Cory wasn't concerned about her impact on the judge. He needed her there as proof she cared about him. He scanned the rows, noting Tracy and a record label executive in the audience.

Searching again, his eyes were drawn to the wooden doors opening. Maybe it was her. When the door fully opened, his spirit soared.

It wasn't Linda but Donny who'd come. Tower hadn't mentioned calling him. Cory's eyes watered when Donny waved to him. His friend had a big smile on his face. Cory wanted to hug him, apologizing for how he'd treated his one and only true friend.

Tower, who'd been huddled with the DA, sat next to Cory. He leaned over and whispered, "I need you to trust me here. Can you do that?"

"Sure, but what's going on? I'm going to get out, right?"

"We'll make our case, but ultimately it's up to the judge."

56

In shock, Cory stood beside Tower in front of the courthouse. A horde of reporters, microphones held high, shouted questions. The lawyer raised his hand, "Justice was done today, and Mr. Lupinski is a free man, grateful to get back to his family and music career. He won't be taking any questions today, as he is anxious to be reunited with his family. Mr. Lupinski will issue a statement tomorrow, before he begins his tour."

Three security guards opened a path, and Cory and his lawyer climbed into a black Escalade.

"I don't know how you did it, but thank you so much."

"That's what I do."

"But how? How did you get me off?"

"Well, you didn't want the news of the blackmailing to get out because it would ruin your career, right?"

"Oh yeah."

"It was all about negotiating with the DA and with Mr. Bonner. Blackmailing is a crime, and right after you mentioned it, I had one of my associates pay a visit to Mr.

Bonner. We wanted to remind him of the seriousness of his extortion."

"You went to see Bonner, in the hospital?"

Tower nodded. "After applying a little pressure and telling him he could keep some of the money he milked out of you, he saw it my way, agreeing to alter his story to line up with our self-defense claim."

"But what about the gun? I went there with a gun."

"Bonner told the DA you didn't pull the gun out until he attacked you. And that was when the gun went off."

"But the DA, they didn't care that I didn't have a permit or anything?"

"That was the easy part. As a public figure, we informed them of the threat you had just received."

"What threat?"

Tower smiled. "Don't worry about the details, okay? The bottom line is you were under a lot of pressure from the divorce and custody proceedings and had been drinking too much. They agreed to drop the illegal possession charges pending completion of an outpatient rehab program."

"I won't have a record or anything?"

"It will all go away."

"I can't believe it. I mean, I shot Bonner. I can't believe he changed his story."

"I'm glad we were able to make him see the benefit of working with us."

"You mean, keeping the money?"

He smiled. "Like I said, let me worry about the details."

"I'm really grateful. If I can do anything for you, let me know."

"Now that you mention it, you're playing Madison Square Garden, aren't you?"

"Oh yeah, it's one of our biggest shows."

"Good. I can use, say, a dozen tickets, up front."

"You got it."

"And backstage passes."

"Okay, I'll get them over to you."

"You're at Soldier Field in Chicago as well, right?"

"Uh-huh."

"Get me another dozen for my boys out there."

"Sure, okay."

Tower's phone vibrated. He answered it. "What's going on?"

"There's fifteen to twenty reporters outside the building."

"Tell Franky to get his men and clear it. I don't want anyone within twenty yards of Lupinski's place."

TRACY SAID, "We have a couple of things to tend to before we leave tomorrow. You have to sign off on the press statement the publicist just sent in. We'll do it as soon as you're done signing the T-shirts."

Cory, Sharpie marker in hand, looked up. "My hand is cramping up."

"Take a break. Here, read this, it's short and sweet. If you're good with it, sign it, and I'll get it out."

Cory read the statement: *I was involved in an unfortunate misunderstanding that led to the unintentional discharge of a firearm. An official investigation confirmed my role was an act of self-defense, and I was released after a brief detainment. I'm grateful for the support you've given me during this incident and look forward to seeing all of you on the tour.*

Cory signed the document. "Here you go."

"I'll get it out. You know the old saying, there is no such

thing as bad publicity? Well, it's true. Since this happened, ticket sales have substantially increased."

"I know. Dave told me, and he said downloads exploded."

"People want to hear what kind of music a gun-toting pop star makes."

"It'd be funny if it weren't true. My hand is killing me."

"Hey, how about I call Carolyn for a quick massage before the photo shoot with the band?"

"Sure. Say, talking about the band. Can you do me a favor and call Donny? Feel him out on coming back."

"But what about Kenshaw?"

"I don't know, we'll figure something out. But I feel bad. I shouldn't have let Donny go. He was the only one there . . . and you, Tracy. Just want to say thanks again, for being there for me."

"Anytime, Cory."

"I appreciate it. What else do I have today?"

"Hairstylist, and you had the three-to-four hours blocked out for a doctor's appointment."

"Oh, I almost forgot about that."

"Everything okay?"

"Yeah, part of the agreement Tower worked out."

"Oh, by the way, I scanned Tower's bill over to Baffa. Tower's good but expensive."

"I know, he said it would run around a hundred thousand."

"It was twice that."

"Are you sure? Let me see it."

Cory autographed a dozen shirts in the time it took Tracy to dig out the bill.

"Here it is."

There were two line items on the invoice. The first, for one hundred thousand, was for legal service rendered. The second line, in the same amount, was described as specialized intervention services.

With the unexpected charge, Tower had soaked up almost half the money he got back from Bonner.

"See? He charged you double what he quoted. You want me to challenge it?"

"No. Forget it, he, uhm, did a lot better than I thought he would."

Cory was troubled by Tower's money grab, but he hadn't expected to get any of the blackmail money back or to get away with shooting Bonner. Everyone liked to say people landed on their feet when they came out on the good side of a bad situation, but none of them walked away with fifty grand and a get-out-of-jail card.

Tracy said, "What are you smiling about?"

"Nothing, just happy for the first time in a long while."

Cory's phone vibrated. It was Tower. "Hello, Mr. Tower."

"How are you enjoying your freedom?"

"Off the charts."

"We need to talk."

"Is something wrong?"

"Come up to the office as soon as you can. I'll be here until seven."

57

Cory wanted to blow off the session with Dr. Bruno. The problem was he respected her, and after the way he treated Donny, he had to tell her in person that he was done with therapy. Tower's office was only ten minutes away. He'd spend a few minutes with her and go see what Tower wanted to talk about.

Getting off the elevator, a woman in her twenties came out of the door to Bruno's office. Seeing the red around her eyes took a bounce out of Cory's step. Just days ago, he'd been so distressed that he had shot someone. Now, excepting the situation with his wife, he was back on top. Walking into Bruno's office, he hoped the young lady would have the turnaround he'd had.

Bruno smiled. "I must say, considering everything that's gone on, you look remarkably well."

"Things really turned around, and I feel good, super good."

"That's wonderful. Would you like to talk about the events?"

"Nah, I'm good, really, I am."

"It might be helpful. Many times, it reinforces things, talking them through."

"I'm okay. It's not necessary."

"May I ask about your drinking?"

"Oh, it's good. I really cut back on the partying, and this time it's for real."

"We never discussed the catalyst for the excessive drinking. We were making progress overcoming your reluctance to discuss it. It would be good to get it out."

"It's not necessary anymore. Everything is good, well, except with Linda, but I'm working on that as well."

"I'm glad things are well, but there is enough research proving that, left unaddressed, the original underlying issues will surface again, especially when undergoing high levels of stress. I wouldn't want you to experience a setback."

"I understand, but I got this. I really feel like I can deal with things. I'm going to be fine."

"Well, I'm proud of you, then." She smiled. "Good for you."

"Thanks. I guess this is going to be the last time coming here."

"Don't be egotistical about things. Whenever you feel the need to talk, don't wait too long. The sooner you address what you're feeling, the easier it is to find a solution."

BEFORE BRENDA OPENED the door to Tower's office, Cory smelled smoke. Ear to a phone and finger circled around a fat cigar, the lawyer nodded an acknowledgment and kept talking. Cory looked at a series of pictures on the wall. He'd missed the winner's circle photos of Tower and his horses when he was here before.

His attorney finished the call with, "Just get it done. I got to go," and hung up. Tower said, "You want a drink?"

"I, uh, I thought you didn't drink."

"I don't, but I know how to take care of my clients. I had Brenda pick up a bottle of single malt." Tower opened a drawer and took out a bottle and glass. "Aberlour. You know it?"

"Not really, I usually drink bourbon. But I'll have some."

Tower poured three fingers of the amber liquid and handed it to Cory. "Thanks." Cory took a sip. "Pretty smooth."

As the lawyer slid behind his desk, Cory took a gulp, relishing the heat it spread. "What did you want to talk about?"

"Retaining my firm's services."

"Retaining? What do you mean by that?"

"That we're ready and available to address all of your legal needs."

Cory sipped his drink. "But I don't have any."

"Everybody, especially a high-profile entertainer like you, needs someone to protect them."

"My record label has a department full of lawyers. They handle all that stuff, like contracts and those things. I can tell them about you and recommend you."

"It's not the business aspect you should be concerned about. I'm referring to protecting you."

"From what?"

Tower said, "Whatever comes your way."

Cory put the glass to his lips. "I don't know about that."

"When you shot Mr. Bonner, did you heed my advice?"

"Sure, everything you said."

"Did I get you out of the jam you were in?"

"Yeah, I still can't believe it."

"Well, my recommendation is for you to retain my firm."

"If you think it's a good idea. I mean, okay, sure."

Tower smiled. "Excellent." He slid a document across his desk. "This is the retainer agreement. Sign the fifth page."

"I'm going to have to read this, run it by my manager. I'll—"

"I'm your lawyer. You can sign it." Tower flipped a page over. "You see right here, section Three B. It says you can terminate the agreement with thirty days' notice."

Cory read the clause. "Anytime?"

"That's what it states. No penalties or costs. You change your mind, you terminate."

"How much is this going to cost?"

"Twenty thousand dollars a month."

"Twenty? That's crazy. Why would I pay that much?"

"Why? Because the next time you get in trouble, if you want me to help, you sign it."

"But I'm not going to do anything like that. I—"

Tower leaned closer. Cory felt the heat of his lawyer's breath as he said, "I saved your ass!"

Cory put his drink down and took the pen Tower held out. "You did."

"Now, go ahead and sign both copies, one is for you."

Cory's hand shook as he signed the agreement.

Tower said, "Good. You know, when issues arise that require my attention, the retainer will go a long way toward covering the costs."

Cory finished his drink. "I got to go. We're heading out tomorrow."

"Make sure I get those tickets I asked for."

Cory got up. "I will."

Wondering what he had gotten himself into, Cory put the agreement on the car seat and made a call.

"Mr. Black, this is Cory Lupinski."

"Hello, sir. What can I do for you?"

"You recommended Barney Tower to me."

"Yes. He performed as expected."

"I know, but he kind of forced me to do a retainer with him."

Black hesitated before saying, "He's got a reputation for being, shall we say, unconventional."

"What's that supposed to mean?"

"He'll use any means necessary to gets what he wants."

"What?"

"I have another call and have to take it. Be careful."

58

The Staples Center audience was on their feet. As the band exited the stage, Tracy handed a towel to Cory. "Wow, that was the best show you've given. They ate you up out there."

"Get someone down to the front where the kids from the Children's Hospital are sitting. Get them backstage passes."

"Sure."

Cory turned to the band. "All right, guys, let's get back out and do the encore. I want to give them two tonight."

The crowd erupted as a jogging Cory led the band back onstage.

Cory came out of the bathroom with a towel around his waist. "What time we flying to Frisco?"

"Just before two. We have to be at LAX no later than one."

"If we do it early enough, we'll have time to make a stop at a hospital."

"It'd be pushing it. You need to rest. Let's wait until we get back to New York."

"Squeeze it in."

"What's the rush?"

"Ava just sent me a text. A Facebook group of kids with cancer reached out to her. Look at this picture, it breaks my heart."

Cory grabbed his phone and showed the image to Tracy. "It's so sad. Let me check for a hospital on the way to the airport, or maybe something close to the hotel."

"Good. And get somebody to pick up a dozen guitars, we'll donate them."

"Will do. I'll get that girl from the *LA Times* to meet us there."

"No, I don't want any reporters."

"You sure? It'll make for nice publicity."

"No. You can post a picture or two on social media. That's enough. I don't want to turn it into a circus; it's not good for the kids."

"Okay if you want, but I don't think the children mind it. I actually think they like the attention."

"Trust me, I'm a father who's made a ton of mistakes. Kids know when you're being genuine or not."

IN THE LIVING room of Cory's Ritz-Carlton suite, Cory and Tracy joined the Zoom meeting. His agent, Dave, said, "Good morning, Cory. How are you enjoying Dallas?"

"All I've seen is the hotel and the American Airlines arena."

"Next time we'll build some downtime into the schedule. Hey, before we get underway, I wanted to tip you off. I just heard from Billboard, and 'Tropical Storm' is back on the charts at number twenty."

"Wow, that's a good way to start the morning."

"We're not done pushing it either. I'm expecting it to go higher."

"That'd be nice."

"It certainly would. Say, let's get this call going. You all know Roger Ball. He's the head of artist development for the label."

"Hey, Roger."

"Hi, Cory, I heard you had a hell of a show last night."

"We got lucky again." Cory laughed. "Things are going a little too well. It's making me nervous."

Dave said, "Roger has some analytical insights he'd like to share. Why don't you take it from here?"

Roger said, "First off, like I said, you're killing it out there. We couldn't be happier the way the tour is going and the rebound we've seen in sales and streams. You're doing wonderfully."

"Thanks. I'm super happy it's working out."

"Now, there are some areas of concern. Sorry, let me rephrase that, opportunities to explore is a more accurate depiction."

"What are we talking about?"

"As Dave mentioned, the sales and downloads are ahead of schedule. But a trend we see in the consumer demographic is a growing number of customers are younger than the pop genre's average. This downward drift mirrors the census of the audiences at each of the stops on the tour."

"Now that I think of it, maybe the audience is a little younger."

"Basically, it's the teenyboppers, on the younger side of the spectrum, that are the growing part of your fan base."

"Why is this a problem?"

"Again, let's not view it as a problem but an opportunity. The other factor to consider is that females make up a majority of buyers and attendees."

"And the issue is?"

"A fan's stickiness. The rate of change in preference and overall lack of allegiance in a younger demographic could impact your career longevity."

Dave said, "Basically, they're fickle. Love you one day and move on the next."

Cory said, "I get it. But I'm not worried about it. I mean, they like what they like, and what could I do about it anyway?"

"Actually, we think you could mitigate the effect and increase the average age."

"How's that?"

"We polled each of the audiences, including last night. Oddly, the songs that resonate with them are the ones you made for your daughter and son. We feel if you were to stop or limit doing them live, it could have an impact."

"They like them, so I should stop playing them?"

"I know it's counterintuitive, but you have to keep in mind the older the fan, the more disposable income they have."

Cory frowned but said nothing.

"It's really up to you, Cory. You have the artistic freedom to express yourself any way you wish. We're just trying to help build you a sustainable career."

Cory was about to tell him what a load of bullshit that was but restrained himself. "I'll keep it in mind. Thanks, be well, guys."

Tracy ended the video call, saying, "It's always the suits against the talent. Don't let them get you down."

"I'm not." His phone rang. "Let me get this. It's my attorney."

"Things are going well, aren't they?"

"Yeah, not bad."

"You're selling out everywhere. My guys said the lines were long at all the merchandise stands. I'm estimating you'll exceed the five million you told me with the next show."

"I'm really not sure. I'm leaving for a rehearsal. What did you call about?"

"Our agreement. It needs to be amended."

"Why?"

"You require more work than I anticipated. We're going to need to go to forty thousand a month."

59

———

Cory's stomach dropped. "What? That's crazy."

"I reached out to your divorce attorney. Gold and I go way back. I've helped him with several thorny cases. Your case is a tough one, but that's my specialty."

"You talking about the custody suit?"

"That and the hang-up in selling a house in Connecticut. I have a couple of ideas on how to resolve these issues in your favor."

"How are you going to do that?"

"I believe magicians handle it the right way; they never explain how they do what they do."

"I don't know about this. You have to tell me what you're going to do."

"You want joint custody, don't you?"

"Yeah, of course."

"Well, then you're going to have to trust me on this."

"If I agree, how long do I have to keep paying the higher amount?"

"Until your kids turn eighteen."

"What? That's ridiculous."

"You think so? If you want to take the chance you'll lose your kids forever—that's your call."

"But come on, Tommy's only a year old. I'm not paying for seventeen years."

"You love your kids?"

"Absolutely."

"You're making a ton of money, right?"

"Yeah, I guess so, but—"

"There's no buts. I'm sending over a supplemental invoice. Get it paid."

The line went dead, and Cory sat on the bed. Who was Tower, and what the hell was going on? Was this just another form of blackmail?

It couldn't be, he thought, because he was getting something for the money. It was overpriced, but people with money always paid more than the going rate. Plus, he was going to get joint custody.

How was Tower going to do it? He'd threatened Bonner, but the extortionist had committed a crime. Linda couldn't be intimidated. Maybe Tower was bluffing. But did Cory want to find out?

"Cory? You okay?"

He opened the door. "Yeah, I'm fine."

"Good. An email from Tower just came in. It's a supplemental bill, for twenty thousand dollars. What's that all about?"

"Uh, he's going to help out on the custody case."

"He does family law?"

"Oh yeah, he and Gold go way back."

"So, I can tell Baffa to pay it?"

Cory walked to the bar area and took out a bottle of bourbon. "Yeah, as soon as possible. And get me some Pappy. This stuff is like rubbing alcohol."

"Will do. But don't overdo it, you have a big show tonight."

He carried the drink back to the bedroom. "I have to make another call."

Cory dialed his divorce attorney. "Mr. Gold, it's Cory Lupinski."

"How are you?"

"Good. Listen, I was told you and Barney Tower know each other a long time."

"Well, you could say that. We've, uh, both been around a while."

"Tower said he was going to help out on the custody battle. What's he doing on it?"

"I, uh, received a call from him, and, yeah, he wanted to be a part of it."

"He sounded confident we'd win. But you said we were going to have trouble. What can he do that you can't?"

"Mr. Tower is, uh, very persuasive."

"He's not going to talk Linda into agreeing to joint custody. What's he going to do?"

"Mr. Tower is, shall we say, unconventional?"

"That's the second time I heard that. What the hell does that mean?"

"I'm sorry, I can't go into it. I have a client waiting for me."

Cory knocked back the drink and walked into the living room. Tracy was at the dining table, talking on the phone. Cory slipped past her and filled his drink up without her seeing.

When she hung up, he asked, "What does unconventional mean?"

"Something that breaks the norm."

"I know, but what does it mean when talking about a person?"

"That they do things differently. You know, a lot of high achievers are considered unconventional. If they did the same things as everybody else, they wouldn't have gotten where they did."

"So, it's a good thing?"

"Yeah, sure. It's responsible for a lot of progress."

Cory Googled "unconventional." A dictionary stated that unconventional people were seen as geniuses, giving him comfort. Another site mentioned something that made him think twice. It said the best thing about being unconventional is the lack of limitations you place on yourself.

Did that mean someone would pursue a goal without regard to the moral and legal boundaries, as he had done with Jay Bird's music? Or was it meant to set aside your fears and hang-ups to go after what you wanted?

Cory scrolled through other definitions, settling on the idea that being different was a positive. If there was a downside to the method of getting joint custody, he'd deal with it somehow.

Cory watched the time on his phone. As soon as it turned 5 p.m., he hit the video call button. On the second ring, a feed of his daughter filled his iPad.

"Hi, Daddy."

"How you doing, sunshine?"

"Good. Where are you?"

"We're in Cincinnati."

"Where's that?"

"Think about it. The same state where Mommy went to college."

"Ohio?"

"Yep. In a couple of hours, we're going to be playing at the Heritage Bank Arena. How's Tommy and Mommy?"

"Good. Tommy, come here." Ava disappeared from the screen for a second. "See Daddy?"

Ava positioned her little brotherfor the camera. "Hey, guy, Daddy loves you. I'll see you in a couple of days."

"Da, da."

Cory's eyes moistened. "Man, he grew like crazy in just two weeks."

"He wrote all over the couch with crayons. Mommy was so mad."

"Don't tattle, Ava. Remember when you scribbled all over the kitchen walls with a Magic Marker?"

"I did?"

"Yep. Everybody makes mistakes. Just keep an eye on him when he's playing with crayons. How is school?"

"Good, I got an A on my spelling test. Mr. Diamond said I was the best speller in the class."

"Wow. You're way smarter than me."

"Than I. You're supposed to say I, not me."

"You're right. Sorry. How are you doing with math?"

"Okay, I'm really trying."

"That's super. Hey, did you like the pictures from the hospital in Dallas?"

"Yeah, I posted them all over."

"You're not putting any personal information out there, are you?"

"No. I never do that, and no pictures of me or Tommy either."

"Good."

Cory heard Linda say, "Let me speak to Daddy for a minute."

"Hi, Linda. How are you?"

"Okay. You?"

"Really good. I'm taking care of myself, and the tour is going better than I could imagine."

"Good. I'm proud that you're doing things for sick children. It really makes a difference and sets a good example for the kids."

"Thanks, I really enjoy it. It was a little scary at first, but now, besides being with my own family, there's no place I'd rather be."

"I, uh, I wanted to let you know that I'm okay with selling the house."

"Really?"

"Yes. Go ahead, I won't stop you."

Cory was afraid to ask why she changed her mind. He wanted to ask her about the custody issue, but Ava was right there.

60

Cory got off the phone feeling like he should head to Vegas. When he told Baffa about selling the house, his manager said he'd just heard from the Realtor, who did a market analysis. The agent said they had someone with a high level of interest in the property.

He wondered whether Tower was involved in that before discounting the idea. Did Tower even have anything to do with Linda agreeing to sell it? He was going to be making good money, so the house was less of a concern. If he couldn't get back with Linda, he had to have joint custody.

The custody hearing was only a week away. Whatever Tower was going to do, it had to happen fast. It seemed crazy, but Cory wondered if the lawyer might find a way to threaten Linda. If he did, that would end any chance of getting back with her. He began pacing the hotel suite. Walking by the bar, he wanted a drink. He stopped but turned around, resisting the urge.

Cory thought bribing a judge was a perfect solution. It would appear he had nothing to do with it. But was that really possible? What was Tower going to do? Cory went to the bar, poured a drink and downed it. He punched in Tower's number and was passed to the attorney.

"Mr. Tower, I've been thinking about the custody case. How are you going to, uh, fix things?"

"As I stated previously, revealing my methods would diminish the uniqueness of my approach."

"But if Linda is going to be threatened or harmed in any way, I don't want to go forward with it. Is that what you were going to do?"

"What kind of a man do you think I am?"

"I didn't mean anything by it. It's just that I don't want her to get scared or hurt."

"Mr. Lupinski, you watch too much TV."

"So, it's going to be okay, then?"

"Absolutely, I've got it under control."

"Okay."

"You're back in the city in a couple of days?"

"Yeah, in two days. I made sure I would be there for the hearing. It's going to be busy. We're playing Giants Stadium and the Garden. I hope the media gives me a break with the court date. I don't want my kids in the spotlight."

"Put your mind at ease. Chances are, there won't even be a hearing."

"How can that be? Gold said it was on the court's calendar."

"Leave it to me."

CORY OPENED the show with "Tropical Storm." The Madison Square Garden crowd went wild, and when the song ended, he said, "Thank you, thank you. It's great to be back in the city. You know, I was born here and can't imagine living anywhere else. It's the greatest city in the world, and you're the best fans on the planet."

When the applause died down, he said, "Truth is, I said the same thing a night ago in Dallas."

The crowd groaned.

"Just kidding. Playing the Garden is always special, but tonight it's super special as we welcome Donny Blake back to the band. Donny and I go way back to grammar school. Take a bow, Donny."

The audience erupted and Cory said, "Okay, Donny, give us some funk and lead us into 'Neon Nights.'"

After two encores, Cory and the band left the stage. Donny said, "Man, that was a lot of fun. It's great to be back."

"Trust me, brother, I'm happy as hell you're here."

"The band's tight and relaxed."

"Don't jinx me, man, things are going good, and I have the custody thing with Linda tomorrow."

"Sorry, man. It must be rough. I can't believe she's actually trying to do something like that."

Cory shrugged.

"Don't worry, I can't see the court taking your kids away.

"I am worried. She's claiming I'm a danger to them."

"What?"

"You know, the knife thing with Stein, and the shooting . . ."

"How you gonna fight against that?"

"I have a new lawyer, Barney Tower, he's expensive as hell, but he's a wizard or something. He's the one who straightened out the Bonner thing."

"Sounds like the right guy."

"I hope so. I'm going to jump in the shower. I'll see you at the party."

In the dressing room, Cory turned his phone on. There was a voice mail from Tower. "Mr. Lupinski, this is Barney Tower. I'm pleased to inform you that the hearing has been canceled. I don't expect it to be rescheduled and consider this matter settled."

Cory looked at the phone and listened again. How did Tower do it? Did that mean he had joint custody? He called Tower. It went to voice mail. He left a message.

The news was better than expected, but he was uneasy. What had the lawyer done to pull this off? How was Linda taking it? He didn't want to solve one problem by creating another. He wanted to call her but was afraid. He decided to text:

Hi Linda, how are you and the kids? I heard the hearing was canceled.

Yes.

I'm surprised but happy. What happened?

My attorney no longer wants to represent me.

He was relieved Linda wasn't the one who backed out. It meant Tower had gotten to her lawyer, not her.

Oh. Are you going to get another lawyer?

I've tried two already. But they won't take the case.

Cory wondered how Tower was able to influence other attorneys.

You'll find one but maybe we can work things out. I'm still doing well.

That's good. I have to put the kids to bed.

Give them a kiss for me.

Relief washed over him, not only was he going to have his kids back, but if her lawyer had quit, it meant the divorce proceedings were probably stalled. The best part was Linda had no idea his lawyer had fixed things for him.

Mind racing, he jumped in the shower, wondering if Tower could somehow get the legal separation killed. He didn't know what to do, but there was an opportunity to get his family back together.

61

CORY WANTED TO ASK TOWER FOR HELP. IT SEEMED TO HIM the unconventional lawyer could fix anything. But he was worried about Linda finding out. He was also concerned about how much it was going to cost.

Mental tug-of-war underway, Cory wished he had someone to talk it over with. There was no one he could trust. If anyone found out, any chance of reconciliation would be stomped out. This was almost as important a secret as his theft of Jay Bird's music.

Considering the secretive nature of the issue brought Dr. Bruno to mind. Anything he said to her was protected by law. Plus, she was about as easy a person to talk to as he ever met. Cory called the doctor and made an appointment.

DR. BRUNO WAS WEARING a tan pantsuit. The lighter color threw Cory off, but he took it as an optimistic sign.

Sitting down, he said, "I know I told you I was done, but I could use your help."

"It's nice to see you. You're always welcome, no matter what you say or how a session goes."

"Thanks."

"How are you doing?"

"Actually, even better than the last time I saw you. The tour is going great, and the custody hearing thing never happened."

"Wonderful. What would you like to discuss?"

"It's Linda. I'd really like another chance to patch things up between us. I know I screwed things up, and it was all my fault, but things are different now. We can get back to where we were when we first met."

"You met as teenagers, right?"

"Yeah, like senior year in high school."

"I understand the desire to go back in time. I'm guilty of that myself, but the two of you are very different people today. Life experiences change us. Becoming a parent alone alters a person's perceptions, reordering life's priorities."

"No, I get all that. I meant getting back as a couple."

"But you realize that while some needs and desires remain the same, others become more prominent. As an example, the children are central at this time in her life, but your career demands significant traveling. Understanding and addressing that so her concerns are alleviated is critical."

"You think she's worried about that?"

"It was an example. You can ask her, but it's better if you can show an understanding before she has to tell you."

"It's hard to talk to her. She doesn't give me much room."

"She's protecting herself. You caused her pain, and she's afraid to open up and get hurt again."

"I think getting back into couple's therapy would help."

"Yes, it could."

"Can you ask her to come back?"

"Sorry. It would be more powerful if you discussed it with her."

"But she trusts you."

"I understand, but she must trust you to have any chance at reconciliation."

"I guess so. Do you have any suggestions for me? Or should I get a flak jacket?"

Bruno smiled. "You have to be yourself. When you suggest it, be genuine. If she's resistant, don't push her. If she feels forced into going, feelings of resentment could impede progress."

"Okay. I'm going to see the kids later. I'll ask her then."

"Good. How are you doing with the drinking?"

"Real good."

"Excellent. That's going to be an important component for her."

Cory stepped off the elevator into Linda's apartment. Ava came running. "Daddy!"

Cory hugged her. "Hiya, sunshine. Boy, did you grow a couple of inches since I went on tour?"

Ava smiled. "I'm five feet one inch now."

"A giant. A super, pretty one."

Holding Tommy, Linda came into the foyer. "Hi."

"How are you?" Cory took his son. "Hey, little man." He inhaled the smell of his son's hair as the child pawed his face.

"You're getting so big."

"Put him down, Dad. Let me show you how he walks."

Standing behind her brother, Ava held both his hands and Tommy plodded into the living room.

"Wow, I can't believe he's walking."

"He's a handful. Getting into everything."

"You need help?"

"I'm okay."

"Look, I'd really like another shot at us. We're made for each other."

Linda looked at her feet. "I'm not ready."

"How about we go back to therapy? We'll work on everything, and you can take as much time as you need."

She looked like she was going to say yes but said, "I'll think about it."

"Okay. That's all I ask."

Linda's face relaxed and Cory said, "Were you able to reserve the rooftop?"

She nodded and Cory said, "Super. If you have any errands to run or you want to do something, go for it."

"I'll probably hang around."

"You sure?"

"Yeah."

"Come on, guys. Let's go up to the roof."

"Daddy, can we play golf?"

"Definitely. But I'm going to win this time."

Less than an hour later, as Cory boosted Tommy onto his shoulders, he saw Linda watching them. He took a couple of steps toward her.

"What's the matter?"

"Uh, nothing, I just wanted to see if the kids needed anything to drink."

Cory knew it was a cover. She was checking up on him.

"I got them a bottle of water from the vending machine."

"Oh, all right, have fun. See you later."

An hour later, Ava held the door for Cory as he carried a sleeping Tommy into the apartment. Cory laid his son on the couch and went into the kitchen. Linda was preparing dinner.

He said, "In two weeks, we're headed to London and then Milan. It'd be a great trip for the kids and you."

Linda shook her head.

"Separate rooms and hotels even."

"Maybe next time."

"Okay. I'll see you day after tomorrow."

"Cory?"

"Yeah?"

"Uhm, I was thinking about what you said about trying therapy again. If you're serious about it, I'm willing to try again."

"Trust me, Linda, there's nothing more important to me."

"Okay, let's try again."

"Thanks. You won't regret it. We'll work it all out."

Cory floated home. For the first time, he truly felt things would work out. They'd take their time, but he was okay with that. All he had to do was end the partying, and he was ready to do it. Entering his apartment, his phone rang. It was Tower. He was finally returning his call.

"I don't know how you did it, but I'm sure glad you did."

"We need to talk."

"About what?"

"Protecting you."

"From what?"

"Your past."

"What does that mean?"

"The material Mr. Bonner had on you."

"Don't tell me he's starting up again."

"No, he's not the issue."

"What is the issue?"

"Keeping the information secret is a very expensive endeavor."

"I don't understand."

"Be at my office tomorrow morning."

62

Cory went straight for the bottle of bourbon, wondering what Tower was talking about. He wanted to cut back on the booze and hesitated. This was a stressful situation, he reasoned, and poured a glass. Was there another copy of the pictures of the stolen tunes? Who could have them? Was it someone close to Bonner?

He wanted to call Mr. Black and ask him to look into it. But he decided to wait until tomorrow. Cory was sure Tower would clarify what the situation was. The lawyer had helped to turn things around. He was sure to have an answer for it.

Cory sipped his drink, thankful he was making enough money to cover Tower's costs. His mood began to rise again. It had been a good day with his kids, and Linda was giving him another shot at therapy.

Cory scrolled through the pictures he took today. It was a little two-hole putting green, but they had fun. He stared at the last image of Tommy sleeping on the couch. He looked so peaceful.

Cory wondered where the switch from being able to sleep in the middle of a noisy place to being woken up by the distant beep of a car horn took place. Cory went to a window and looked at the sky thinking it wasn't only innocence that children lost.

Seeing the stars that made up the Milky Way gave Cory a song idea. He retreated to the studio and sat at the piano. He started composing a kid's song in the key of C. The simple melody was nothing more than starting on the third note and going up the next three, then back down one and repeating it for another bar.

He wrote down ideas for lyrics, knowing he wanted the message to be hope. He was amazed at how quickly the process went. The words came easily. Excited by it, he wanted his kids to hear it. It was too late to call, so he recorded what he had on his phone and sent it to Linda.

SIPPING COFFEE, Cory left a message for Dr. Bruno. He asked for a couple's session as soon as possible, even today, if she had availability. He was going on tour and there was no sense waiting in case Linda changed her mind.

Looking out the window, the sun was shining. He knew it was going to be a good day. The sky made him think about the song he'd written last night. He went into the studio and picked up the sheet music. Humming the melody, he thought of his kids and Linda. He couldn't believe he was getting another chance to be a family again.

It would be nice if they could take a vacation. He felt it could fast-forward the reconciliation. His schedule was hectic, but at the least, they could spend a few days in Connecticut.

He dialed Baffa's office. His manager was out, but he left a message telling him to hold off selling the house. Cory went back to the kitchen, popping another pod in the machine.

He couldn't get the melody to "Milky Way Express," the song he wrote last night, out of his head. Linda said the kids really liked it. Cory wondered if there was anything he could do with it, or was it just something for his kids. He'd check into it when he came back from meeting Tower.

As the SUV pulled up to an office building, Cory's attention shifted. "Wait here. I don't think this is going to be more than half an hour."

Tower didn't get up when Cory was shown into his office. "Have a seat."

Cory eased himself into a chair. "What's going on?"

"The value of the compromising material obtained from Mr. Bonner tracks the success of your career. You're rising, climbing the charts, and selling out venues. Naturally, anything that would jeopardize the revenue stream you're producing needs to be tightly contained. You understand that, don't you?"

"Sure, but you said Bonner isn't a problem."

"He may no longer be, but the images are digital, and there is simply no way to know, with any certainty, that copies have not been circulated."

"But that's always been the case. We never knew if there were duplicates out there, and we were okay with that because nobody came forward."

"Yes, that's true. But it doesn't remove the threat."

"I'm sorry, I don't understand what's changed."

"The value of what would be career-ending information has changed."

"What difference does that make? And to who?"

"To me and my firm. Safeguarding such critical information is a difficult and expensive endeavor."

Cory swallowed. "Has someone said something to you?"

"No. There is no known threat, but we must remain vigilant. Museums spend enormous sums of money protecting works of art without being aware of any specific dangers. It's the price of deterrence."

"How much more a month?"

"It's time to set aside the idea of a monthly payment. It has an adversarial feel to it. I feel our agreement should be one that perfectly aligns our interests. That makes more sense, doesn't it?"

"I guess so. What are you talking about?"

"My proposal is to split the revenues in the middle. Whatever you net from touring, appearances, sales, and downloads, we split right down the middle. Half for you and half for my firm."

Cory's face heated up. "What? You want half of the money I make?"

"Correct."

"That's way too much."

"No, it's cheap in comparison to what you'd lose if the evidence leaked out."

Blood pounded in his ears. "You're threatening me?"

"It's not a threat. The reality is you have no choice."

"I . . . I got to go."

Cory's hand trembled as he hit the lobby button. He couldn't think straight. Tower, the man who saved his ass from going to jail, was trying to extort money from him. He was no better than Bonner.

Climbing into the SUV, the driver asked, "You all right, Cory?"

"Yeah, just got a lot on my mind."

Back in his apartment, Cory poured a glass of bourbon and kept rolling around what Tower said. He'd asked if there was anyone who might have known that he stole the music that made his career. The answer was no. There was no doubt it was Tower threatening to release the damaging photos if he didn't partner with him.

He couldn't be blackmailed again, especially in the amount Tower demanded. Cory considered coming clean. As he finished his drink, he thought it could be time to get it out there and end the madness.

It was the only way to get true freedom. It was the right move, but the problem was his family. If Linda found out what he'd done, it'd be another setback. He felt it would be the end. How would he explain it to her? To Ava? They'd be crushed and embarrassed.

Cory picked up the bottle of bourbon and stared at it. He needed a little taste. Just enough to soothe his nerves. Grabbing a glass, he poured a finger's worth. He lifted the drink, pausing before downing it.

It felt good. Thinking how tough Tower was, he poured another drink, this time two fingers. Cory picked up the bourbon, wondering if his all-or-nothing plan would work with the cagey lawyer.

He set the glass back down and picked up the bottle. Cory held the bottle upside down over the drain, emptying it. Tower was tough. Cory would need a clear head if he was going to walk the plank.

63

A FEELING OF SATISFACTION WASHED OVER CORY. HE SMILED. "That was great, guys. My friend Tracy has some cool stuff for everybody. Who wants a T-shirt and hat?"

Every one of the kid's hands shot up. "I don't think we have enough to go around."

A chorus of groans rang out.

"Just kidding, guys."

Cory was chatting with a girl in a wheelchair as Tracy distributed the giveaways. Cory's phone rang. It was Bruno. "I'll be right back, I got to take this."

He stepped into the hospital's corridor. "Hello, Dr. Bruno. I did what you said, and guess what? Linda said yes. How soon can you fit us in?"

"Wonderful. I have a slot available on Thursday, noontime."

"Perfect. Say, I need a few minutes alone. Something major came up, and it'll affect Linda and the kids. Can I sneak in today?"

"I'm sorry. There's no room in my schedule."

"I only need ten minutes, max."

"There are protocols—"

"Please, Doc, it's super important. As a friend, I'm asking."

"Come in during my lunch break."

STEPPING into Dr. Bruno's empty waiting room, Cory said, "Hello? Dr. Bruno?"

"I'm in my office."

A Tupperware container full of salad was centered on Bruno's desk. "Sorry to bust up your lunch."

"It's fine. Sit down. Tell me how I can help."

"Thanks, uhm. Well, you know, things are going well, as I told you. I'm super excited about Linda agreeing to do therapy, and I want everything to work out."

"What concerns you?"

"There's something I don't want her to know. I mean, I want her to know, but I'm afraid it's going to change everything and ruin things."

"Does it involve your relationship? Another woman?"

"No, it's my career. You see, I did something I'm not proud of, but, well, I did what I did. It's been tough to deal with, but I had everything under control until it came back to haunt me."

"Burying troubling experiences delays their resolution. Eventually they surface and must be dealt with."

"I know, but the timing is all wrong. I'm just getting a chance with her, and I can't screw it up before we start. I want to tell her, but can't I wait until we get back on track?"

"Honesty is fundamental to building the trust necessary for a lasting relationship."

"I know, but I need to start things back with Linda, otherwise there's no relationship at all."

"You want to find a way to delay telling her until you're on solid footing with her?"

"Exactly."

She shook her head. "Honesty isn't something to be postponed. If she were to find out before you had a chance to tell her, it could backfire on you."

"Yeah, but telling her upfront would kill any chance of getting back together."

"Telling the truth may have consequences, but it wouldn't undermine trust. Additionally, you'd be able to finally get the demon out in the open."

"The timing isn't right."

"It often never is. Can we discuss the issue? You're safe here. You can tell me anything, and it can't be repeated, not even to law enforcement."

"Somebody did something to me, and I can't believe it."

"You're feeling betrayed?"

"Damn right, I am. My manager screwed me, and now this."

"We must rely on others at times, but we also must exercise personal responsibility. You can't outsource certain things. You don't have to answer, but given what happened with your former manager, is this a financial matter?"

"Part of it is, but the other thing is it won't make me look good."

"Money is made and lost but doesn't influence happiness, love, or relationships. Most of my clients are considered wealthy, yet they have problems. In many cases, money complicates matters, and I've yet to see it solve the issues that bring them here. I would focus on the issue's impact on the people that you love."

"You're right, but I just can't say anything now."

The timer on her desk sounded. "I'd like to discuss this further, but I've got an appointment in five minutes."

TOO MANY THINGS were running through Cory's mind. He put sunglasses and a baseball cap on and went for a walk. Bruno was right about coming clean, but he knew Linda; she'd shut down, and that would be it.

He couldn't fault her. What he'd done was despicable and would bring shame to her and his kids. Waiting to cross Madison Avenue, a woman to his right stared at him, putting her hand to her mouth. He smiled and turned up the street instead of crossing.

He wished there were a way he could tell his wife, explain that he wanted a better life for them, but how?

Mid-block, a mother came out of a building holding the hand of a girl in leg braces. "Howya doing today, ladies?"

"Oh my God! Mom! It's Cory Loop."

"Can we take pictures?"

"Absolutely, go for it." Cory put his arm around the girl, and the mother took pictures.

"Can I have an autograph?"

"Of course."

The mother rifled through her bag, handing him an envelope that he signed. "If you want, send an email to FanofCory.com, and we'll send you a signed picture."

"Really?"

"Absolutely. Have a good one, I got to go."

Cory felt good. Cheering up kids, especially those with challenges, touched him in a way that even music didn't. He knew they got a charge out of him because of who he was, but he also got something out of it.

Cory remembered that as a teenager, his father thought he was obsessed with practicing. He never understood the inner joy and fulfillment Cory got from playing. It wasn't the same with helping kids, but they both generated a deep sense of satisfaction.

Cory realized that not one of the things he got with the money, including the Connecticut house and high-end apartments, came close. Cory believed he could do without wealth, but the shame and damage to his reputation would ruin his ability to help children.

He would pay Tower, if he had to, at least for a short time. But he had to find a way to get out of his grasp because giving up half his income would be impossible to hide for long.

Cory turned around and headed back to his apartment. A block away from his apartment, he stopped short. An idea hit him. He thought it through. Could it work?

64

Cory finished telling Baffa what he wanted to do. After ten seconds of silence, his manager said, "Are you sure about this?"

"Yes. I feel strongly about it."

"You're aware this is going to require changes, large ones?"

"Yeah, I get it, and I'm super okay with it."

"We'll have to advise the label about this."

"You think they'll be a problem?"

"They may not like it, but the reality is they don't have a choice; it doesn't affect them."

"Good. How long is it going to take?"

"A couple of days, maximum."

"Super."

"You really want to go ahead, then?"

"Absolutely."

"You realize there is no going back after this?"

"I get it, and I'm fine with it. Get it done."

CORY HUNG up with Tower and shut his phone. He took a couple of deep breaths and stepped out of the bathroom.

Tracy said, "You okay?"

"Never been better. Let's get this going."

Cory walked down the hallway into a roomful of reporters. He sat behind a microphone-covered table. Cory smiled.

"I want to thank everyone for coming this morning. I'm hoping that today marks the beginning of the end of suffering for millions of children. It's time that we truly commit to finding a cure for childhood cancer.

"It's not an easy battle to fight, but I believe we can win it. In an effort to show my commitment, I have created an irrevocable trust. The Reach for the Stars Trust will provide money to researchers to treat and cure this devastating disease.

"I'm hoping others will agree to contribute to this effort. To get things started, I'm going to do my part. Effective today, three-quarters of all my earnings, including touring, record sales, downloads, and merchandise, will go into the trust.

"There are no loopholes in my commitment to this battle. All my contracts with the record label, agent, and management are ironclad. Seventy-five cents of every dollar will go to the fight against childhood cancer. That's a good reason to buy my music, even if you don't like it."

Cory laughed before turning serious. "I can't do this alone. I'm hoping the steps I'm taking will set an example for others with similar resources and profiles. It's important to take a stand, and I'm hoping others will follow my example.

"This is not an easy challenge, but I believe with all my heart that, together, we can do this.

"I can see a cancer-free world. It's not that far ahead. Can you help us get there?"

As the SUV headed down Broadway, Cory powered up his phone. There were four missed calls. All from Tower.

Cory would have preferred to talk to Tower on the phone, but doing it in person was what Dr. Bruno would have wanted. He was afraid to see him alone, but Cory couldn't allow anyone to hear the conversation.

The SUV pulled up to his lawyer's office. Cory said to Tracy, "If I'm not back in twenty minutes, come up to the seventh floor and get me."

"Who are you meeting?"

"It's a personal thing."

Cory swallowed hard as Brenda showed him into Tower's office. The lawyer had both feet on the desk and a smile on his face.

"You think you're pretty cute, don't you?"

"I had to do what I did."

Tower swung his feet off the desk. "Do you really want to go head-to-head with me?"

"Look, you got greedy, wanting half my earnings. End of the day, you were no better than Bonner."

"I earned it. You got a bargain on the shooting incident; you have to make it up."

"I'm done with blackmailing. The money you wanted is going to help kids with cancer."

"If you go through with this scheme, the pictures will get out and you'll be ruined."

"If they do, I'll get you disbarred. You'd be breaking attorney-client confidentiality."

Tower laughed. "Who counseled you on that? You think I won't get the charge dropped?"

"I'll tell the press everything. That you made a deal with Bonner and paid off half the divorce attorneys in the city not to represent my wife."

"Incentives are very effective."

"It's illegal."

"Try and prove it. They were paid to research your assets, and that conflict prevents them from representing your wife."

"You got an answer for everything, don't you?"

Tower smiled. "I appreciate the compliment."

"Yeah, well, I'm taking you down."

"Listen, you little smart-ass, before you threaten me, you better have evidence, hard evidence. Otherwise, get back in the playground."

Cory took his phone out and waved it. "Is a recording of this meeting hard enough for you?"

"You're recording this?"

Cory tapped on his phone. "Yup, sure am."

"Give me that phone."

Cory tapped his phone. "The audio file is on its way to my manager. He has instructions to release it if anything happens to me."

"I'll destroy you. Don't fuck with me."

"I have nothing to lose, and I'll take you down with me."

65

Cory steered the SUV onto the ramp for I-95.

"Mom and I wanted to tell you something. We just started working with a Realtor, and we're going to be moving out of the place in Manhattan as well."

"Moving?"

"Yes, I know you like the apartment, but we're going to move into something smaller."

"How come?"

"Well, we can use the money we'll save to help find a cure for childhood cancer."

"Mary said you were giving all our money away."

"Not all of it. Just a good piece of it. But we'll still be more than fine. At this point, it makes sense to save as much as we can and see how things go."

"But where are we going to move to? Back to our old place?"

"Nah, we're going to stay in the city. You won't have to change schools. There's a lot of new buildings we're looking at. The apartment will just be smaller."

"Am I going to have my own bedroom?"

"Of course. And one for Tommy and a place for grandma when she stays over."

"Okay. I'm really glad you're helping sick kids, Dad. It's nice of you."

Cory smiled. "It's the least I could do."

Linda said, "Your father is a good man. He knows that helping others is really important. Doing something for someone else gives you a great feeling."

"I know, Mom. I like to help people too."

"I know you do. You're always helping me."

"How long till we get there?"

"Navigation says ten minutes."

Cory pulled up the driveway of a cedar-shingled cottage. "This is it, kids."

Ava said, "It looks pretty old."

"It needs a little fixing up, but it's got a lake out back."

"Really? Our own lake?"

"It's not ours. All the houses around it use it. And the best part is the owner left a little boat for us."

"With a motor?"

"Yup. It's nothing big, but it'll be fun."

"Look, there's some kids riding bikes over there."

Linda said, "Most of the families here have children your age and younger. That's why we decided on this house."

"That's cool. I never had anybody to play with at the other house."

Cory patted Linda's thigh. The move from the Connecticut estate was going to work out. Despite how badly Cory had handled success, Ava's value system was intact.

CORY CAME off the elevator and stepped around the boxes filling the foyer. Linda was in the kitchen.

Cory kissed her cheek. "What are you making?"

"Shrimp and veggies. How'd it go?"

"Good. There's this one kid, he's got leukemia, he picks up anything I show him. I had to give him some diminished scales to occupy him."

"A prodigy?"

"Maybe. Dave called, and Disney is interested in 'Milky Way Express.'"

"What? Oh my God, that's great."

"They're about to start an animated movie where the characters are figures from the constellations. It's a pretty cool concept. They have high hopes for it, signed up a bunch of big actors for the voices."

"It sounds like it could be a winner."

"Dave said that because all my contracts have genre clauses, that I can keep this outside of the trust, and we can keep whatever it makes."

"Really?"

"Yeah, but I told him no. It wouldn't be the right thing to do."

Linda smiled at him. "I'm proud of you."

BRUNO WAS RIGHT. Holding a secret was mind poison. Even though Tower had left him alone, Cory needed to get it out. He needed to be honest with Linda. And he wanted to tell his kids. Tommy was too young, but for Ava it would be one of the most important life lessons one could learn.

Linda came out of the bedroom. "He's finally asleep."

"He was overtired. Maybe we shouldn't have taken him to the show."

"No way, he's your number one fan."

Cory shrugged. "Look, I have something to tell you and Ava."

"What?"

"It's a long story. Get Ava, and I'll tell you."

The next book in this series is, Cory's Flight: Facing the Music. Find it in eBook & Paperback.

I hope you enjoyed reading this book as much as I enjoyed writing it. If you did, I'd appreciate it if you would write a quick review on Amazon or your favorite book site. Reviews are an author's best friend and even a quick line or two is helpful. Thanks, Dan

OTHER BOOKS BY DAN

Complicit Witness

Push Back

Ambition Cliff

You can keep abreast of my writing and have access to books that are free of discounting by joining my newsletter. It normally is out once a month and also contains notes on self- esteem, motivational pieces and wine articles.

It's free. See bottom of my website: www.danpetrosini.com

ABOUT THE AUTHOR

Dan is a USA Today and Amazon best-selling author who wrote his first story at the age of ten and enjoys telling a story or joke.

Dan gets his story ideas by exploring the question; What if?

In almost every situation he finds himself in, Dan explores what if this or that happened? What if this person died or did something unusual or illegal?

Dan's non-stop mind spin provides him with plenty of material to weave into interesting stories.

A fan of books and films that have twists and are difficult to predict, Dan crafts his stories to prevent readers from guessing correctly. He writes every day, forcing the words out when necessary and has written over twenty-five novels to date.

It's not a matter of wanting to write, Dan simply has to.

Dan passionately believes people can realize their dreams if they focus and act, and he encourages just that.

His favorite saying is – "The price of discipline is always less than the cost of regret"

Dan reminds people to get the negativity out of their lives. He believes it is contagious and advises people to steer clear of negative people. He knows having a true, positive mind set makes it feel like life is rigged in your favor. When he gets off base, he tells himself, 'You can't have a good day with a bad attitude.'

Married with two daughters and a needy Maltese, Dan lives in Southwest Florida. A New York native, Dan has taught at local colleges, writes novels, and plays tenor saxophone in several jazz bands. He also drinks way too much wine and never, ever takes himself too seriously.

He puts out a twice-a-month newsletter featuring articles, his writing and special deals and steals.

Sign up at www.danpetrosini.com